# A CORPSE IN
# THE KORYO

# A CORPSE IN
# THE KORYO

# JAMES CHURCH

Thomas Dunne Books

St. Martin's Minotaur    New York

THOMAS DUNNE BOOKS.
An imprint of St. Martin's Press.

A CORPSE IN THE KORYO. Copyright © 2006 by James Church. All rights reserved. Printed in the United States of America. No part of this book may be used or reproduced in any manner whatsoever without written permission except in the case of brief quotations embodied in critical articles or reviews. For information, address St. Martin's Press, 175 Fifth Avenue, New York, N.Y. 10010.

www.thomasdunnebooks.com
www.minotaurbooks.com

Library of Congress Cataloging-in-Publication Data

Church, James.
    A corpse in the Koryo / James Church—1st ed.
        p. cm.
    ISBN-13: 978-0-312-35208-0
    ISBN-10: 0-312-35208-5
    1. Korea (North)—Officials and employees—Fiction. I. Title.
PS3603.H88C67 2006
813'.6—dc22

                                    2006045471

10   9   8   7   6   5

Names, places, even mountains change. But people remain. They are real. This story is just that, a story for anyone to read. The book, though, is for the people of North Korea, and especially for the little girl, crying in the field.

# ACKNOWLEDGMENTS

Thirty years is not a long time, yet in that period one comes in contact with a lot of people. Some of them are formally introduced with name cards. Some sit beside you on long trips over the Pacific. Others brush by on the street, or wave from the side of a dirt road, or stroll with you around a temple complex. Many have spent countless hours, decades really, patiently explaining Korea and Koreans, and in that process have transferred to me their love of the place, its constant beauty, and its clear, if sometimes melancholy, inner song. I am deeply grateful to them and can only apologize where I have fallen short as a student. There is always more for the heart to learn. To turn ideas into a book takes a great deal of encouragement and good advice along the way, not to mention an agent who is dedicated (Bob Mecoy), and an editor who is skilled (Pete Wolverton).

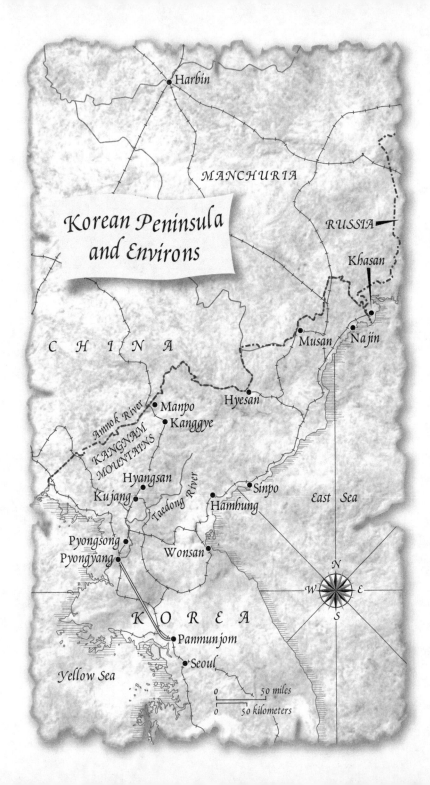

# PART ONE

At dawn, the hills wake from the mist,
One row, then another,
Beyond is loneliness
Endless as the distant peaks.

—O Sung Hui (1327–1358)

N o sound but the wind, and in the stingy half-light before day, nothing to see but crumbling highway cutting straight through empty countryside. Laid out straight on a map thirty years ago, straight was how it was to be built. The engineers would have preferred to skirt the small hills that, oddly unconnected, sail like boats across the landscape. Straight, rigorously straight, literally straight, meant blasting a dozen tunnels. That meant an extra year of dangerous, unnecessary work for the construction troops, but there was no serious thought of deviating from the line on the map, pointing like Truth from the capital down to the border and drawn by a Hand none would challenge. Alas, to their regret, the engineers could not completely erase the rebellious contours of the land; in places, the road curved. For that, the general in charge, a morose man of impeccable loyalty, caught hell. Cashiered one afternoon, by evening he was on his way to the northern mountains to manage a farm on land so bleak the grass barely grew. Eventually, he was let back into the capital to serve out his years planning new highways—all straight as arrows, and none of them ever built. By then the mapmakers had learned their lesson. Every map showed the Reunification Highway running ruler-straight and true, and that was how people came to think of it. Hardly anyone traveled the road, so few knew any better.

My orders didn't say where to look, only to be on the lookout for a car. No color, no description, just "a car." This was routine. As the English poet said, it was all I needed to know.

Frankly, I had no interest in knowing more. At this hour, if a car did appear, I figured it would be moving fast from the south. Why a car would be coming up from that direction was an interesting problem, but I wasn't curious. It wasn't my business, and what I didn't question couldn't hurt me.

Take a picture, they said; that's all I had to do. I looked through the viewfinder to find the range, then put the camera down on the grass. My vantage point was no problem—good angle, the distance fine for the lens, the lighting sufficient given that sunrise wouldn't be for another half hour. I knew the road emerged from a short tunnel a kilometer away. The sound of the engine echoing against rock would reach ahead, giving me time to get ready before the car slammed into view. The driver had probably been running without lights; he would be tired from peering through the windshield into darkness, fighting to hold the center of the highway for the ribbon of good pavement that remained. He wouldn't be looking up a hillside for anyone with a camera.

Now, though, nothing moved. No farmers walked along the road; not even a breeze rustled the cornfields bleached from too much summer and not enough rain. The only thing to do was wait and watch the line of hills emerge from the misty silence.

"Status?" It was turned low, but the sound of the radio still shattered the tranquility. I checked my watch. Every thirty seconds from now on the radio would spit out, "Status," "Status," "Status," unless I turned it off.

The voice began again, then strangled on its own static. I left the dials alone. A better signal would only invite more noise. Anyway, no response was necessary. Nothing was happening, and I was already convinced nothing would happen. If a car hadn't appeared by now, it would never show up.

I sat back to watch the third row of hills take shape, a dark ink wash against the barely light western horizon. The contours were smooth, not earth and rock but the silhouette of a woman lying on her side. Up the road, smoke curled toward the touch of morning. Probably from the village that worked the fields spread out below me. I turned my attention back to the highway and flexed my knees to keep my legs from falling asleep. A stone rolled down the hill from behind me. A split second later, I heard a bird cry and then the sound of its wings beating against the grass as it rose into the sky. This sort of surveillance always made me jumpy. I wanted a cup of tea.

The radio crackled back to life. "In case you've forgotten, you're supposed to click. How many times do I have to tell you. Once for affirmative, twice for a negative." The briefest pause, and I knew Pak was softening. "All right. It's busted, come on in."

"Save some tea." I spoke softly into the handset, though there was not a living thing in sight.

"Can't. The kettle's gone. The red one. It disappeared." Just from his voice, I could sense the trace of a smile on Pak's lips.

"From a police station? How do we boil water without a kettle?" I should have brought my flask. A little vodka would have helped pass the time, especially if there was to be no morning tea. The office didn't own a thermos. The Ministry had a few but refused to supply them, not even in the dead of winter, much less on an August morning like this. No matter that getting in position meant climbing a hill in the dark and sitting on wet grass until sunrise. The answer was always the same. "You want tea, Inspector? Perhaps we should offer rice porridge and pickles as well?" The supply officer had been around for years. When he talked, he simpered. Unfortunately, he kept impeccable records. Though we tried several times, no one could catch him taking a bribe. It was impossible to get rid of him.

Pak's voice turned unusually official, signaling there was someone else in his office listening to our conversation. "Stop moaning. And turn off the radio. If we have to replace the battery—"

I heard the sound of an engine. "Car coming," I broke in, no longer bothering to whisper. "Fast. Down the center of the road." I grabbed the camera, framed the big Mercedes, and pressed the shutter. No click, no whir, no picture. Horn blaring, the black car stormed past. One minute it was flying toward me; the next it was disappearing, pale blue wild flowers along the roadside flattened in its wash.

I watched the car drop out of sight over a small rise, then threw down the camera in disgust. The battery was dead. But even a perfect picture would have been useless. The car had no plates.

# 2

*The clock on the wall next to the window said 2:40, but that wasn't right. It was dusk. At this time of year, in midwinter, the sun set early, but not that early, not even here. Just neglect, I figured. If the apartment wasn't used often, the clock must have run down. On the opposite side of the room was a floor lamp shaped like a piece of bamboo. The shade had green fringe along the bottom; it was open at the top, and the bulb threw light pretty far.*

*The man on the couch had closed his eyes and raised his chin, as if he were on a beach, sunning himself. "Not very illuminating, that," he said. "A pretty enough picture with those flowers, I'll admit. Too bad I didn't come to hear a travelogue." Stilted Russian; it was barely understandable. His eyebrows were red, flaming red on a milk white face. He was big, bald as a monk. To look at him, you had to think there had been a mistake assembling the parts. He wouldn't blend in with a crowd. Not in any city.*

*"You told me to describe a day in my life," I said. "I just did. Next, you'll be asking me what kind of phones we use. I won't tell you. You'll want to know the color of the upholstery in the duty car. I won't tell you*

that, either. I'd say this has the makings of a long night, but maybe you'll learn more Russian vocabulary before it's over."

"Suit yourself." He said it in English.

"You're not American, not with that accent."

"Irish."

"What do the Irish want with a North Korean?"

He moved his head in a slow arc, stretching his neck muscles. "You know, some people say the Irish and the Koreans are alike."

I snorted. "Don't fool yourself. It's an insult to one of us." I took another look at the clock on the wall. "Let me guess. You work for British intelligence. What do they need with me?"

"No one needs anything, not from you, anyway, friend. We're not even sure who you are. I couldn't care if you float away on the Vltava with the rest of the trash. In case you've forgotten, you set up this meeting. You're here. So the question is, what do you want?"

"I didn't set up anything. I just made a phone call to a friend."

"Maybe your friend got in touch with us."

"I don't think so. I think you're listening in on conversations that don't concern you."

"You're here. We're here. Maybe a mathematical improbability. Two bodies on different vectors in the same place at the same time."

"I'd call that a collision."

"That would be up to you, wouldn't it?"

"You know what? Your problem is you think you've got a real live North Korean on the hook. But you don't know why. You're thinking to yourself, maybe the guys wants to defect, maybe he has the crown jewels."

The Irishman looked me over very deliberately, like a man about to buy a piece of used furniture. Finally, he said, "No, I don't think you have the crown jewels. Because if I did, you'd already be out the back door and into a car. Maybe I was interested when you walked in. Now, I'm not so interested."

"What do you want?"

"Like I told you, we don't want anything from you. Not a thing."

"So, enjoy your night." I started to turn away.

"Someone said they thought you knew something. About somebody. Do you?"

I almost left right then. Maybe I should have. Instead, I turned back toward the Irishman. "Why do I keep having the feeling you're listening in on conversations that are none of your business?"

"I'll tell you how this is going to go. Every time I ask a question and you change the subject, I get a point, alright? If you answer, you get a point. As of now, you're behind. Want to get back in the game? Let's try it again. Do you know something about somebody?"

I didn't say anything.

The Irishman bit the inside of his lip, barely enough to notice, but I saw it. You just lost a point, I thought, whether you know it or not. "Another thing." His Russian was so bad I was getting annoyed. "Silence is like running over the referee. Be careful, you might do it once too often. Let me try this a different way. You said you knew about Kang."

"You're interested in Kang?"

"Cut the crap."

"He's dead."

Not a lot of noise, suddenly, except for a bus in the distance and a bicycle bell ringing nearby. "Really?" He was speaking carefully. "We hadn't heard. We heard he was here, in Prague."

"Not likely. Last time I saw Kang, he was slumped against a tree, staring into space, a little hole right there." I walked over and put my finger between those red eyebrows.

He looked up, daring me to leave my finger where it was. I shook my head, but I didn't move away. Finally, he leaned back slightly. "Why should we believe you?"

"Maybe you shouldn't. Maybe you're not really interested." I took a step backward, toward the door. "Wasting your time, maybe."

"My name is Molloy. You can call me Richie." He pulled out a pack of cigarettes. "Smoke?"

"No. Thanks." I backed the rest of the way to the door and stood there, looking bored.

"A drink, then. Vodka?"

"No."

"Christ, a bloody nun." He pointed to a round table in the middle of the room, with a tin coffeepot on it. "Alright, pour yourself a cup. Maybe it will make this less of a battle. Sort of friendly, like."

"Tell me what you want, or I'm out the door. If this isn't going to lead anywhere productive, I've got better things to do."

"Like what?"

"Like finding something to eat, then going to bed."

"Why are you people always so difficult?"

"Difficult? I think I've heard that before, somewhere. You'll accept my deep apologies, won't you? Must be a lack of breeding. Or civilization, maybe. Yes, probably that, lack of civilization on our part. You are the civilized ones. Obviously, we must learn from you."

He moved his head from side to side, as if he had fixed the problem with his neck but now his shoulders were sore. "Go ahead, leave if you want. Makes no difference to me."

"Will you be going out the front or the back after I'm gone? The front of the building is being watched. We always thought it was yours but weren't sure. Now we are."

His head stopped moving. I could tell he didn't know I had been watching the building for the past few days. Simple surveillance, straight from the Ministry's training manual. I'd seen the technicians come in to get ready for the meeting. I decided to push him a little. "We have a list of every license plate of every car you and your friends have in this city. And when you change plates, which you do from time to time, we know the numbers of the new plates before you receive them."

*He was sweating, not much, but the light from the lamp picked it up. I didn't have any list, but it was worth the bluff.*

*"Piss off." He kept his voice low.*

*"Tell me, are there any mountains in Ireland?"*

*This relaxed him some because he suddenly realized what I was doing. Getting ready to dance. The decision was his: He could tell me to leave, or he could join in. "Hills, yes, finer than girls on a sunny day." Good, he was in. Then he seemed to reconsider. He looked thoughtful, rubbed his chin. I thought I'd lost him. "Though I couldn't say if any of our hills look like an Irish woman lying on her side. An odd thought, that." He laughed gently, barely a laugh, more at a memory than at anything I'd said, but that was alright. I knew we were past the first barrier.*

*"Ever been to Finland?"*

*The big face cracked a smile, but the green eyes were steady, eyes like I'd seen once on a cat. "So, we're back to Kang. A long way around to get to the subject at hand, but here we are. You really did know him?"*

*"I did. I didn't kill him, though I should have. Anyway, he's dead."*

*"And you? What are you doing in Prague?"*

*"Nothing. I just happened to get off the train. There was a message for me at the hotel from my friend. I gave him a call. He talked to me, I talked to him, and your transcribers wrote it all down. How did you know I'd be in town, by the way? My orders are for Budapest."*

*"Not my concern, figuring out how we know what we know, or why we do what we do. I don't guess about such things. Big man like me, I just show up where they tell me to. I take notes, listen real close when people talk. You never know what they mean until you hear what they don't say. Simple guy, that's what people call me. You, you're more complicated."*

*His cell phone rang. He answered it, softly. "Right. Right." He turned off the phone and gave me a long look. "Right." He walked past me to the window, moved the curtains aside, and peered outside. "You're wrong, but you knew that." He turned to me. "The front of this place isn't covered."*

*"Does this mean you throw me back into the Vltava?"*

"*Your friends would yank you out and put a bullet in your eye.*"

"*Don't worry yourself. No one knows I'm here, though they may be curious by now where I went.*"

"*No one is trolling you?*"

"*No, nothing so crude or well planned.*"

"*Excuse me, but I'm not convinced. You're out of your country, rolling around Eastern Europe like a billiard ball, and no one knows where you are? Sorry. I'm not in the market for a story like that. And you know what? If I don't believe you, we don't have a meeting. You go your way, I go mine. Good-bye, see you in a ditch.*"

"*You want the truth? They don't care who I meet.*"

"*You don't get it, do you?*" He closed the briefcase that was beside him on the floor. "*I'm only going to give you one more chance. Then I'm gone.*"

*I didn't say anything.*

"*See, I'm a trusting fellow, but I'm not stupid. Let's say I hand in my notes. First question I'm going to get is, 'What was the SOB doing in Prague if his orders called for him to be in Budapest?' And I'm going to say, 'Wow, good question. It didn't occur to me to ask. I was thinking of hills and girls on their sides.'*" He clicked the lock on the briefcase. "*Like I said, see you in a ditch.*"

"*Go to hell. I'm only a police inspector. Sometimes they need someone unmarked. They hand me my passport, tell me to go somewhere, see someone, do something. Nothing complicated. I'm like background noise. No one looks twice at me.*" I glanced at the red eyebrows. "*Anyway, as far as they're concerned, I don't know anything that will do anyone like you any good. Even if you chop off my fingers one at a time, I've got nothing to tell.*"

"*We're not into fingers.*" He settled back on the couch. "*Not this week.*"

"*You asked about Kang. Still interested?*"

*He gestured toward the table. "Sit down, if you want. You got something to say, I'm listening. I doubt if it's worth a lamb's tit. We'll have to see. If it makes any sense, I'll take out my notebook. Otherwise*"—*the red eyebrows jumped on his forehead, then settled back into place*—"*I have a date.*"

*"The man's dead. Why would I make anything up?"*

*He clicked his pen twice. A nervous habit. He wasn't trained very well, I thought, and his Russian was getting worse the more we talked. I walked over to the table and sat down. "You ready?"*

*"Yeah." He turned on a tiny silver tape recorder and put it on the low table in front of him. The table was dark wood, maybe black walnut, covered by a white cloth with blue and red birds embroidered around the edge. They all had sharp, bright yellow beaks. The cloth was new; you could still see where it had been folded. "Just a nice narrative, a bedtime story. Clean and simple. I don't need anything too Oriental." All of a sudden, his Russian was perfect.*

# 3

I didn't knock. Just opened the door, tossed the camera on Pak's desk, and pulled up the only empty chair left in the room. My trousers hadn't dried from the wet grass; the camera hadn't worked; nothing had been accomplished. I was plenty irritated, and I wanted Pak to know it. I could tell he was annoyed as well. He ignored me. He kept writing on his blackboard, making a clicking sound with the chalk as he lifted it and then attacked the blackboard again. He battered the blackboard pretty good, pretending to be deep in concentration before saying, "Please come in, Inspector." There were two other men in the room. Neither one spoke. Finally, Pak turned to me. "Inspector O, you know everyone here." His face took on the slightest hint of warning. "Or maybe you don't. This is Captain Kim, from joint headquarters."

I had never run across Kim, but I didn't have to look twice to know we weren't meant to be friends. He had short hair, unevenly cropped, a thick neck, and a dark face with an expression that might have been sullen except that his eyes were quick and sharp, like little paring knives. His summer uniform was good quality, better than his haircut, and someone had spent a long time shining his boots. He gave me a dismissive glance, then turned to frown at the camera on Pak's desk. No one had to tell me, it was pretty clear he was connected with the surveillance.

"No pictures," I said. "Battery's dead. Anyway, there were no plates on the car." I flashed Kim a grin meant to suggest we were about to share something that would amuse him, but his little eyes stayed metallic, and I could sense he only laughed when he was the one making the joke. Off to the side, I could see Pak bracing himself. "You may not believe this, but the bastard honked the horn as he drove by."

The man next to Kim sat back and folded his arms. "What?"

Before I could reply, Pak took my elbow and walked me to the door. "You'll be wanting some tea, Inspector."

"No, he needs to answer my question." I recognized the tone of voice. It was like the tip of a whip being dragged slowly back along the floor, just before it cracked through the air. A certain type of party official used that tone. Not mean, but quick and always decisive.

"Actually," I said, "I would like some tea." Pak shut his eyes. He did that when he was embarrassed. Whether he was willing himself into an incorporeal state or hoping I might disappear if he could no longer see me was never clear. The man in the chair shifted his weight and stretched his legs, seemingly unhurried and at ease, but watching me the whole time. He put his fingers together, tapered fingers with well-manicured nails. Not someone who had recently been out helping the farmers. I knew what was coming.

"I see, Inspector, that you are not wearing your portrait of either of our great Leaders." The man paused for a fraction of a second. Captain Kim's polished right boot tapped the floor lightly, just once, like the flick of a cat's tail. Everyone pretended not to notice. "Can I assume there is some reason you choose not to wear one, unlike your fellow citizens in the capital?"

"We don't wear pins in the field," I kept my tone matter-of-fact. Pak's breathing had become dangerously slow. One of his standard warnings to me, repeated endlessly, was, "Never call the small picture of the Leader a pin." But every time I put the little round badge on, it pricked my finger. Same place, every time. As far as I was concerned it was a nuisance, a sharp point in my life I didn't need, a pin. I shrugged. "I haven't been home in three days. It's in my top drawer, on the left. Actually, the top drawer is my only drawer." I could not resist what came next. "But you probably already know that."

"Inspector, this is Deputy Director Kang from the Investigations Department." Pak was back with us. His eyelids flew open, and he put a smile on his face, though his lips didn't take part. "We rarely get a Central Committee visitor to our small office. This is an honor."

Kang smiled in return, not to be friendly but to show me his teeth. He had on civilian clothes. His trousers were a little too long and wrinkled; the white shirt, open necked, looked like it was worn for a week at a time. His belt and his shoes were from overseas. Carefully chosen, not too stylish. The shoes were nicely scuffed, almost in deliberate counterpoint to Kim's boots. "I asked a question," he said evenly. "I'm still waiting for an answer."

"What I said was, the bastard honked."

Captain Kim broke in. "Who did? You mean the driver?"

This caught my attention. I had assumed the two of them were cooperating, until Kim interrupted. Even in a session as informal as this, interrupting threw off the rhythm. Questions weren't the key to an interrogation; it was the rhythm. Lose that, you lose everything. Then you have to start all over again. Good teams wouldn't do that. Even bad teams observed basic rules.

"How do I know who honked?" I relaxed. These two, whatever they were doing in Pak's office, were pulling against each other. "The windows were smoked, and the car was moving so fast it was a blur."

"So how could you be sure it had no plates?" Kim picked up the camera. Unlike Kang's, his hands were calloused and hard. Not from helping farmers but from breaking bricks and boards. Maybe bones, though I wasn't going to ask. Kim's voice emerged from inside a dark cave, where even simple questions were mauled and came out nasty. "How do we know you didn't fail to take the picture on purpose? How do we even know you really tried?"

"Look." My voice got an edge to it sometimes when it shouldn't, and this was one of those times. I put both hands on Pak's desk and leaned toward the two strangers, moving slowly, deliberately. It was either insubordinate or rude, I didn't care which. Kim's face darkened even more. He wanted a sign of deference, maybe a touch of fear, something to show I acknowledged his status, but I wasn't in the mood to be deferential. Kang was almost the opposite: He didn't seem to care. He didn't change expression; his eyes followed me like a bear watching a rabbit. Not interested, not uninterested, just watching.

"I don't know about you, but I got up early to go sit on a hill in the dark, and for what? The battery in that camera is dead, like most batteries they issue us." I paused. "The car, a big black Mercedes, was waxed and shining, no mud on the sides, new tires, no identification plates. None, not front, not back. It was coming from the south, incidentally, though no one has bothered to ask." I paused again. Every time I paused, Kim got angrier. The metal in his eyes took on a dull sheen like the sky before a bad storm. "And the driver honked. A real nasty blast, more like a sneer. Why, in the middle of nowhere, on an empty road at dawn, would he do that? Lots of coincidences for just one morning, don't you think?" I glanced at Kang. His face was still blank. "Now, if no one objects, I'm going to find some tea."

Pak moved to the blackboard and began erasing what he'd written. "I want a report on my desk in one hour, Inspector. Turn in that camera to Operations, and tell them to check it. And turn in the radio to Supply." He blew the chalk dust off his fingers.

Kang tore a page out of a small notebook with a leather cover. Nothing like what we were issued. "This is my number. Call me this afternoon. Two o'clock." If I told the supply officer to get me a leather-bound notebook, he would laugh in my face. "Inspector," he would simper, "you're a riot."

I took the paper and put it in my pocket without looking. Kim had put the camera down on the desk, but he was still holding the lens cap. He bent it double between his fingers, gazed at it thoughtfully, then nodded slightly and handed it to me.

"Do you think Operations has a kettle?" I turned to Pak, who was sitting at his desk again, pretending to study the first page of a long-out-of-date Ministry personnel manual.

"I want that report, Inspector." He didn't look up as I walked out of the room and down the hall to Supply. I pulled the radio off my belt. It was switched on. That meant the battery had died, because otherwise it would have been popping and spitting throughout the meeting. I wondered if the third row of hills had disappeared in the haze of the August day.

# 4

The report didn't take long to write. There wasn't much to say, and I knew Pak wouldn't want much detail. Details invite questions. Questions demand answers. Answers get twisted, or misinterpreted, or used as weapons. When I finished, I made sure Pak was alone. His door was wide open, but this time I knocked.

"Come." Pak was facing the blackboard, but it was blank. Two personnel dossiers lay open on his desk. One of them was mine, with an old picture of me stapled in the corner. I had a frown on my face. I drank too much in those days, and bright lights gave me a headache. I always frowned in front of cameras, waiting for the flash.

"So, Inspector O, what have you to say for yourself?"

"Sorry?"

"How about, 'Very sorry, Chief Inspector, for acting insubordinate to your visitors.'" I couldn't see Pak's face, but I knew his eyes were closed. He was wishing he was somewhere else. "You weren't drinking that damned Finnish vodka on that hillside, were you?"

I ignored the question. "Visitors? Visitors are meek. They murmur soft compliments. Those two weren't visitors. Those were aliens. Being in the same room with them, it made my skin crawl."

"Please, Inspector." Pak finally turned around. His face was drawn in a way I'd never seen before. "We're in so much trouble I can't count that high." He looked at his watch. "And it's not even noon."

I moved over to my favorite spot, where I could look out the window. It wasn't much of a view. In the course of a year, the courtyard below alternated between dust and mud. At one corner sat a pile of bricks meant for a sidewalk between our offices and the Operations building across the way. Years had passed, but the walk was never built. No one raised the lack of progress with the Ministry; it would have done no good. We expected the bricks to disappear, a few here, a few there, two or three taken home, a dozen showing up for sale in the street market a few blocks away. Miraculously, no one touched them, and the brick pile was transformed into a permanent monument, useless but familiar.

One summer, a junior officer in Operations had used the bricks as a bench, sitting there at dusk and singing up to a young telephone operator who worked the third-floor switchboard with her window open. She leaned her elbows on the windowsill and looked dreamily out at him, leaving calls to pile up. Her uncle was a colonel general in the army; otherwise she wouldn't have lasted the several months it took for the Ministry to muster the courage to transfer her back to her hometown. She was pretty, a cheery sort, and I was sorry to see her go. No one sat on the bricks after that.

I counted the bricks whenever a Ministry directive got under Pak's skin. He would read the offending paper a few times, call me into his office, and then start writing furiously on his blackboard. Usually he would mutter only a word or two that I could catch—"idiotic" was common—but on occasion he would launch into a full-blown lecture. It took me a while to realize I wasn't meant to respond. I only needed to stand at the window and tally one brick with each click of the chalk. Pak would finish his lecture and say, "What do you think?" I would reply, "Incredible, all there."

Pak liked the window, view or no view. He said it let in extra light on overcast days. In autumn, across from the brick pile, two tall gingko trees turned a brilliant gold for several weeks before the wind and cold November rains took away the leaves. Pak seemed happiest in early October. He would restlessly look out his window to spot the earliest touch of color on the trees. Finally, he'd call me to his office, and when I poked my head in, he would point to the window, a faraway look of quiet pleasure in his eyes. Now we were in the grip of summer, too soon for golden leaves.

"What's got you so upset?" I asked. "A dead battery kept me from taking a picture. Tell me, who the hell cares? Those two acted like it was a national crisis, like MacArthur had landed again."

"Maybe not so far-fetched." Pak lowered himself into his chair. "A simple operation, really. Sit on a hill surrounded by the nice flowers at dawn—your favorite time of day, you always say—snap a picture, two maybe, and come home."

"Not my job." Pak and I had been over this ground many times before. It wasn't an argument. We each knew where it was going. "I don't get paid to take pictures out in the countryside. I'm supposed to keep the capital in good order, at least my sector of it. That's what I do. You heard complaints?"

"Inspector, when was the last time you were paid?"

"Okay, so they haven't paid us lately. So, we aren't paid to do anything."

"Good, because that about describes what you do."

From someone else it would have sounded cruel, but I knew Pak didn't mean it. He and I got along fine, mostly. Ten years working together had worn away the rough edges. He was worried about something, I didn't know what, and when he worried he got testy. But this time, I was testy, too. I was the one sitting on wet grass before daybreak, and now I was on the hook to call a party official who wanted to harass me about my pin. "I don't take pictures in dim light of speeding cars without plates. I especially don't do it with a bad camera." I turned away from the window. "And why can't we have a thermos when we have to wait around doing nothing at the crack of dawn?"

"Did they see you?" This, too, was typical of Pak. For no reason I could see, he would get mad, then cool off quickly and focus back on the main problem.

"Nobody saw a thing." I was sure no one could have seen me from the road. I had been on a small rise, with another hill behind me. Anyone who looked up from the highway would have focused on the crest of the hill. People did that. You could send a marching band along the flank of a hill and no one would notice. They always eyed the line where earth and sky met. "Even when I was trying to take the picture, I was hunched down. Anyway, I had on a farmer's hat. If the driver took his eyes off that lousy road—which he would have been crazy to do at the speed he was traveling—he would have thought I was Kim Satgat."

Pak shook his head. "Don't tell me. I don't want to know."

"Fine."

"Alright, who is Kim Satgat? Is he on file?"

"Probably, at one time. His real name was Kim Pyong Yon. Wandering poet from the old days."

"That's it?"

"Long story, but he accidentally criticized his grandfather. Badly unfilial thing to do. He went into hiding, wore a bamboo hat to cover his face."

"So, if they couldn't see Kim Satgat, why did they honk?" Pak bobbed his head back and forth a little when he already knew the answer to a question he was asking. He waited, until he sensed I knew it, too. "Yes, the radio."

"That car was monitoring frequencies? No one gets equipment like that without piles of paperwork." I thought it over. "Unless it came from the outside. Who are we talking about here?"

Pak shook his head. "I don't know. And don't ask."

"That stone head Kim isn't from any joint headquarters, is he?"

"Inspector, drop it."

"I thought so. His neck is too thick. Not pretty enough for a head-quarters billet."

"Drop it." Pak held up his hand. "Stop, drop it, enough."

"I don't like this operation. Kim I don't like. Kang I really don't like. You notice? He never changes expression. It's like watching a trout on your dinner plate, staring up at you." We were both silent for a moment. "Did you see Kim tap his foot?"

Pak's chair squeaked as he swiveled around to face the window. He slumped and put the tips of the fingers of both hands together, making small diamonds for the sunlight to shine through.

"They're not working together, are they, those two aliens?" Pak pretended to ignore me, which meant I was right. "I don't suppose anyone checked. Was there even a battery in that damned camera?"

Pak sat up and the chair squeaked again. "You go home." He turned to face me. "You put on a clean shirt, if you can find one. Maybe some new trousers, too. You get a cup of tea and something to eat. Then, as fast as your little legs can pedal, you get back here. No visiting friends. No stopping at markets. No sitting under a tree, gazing at the summer sky." He looked at his watch. "It's 11:30. You got up early. Take a rest. Be back here at 1:45, in time to call Kang."

"What does he have to do with this, anyway?"

"Out. Now!"

I got one foot out the door, and Pak called after me. "Inspector, don't forget."

"I know." I said. "The pin."

# 5

The day had turned into a summer steam bath, not good for pedaling a bicycle, especially with the back tire almost flat. Every morning, I put air in the tire. It leaked out a few hours later; no one could discover from where, or why it always stopped leaking by noon. Every couple of weeks, I brought the tire to an old man who fixed bicycles in the shade of a pair of chestnut trees not far from my office, until he finally told me in disgust not to come by anymore, it took up his time and ate into his profits. I asked him what happened to the spirit of cooperation among us working people, but he snorted and turned his attention to an old Chinese bike that had been hit by a car. "Now that," he said, "will pay for dinner."

"This is a controlled intersection." I turned toward a traffic lady standing a few feet away, her whistle held close to her mouth. "And I control it. No bikes. No pedestrians. Just cars." There wasn't a car in sight. Sweet-looking girl, tough as nails. She had pouty lips, like all the traffic ladies did. Soon after I was assigned to the office, Pak and I had a long discussion about whether they selected girls with those lips from the start or trained them to look that way, extra lipstick or something.

Pak told me it didn't matter; either way, he wanted me to keep away from them. "They're off-limits. Each one of them is special issue." He paused. "Let me rephrase that. Each one of them is to be respected. No leering, no clucking your tongue as you stroll by, no comments on their sweet blue uniforms, or their pertness, or anything. You get me? Everything about them has been checked out at the top. The top looks very kindly on them, and not very kindly on one of us if we ruffle their little feathers."

I didn't dismount. I'm not short, but sitting on a bike makes me look taller, and getting off the bicycle would make her think she had some authority over me. "Yeah, I know the rules, but I'm in a hurry. Official business."

"There's an underground passage." She pointed to the corner. "Use it."

"In this weather, a fifty-six-year-old man has to carry a bicycle up and down those stairs?" I didn't figure she would back down, but I wanted to see her smile.

She didn't smile, not even close. "You don't look that old to me." Someone guffawed in the crowd that was forming.

"Well, I'm in pretty good shape."

She looked me straight in the eye. "I wouldn't know." This provoked another guffaw. One old woman put her hand over her mouth. "And I don't care."

My shirt was soaked with sweat when I emerged from the stairs on the other side. Still no cars. It did not improve my mood when I saw that the traffic lady had moved out of the sun into the shade. She was watching me casually, her uniform crisp and unwrinkled, her black boots gleaming as if there were no dust for a mile in any direction. I thought I saw a smile flit over her pouty lips, but I didn't feel like chatting anymore. A man on the corner looked up and waved as I passed by. "Bad tire. Get you a new one?" I coasted under the willow trees that lined the river, trying to catch a breeze, then gave up and pulled onto the old Japanese-built bridge that led to my street in the decaying eastern part of Pyongyang.

Inside my room it was no cooler, but with the shades down, the sun no longer glared in my eyes. The apartment house was already falling down when I moved in years ago. It was one of four buildings set around a square in which several small flowering bushes grew according to no particular plan. The apartments had been constructed from blueprints the East Germans brought with them in 1954 as part of their offer to help rebuild a Korean city after the war. They ended up restoring Hamhung, on the east coast, but the architecture was so appealing to someone in Pyongyang that the plans were "borrowed" and used for a number of offices and apartments in the capital. Later, to no one's surprise, it was decided that buildings in a "foreign style" were not a good idea. After the fact, special work teams went back and modified all of them, including my group of apartments, adding touches that would make them "our own."

The floors of the balconies had crumbled beyond repair, except for a mysterious few that survived and were crowded with plants. Much of the building's yellow facade on the first two floors had fallen away, leaving stained concrete that for some reason turned a deep green when it rained. An East German police official I once drove around the city told me the apartments were "Bauhaus style," but he said that the tile roofs were nothing quite like they had in Berlin, and the designs on the balconies were— here he paused a moment looking for the right word—"interesting."

You could still see where the new exterior designs had been added, one marking each of the six floors and all topped by what had once been an intricate, probably very attractive molding just below the roof line. Whole sections of tiles had come off the roof, which was why the stairway always smelled dank.

I liked the place. People said hello when they passed you in the hall, partly to make sure you didn't knock them over in the dark corridors, but also from friendliness. A group of old ladies, widows of war veterans, was assigned rooms on the lower floors so they wouldn't have to walk up so many stairs. In good weather they sat outside and watched the road that ran in front of the building. They enjoyed the idea of having an inspector from the Ministry of People's Security living in their building; they thought it gave the place a certain status and imagined that if word spread it would keep the area free of burglars.

Soon after I moved in, a few of them cornered me to insist it was not right that I was unmarried. They waved aloft a list of girls for me to meet. Heading the list, they said, was a beauty from Kaesong, a good cook whose noodle dishes were worthy of the country's old capital and would be waiting for me each night. I told them that if I got married, it would mean moving out of my tiny single room, and if I moved away, which I certainly would, they would be left without a resident police inspector. I never saw the names of the girls, nor heard again of noodles.

My apartment was simple, but it was home and it was enough. For a while, I kept a small altar for my parents near the door. I even had a vase with a flower to remind me of the countryside where I had grown up, a small valley an hour's walk from the nearest town, with nothing but dirt paths and rice fields shimmering in the afternoon sun. My balcony was unsafe to stand on; the birds perched on what remained and chattered at sunset. The couple next door, though, had a good balcony. Our side of the building faced south, and in the sunlight they grew flowers in pots of every size and description. On Monday mornings, rain or shine, the wife left a fresh red flower outside my door. She had plenty of colors to choose from; she always gave me red.

Against one wall of my room I had a small, single-drawer pine chest, inherited from my grandfather. He had built it for his wife when they were first married somewhere in the mountains near the Amnok River, hidden away from the Japanese patrols in the early 1930s. I called it my Manchurian chest and kept a clean uniform in it during the years when we were issued extras. There was an icebox—but I never bothered to plug it in—a burner where I boiled water for tea, and a Chinese-made rice cooker I'd brought back from Vladivostok, which always undercooked the rice. On the floor was a blue kettle with a wooden handle. The water in it was from three days ago, but the tap wasn't working. There was still vodka in a bottle sitting on the icebox. The vodka was from Finland, and as I took a couple of swallows, I closed my eyes and imagined what it was like in the Finnish summer. Twilight that stretched forever—a soothing idea. Whenever I mentioned it to Pak, he replied that only meant the day shifts must be hell. I liked Pak, but he had no poetry in his soul.

The altar was long gone, as was the green celedon vase, cool and smooth to the touch. The vase had been my grandfather's. When I was young, it sat on a bookshelf in his house. I had stared at it on many quiet afternoons, imagining the white cranes painted on the sides were lifting themselves in flight to somewhere I could barely picture. I don't know when it was, but at some point I began to doubt that the cranes knew where they were going.

One night soon after moving into the apartment, I came back from the office to find the altar knocked over and the vase on the floor. It wasn't necessary, and it wasn't an accident. Just a rude calling card. There was nothing else to disturb, no books to scatter about or pictures to pull down from the walls, but if there were flowers, they had to knock them over. Otherwise, what was the point of rousting the room? Once I saw the vase hadn't been damaged, I decided to forget the whole thing. Having the room searched didn't bother me. Whoever did it wasn't trying to be subtle. I figured maybe it was a drill, to show me how rooms looked after a search if you didn't do your job right. Or maybe it was a mistake: The wrong file got pulled, and when they walked into my room they realized they had made a trip for nothing, so they let off some steam.

The second time I found the vase on the floor, I wrote them a note. Pak called me into his office and told me that had demonstrated poor judgment, but I heard no trace of anger or warning in his voice as he stood behind his desk to deliver the scolding. After the third time, I just took the vase to work and put it away in my file cabinet.

# 6

I was back in our building at 1:45. I stood in the doorway to Pak's office, smoothing an oblong chip of persimmon wood with my fingers while I waited for Pak to get off the phone. I always carry a small piece of wood, the size of a matchbook, in my pocket. If you roll a piece of wood around in your fingers, eventually it finds the shape it wants to be and then starts smoothing itself. Every type of wood is different. Some take months to settle down; some can't wait to slough off the bad years.

I started doing it on sentry duty in the army to keep the circulation in my fingers. After I began work in the Ministry as an inspector, I discovered that while I was sitting at my desk, reviewing a file of unrelated facts, it helped me focus. Some people find it amusing; they call it my dirty habit. Other people can't stand it, which can be useful during an interrogation. I just have to lean against the wall, not saying anything, turning the wood over in my fingers, and they get nervous.

Pak was pleased to see me, until he glanced at my lapel.

"Don't blame me," I said. "They took the pin. Kang probably has it on his desk. Look, I don't want to get you in trouble. Why don't I put in for a transfer, maybe up north, to Kanggye?"

I put the persimmon wood back in my pocket. I'd been working it for a couple of months and it was only just getting calm. Persimmon usually goes faster than that. It's pretty wood if you treat it the right way. Otherwise it tends to be gaudy. You can't be sure you've found the heart with persimmon; it just wants to please. Walnut is different. My grandfather used to tell me that walnut couldn't give a damn. If you were going to match wits with walnut, he'd say, you'd better be serious.

"Pyongyang is getting too bourgeois. The traffic ladies won't even let you ride across the street. Incidentally, I think one of them almost smiled at me."

Pak ran his hand through his hair, a nervous habit he developed after his son died a year ago in a military training accident near the front. Pak was going gray, though he wasn't that much older than I was, maybe five or six years. His hair was too long for a chief inspector. Recently, notes about "grooming" had been showing up in his file during the quarterly evaluations, but he didn't care. Ever since his son died, he had been stepping on rules.

I never met Pak's son. When he was still little, I returned from a liaison trip abroad with a present, a boxed set of tiny metal cars made in Japan. One of the cars was yellow; it was a bus. The others were red. The tiny doors even opened, and the black tires went around. Pak thanked me and said he was sure the boy would enjoy the cars, but a couple of weeks later I found the unopened box in the trash. I knew Pak wasn't worried about having goods from the outside, and I knew he was fiercely attached to the boy, always wanted the best for him. I didn't mention it, but that was the last time I brought back any gifts from a trip. Right after the boy died, I could sense Pak wanted to tell me something. Once or twice a week, always when the sun was getting low in the sky, he'd show up at my door and start a conversation, then fall silent. "Nothing, forget it," he'd say at last. "You got any of that damned Finnish vodka around?"

"Kanggye?" Pak said now, a surprised look on his face. "No, not Kanggye. Kanggye is full of hicks and crooks. You'd drop dead of boredom, or worse. Let's go for a walk."

We went down the stairs into the street. "Ever notice the way the sunlight dances on the river, Inspector?" The river was several blocks away, hidden behind buildings that were empty and served no purpose except as a source of shade for crowds waiting for a bus in the late afternoon. Pak couldn't see the river; he was just keeping up a one-sided conversation. "You should try your hand at poetry, Inspector. Maybe join a club studying ancient dance."

Pak leaned forward when he walked, sailing into a wind no one else could feel. For someone who examined ideas seamlessly, his thoughts gliding like a razor cutting silk, he moved with a surprising lack of grace, shoulders hunched, arms swinging fitfully just out of rhythm with his steps. He never looked comfortable with gravity; it was a concession he seemed unwilling to make. As a man, Pak was handsome. The shaggy gray hair made his crisp features seem more delicate and finely wrought. Everything fit perfectly on his small face, even the hint of a frown that rested almost constantly on his lips and the elusive sense of worry that never left his shining eyes.

As we walked, Pak fell silent. Then he was no longer beside me. It happened so abruptly that I went several steps before I realized he was gone.

"Inspector!" I looked around to find him down an alley, sitting under a willow tree whose branches drooped onto a rusted swing set. "Marvelous how we provide for children, the little princes and princesses. Nothing too good for them, eh? Care to guess the last time this was painted?"

I settled next to him. "If this is a social criticism session, I have nothing to say. It only gets me sour looks."

Pak hummed to himself, a folk tune about a young couple separated by a river no one could bridge. They would have drowned themselves, but before things got that far, Pak turned to me, speaking quietly. "Kim is not a captain."

"Figures."

"He's not from any joint headquarters."

"Army?"

"Close enough. He's from the Military Security Command, a colonel."

I didn't say anything. Pak coughed, another nervous habit. He lowered his voice another notch. "I'm not supposed to know where he's from, and neither are you."

"The car?"

"A picture. One lousy picture, Inspector, and Kim would have gone away happy."

"That's what I figured, he was the one who wanted the picture. Those types are never happy, you know that. Happiness doesn't sit well with their sort of noxious purity. They give loyalty a bad name. If the Center mentions it wants a dark night for a drive, Military Security looks for ways to erase the moon." Pak puffed out his cheeks, a sign I was going off on a tangent. I backed up. "Okay. The picture. Don't they have their own camera, something expensive? Or are they too dumb to know how to use it?"

"Inspector!" Pak's tone was always friendly, even when he was irritated with me, but now it was deadly cold. "Don't underestimate them. If you'd pay attention once in a while, like the rest of us, you'd know that. Don't even think about underestimating them."

"What do we do now?"

"We go back to the office so you can call Kang."

I looked at my watch. "It's early, and you didn't really answer my question."

"At the moment, it will have to do. We'll tiptoe until Kim retracts his claws and pads away. Just hope we're too small for him."

"He may want us as a snack."

"Not if he can't see us, or hear us, or smell us. For the next ten days we fade into the background. See this swing set? It's colorless. Blends in with the dirt. Moves ever so gently when the wind blows. Even the birds won't shit on it, because they don't believe it's here. That's us. Do I make myself clear?"

"I bet they don't have swing sets in Kanggye."

"Inspector"—Pak got up and dusted off his trousers—"notice how the sunlight dances off the sunglasses of that guy on the corner?"

"Yeah?"

"Let's hope the battery in his camera isn't working, either."

# 7

The number on the piece of paper was only a switchboard. I told the operator I wanted to speak to Deputy Director Kang. "Everyone here is a deputy director," she said. "The lot of them. And I have three Kangs. So you'll have to be a little more specific."

"How about the Investigations Department?" I asked.

"Better." I could tell she was reading something, and it wasn't a telephone book. "I do have a Kang in the Investigations Department."

"That's fine," I said. "You suppose I could talk to him?"

"Could be, but you'll have to be patient. This switchboard is being upgraded, and they've got wires crossed all the way from here to the border. Yesterday I tried to connect to a Kang and you know what I got?"

"No, what did you get?"

"Kanggye."

"Ouch."

"In case I lose you, what's your ID so I can call you back?"

I gave her my name and number.

"Okay, Inspector, hang on, here we go." The phone buzzed and clicked for a few seconds, and then another voice came on. "Hello."

My watch said 2:05. "Inspector O here, calling for Deputy Director Kang. Official business."

"Inspector, I know who you are, and you're late."

"Blame the switchboard."

"I've been reviewing your file."

This is rarely a good sign, but it helps to sound unconcerned. "I'm sure you found it fascinating. Especially my poor performance in photography class."

"Your chief inspector rates you highly."

"That's just for the file. He needs that in case he ever wants to get rid of me. If he gives me a low rating, no one will take me."

"No, he's very specific. You have solved sensitive cases involving high-ranking cadre. You have protected your Ministry from disturbing developments. And you have a reputation for following orders in a discreet and sensible manner, with excellent results. What does that mean, I wonder?"

"I wouldn't know. You'll have to ask Pak."

"I might do that."

"Kang, we're each of us busy, in his own way, and I'm glad to have reached you. But my office is hot, I still haven't had any tea, and it will probably take me all afternoon to track down a battery for that camera."

"Exactly why I like your type, always charging ahead to protect the people of the motherland."

"I'll tell you what, Kang, why don't we have a beer?"

A slight pause, then a short laugh. "I thought you'd never ask, Inspector. I'll meet you at the Koryo Hotel, say at six o'clock. Precisely."

"Good." I hung up and walked across the hall to Pak's office. Pak looked up warily. "He wants to have a beer."

"Where?"

"At the Koryo."

Pak raised an eyebrow. "Funny place to have a meeting. Not an accident, as the Russians used to say, even if you did mention it first." A smile quickly passed across his face. "Quiet day. Thin walls. Watch your step. And Inspector"—Pak walked over to the blackboard and began beating on it furiously with the chalk—"mind your manners."

# 8

Kang was sitting on one of the benches at a wooden table in the beer hall at the front of the Koryo Hotel. As it usually is, the hotel was quiet and cool. I never figured out where the coolness came from. There was no air-conditioning. Maybe it was all the marble—the floors were marble, and so were the pillars where they weren't mirrored. The marble was too dark for my taste, mostly black and gray, but if it kept the place cool in August, I wasn't going to lodge a complaint on aesthetic grounds.

When the architect first presented the plans for the hotel, they probably looked grand. Two towers side by side, a revolving restaurant on the top, a marble lobby with high ceilings. The scale model must have been fantastic. Scale models usually are. One of my first assignments when I joined the Ministry was to investigate the disappearance of funds from the central offices of the Union of Architects. There were little models everywhere, models for government buildings, movie theaters, apartment houses with perfect balconies and intact facades, parks with winding pathways and beautiful landscaping. Architects make good scale models, but they make lousy thieves. The key to a suitcase was hidden under a marble kiosk in one of the model parks. It wasn't so hard to find. Who ever heard of a marble kiosk? Once I had the key, finding the suitcase was no problem. The key was for French luggage. None of the architects had been to France, but one of them, the deputy chief, had been to Beijing recently. I paid a call on him at his apartment, late at night. He had a lot of second-rate silk scarves and windbreakers lying around, draped over chairs and on the bed, along with a woman he said wanted to learn about masonry structures. He said the goods were for family members, and I told him he was under arrest unless he showed me the French-brand suitcase he used to carry all that stuff back from China. The key fit; the money was inside, wrapped in a red and white jacket. The woman got dressed in the meantime and left. I saw her a few weeks later while I was walking down a street in my sector. She was wearing a green scarf, but she didn't say hello.

A white player piano at the entrance to the Koryo's beer hall provides a contrast to the dim, muffled mood that otherwise settles over you as soon as you walk past the doorman into the hotel. The doorman acts friendly and touches the brim of his scarlet hat if he recognizes you or guesses you are important, but he closely questions anyone or anything that looks like it doesn't belong. The piano had arrived by truck one rainy morning. The doorman was about to wave it away until he glanced in the back and found a ten-dollar bill.

At first, the hotel staff only put classical music rolls in the piano, mostly heroic-sounding pieces that made people stride quick-step across the lobby. Now the invisible hands at the keyboard were playing a Beatles tune. I didn't know the title, but I knew it was from the Beatles. The song was the staff's idea of a joke, a pinprick for the puffed-up types who strut past the doorman, stand around the lobby swaying in time with the music, and then stop abruptly when it occurs to them that whatever they are hearing isn't familiar and could, conceivably, get them in trouble. I know it was meant as a joke, because I gave the staff the idea. I also gave them the piano roll, which I'd found by accident in a bin filled with piano rolls outside a small music store down a narrow side street in Berlin. I was looking for Mozart. I came home with the Beatles. Procurement trips were often like that.

Most people would have waited until I arrived, but Kang hadn't. He was already sipping a beer. It might have been bad manners, but I was sure it wasn't. With someone of his rank, it was bound to be calculated, an effort to make me uneasy, to show he didn't care what I thought of him. I stood beside the table, waiting for acknowledgment of my presence.

"Inspector, have a seat." He took a sip from his glass but didn't look up. "I hope you don't mind, but I started without you." I just stood there. Until he looked at me, I wasn't going to move. Finally, he turned his head and nodded for me to sit. "It's hot in my office, and I was thirsty." This was unexpected. People like Kang don't usually explain themselves.

"Glad you did," I said, and slid onto the bench opposite him. "I'm a little late." Kang looked at his hands. He was older than I was, and senior. I needed a touch more deference. I hadn't shown any during our first meeting this morning; it wouldn't hurt my case to throw in a little now. "I'm sorry, traffic can be a problem. Used to be, we could zip anywhere we wanted. Just hop in the car, pick any lane, and there you were. Never even had to flick the turn signals on. No one to see it anyway. Now, cars and buses and trucks all tangled, trollies holding things up. This isn't progress." He was still examining his hands. I switched gears. "I hope I didn't keep you long." I paused. "Sorry."

Kang looked up. "There are two kilometers between your office and the hotel. This isn't downtown Tokyo. Try leaving five minutes early next time. It's only going to get worse, or better, depending on your point of view." Some people would have smiled when they said this, to cover the ambiguity. Kang didn't change expressions. He didn't even blink.

I nodded to the waitress, who knew I ordered only Pyongyang beer when meeting someone from the party. She raised her eyebrows, her way of asking if she should bring a plate of dried fish. She knew I never got it for myself; it was too salty. I nodded again.

"You seem to know the staff here pretty well." Kang had changed his shirt since I had seen him in the morning. "That's good. Staff can be quite observant, very useful for information." Still his face was blank. Not a muscle twitched; there was nothing to read. He wasn't holding a conversation, he was just watching me.

"Mmm, hadn't thought of that. I'll see that it gets in our duty manual." I was going to get riled in a minute, which might be what he wanted. There was no sense in playing his game, so I changed the subject. "Hotel seems pretty full." At that moment the piano began a new song. I pretended not to recognize it. "Pretty, might be Russian," I said.

"Not Russian. You don't know the tune, Inspector?" I shook my head. "It's the theme song to *The Godfather*. I brought the piano roll to the staff a few months ago from Berlin. Funny store. All the piano rolls thrown together in a big bin out in front."

According to this game, my next question was supposed to be, "What's *The Godfather*?" But I wasn't about to spar endlessly with the man. "Ah, that's why it sounded familiar." I laughed. The man's face was never going to give me a clue, so I moved my attention to his hands. "I remember, I saw it in Prague." It's hard for people not to react at all. If they keep their faces under control, they often do something with their hands. Just a finger lifting off the table, one thumb tapping the other, nothing you'd normally notice.

In fact, at that point I'd never been to Prague. I had seen the movie, though, in Budapest. If Kang had done anything more than flutter the pages in my dossier, he'd know I supposedly passed through Prague last year on official business. He might even have skimmed some of my reports, filed from the embassy in Prague thanks to a family friend who worked there and agreed to cover for me after I ignored my orders and went to Hungary instead. Eventually, I figured, I'd get to Prague, maybe the next time I had orders to Budapest. We had a lot of trouble with the Hungarian security ministry; it didn't put up with much, so liaison visits were often necessary to straighten out "incidents."

Precisely because they were unauthorized, my two short days in Budapest had been sweet, the Tokaji warming my blood after dinner, the smell of morning pastries waking me even before room service knocked on my door. Even the constant rain, melancholy as it dripped off the old stone houses, was a welcome change from the relentless downpours that left buildings at home looking sodden and cold. The rain couldn't dampen my spirits, so I was surprised to find what did. What made me lonely was the sound of the signs above the shop doors, creaking and rattling in the wind. There is nothing like it in Pyongyang; the wind blows, but there are no signs.

After I mentioned Prague, Kang sat completely still, his hands resting on the table, not a peep from them. Then, with a strange smile, he turned his beer glass and held it up to the light. "German beer is quite good," he said, "but the Hungarians only make good pastry. Now, why is that, do you suppose, Inspector?"

My stomach gave a little warning lurch. Kang was better than I thought, maybe deeper than I'd guessed. I shrugged. "Something tells me we're not here to discuss pastry, or to compare notes about the outside."

Kang's eyes went from expressionless to dead. It must have been something he had practiced, because he was very good at it. It was as if a clear lens several millimeters thick had come down over them. All of a sudden, his eyes didn't reflect the light; they didn't react to what they could see. His voice stayed smooth, no hint of threat, but without anything in his eyes the overall effect was disconcerting. I knew he had finished sparring. He was going into battle. "What time did you leave the surveillance site this morning?"

"It's in my report." I took a piece of dried fish without realizing it. "Must have been about 7:00 A.M."

"How about 6:30?"

"If you say so."

"No, Inspector, when do you say it was?"

"I'd say it was when the sun had just burned through the mist. Third row of hills was soft against the horizon." I was getting annoyed. The fish was salty, and I didn't know what Kang was up to.

"Very poetic. But to be a little more precise, what time might that have been?"

"Six fifteen. I looked at my watch when I got into my car. I may have sat there a minute or two before I turned on the engine. By 6:45 I was back in the city."

"At 7:10 you walked into Pak's office. I looked at my watch when you threw the camera onto the desk. You made good time. No traffic problems at that hour?" He smiled faintly. I smiled back. There was more to this than just checking my progress into the city. I'd let him string it out, if that's what he wanted to do. Intelligence types never liked to get right to the point.

"At 6:40, a farmer walking along the highway found a body. He had a watch, too—the farmer, I mean." Kang paused, waiting for my reaction. I said nothing. "Just up the road there was a car in the ditch. Rear tire had blown. The left front window was shattered." I sat back from the table so I could see him better. "Want to know what color the car was?" Kang's eyes were coming back to life. "It was black. No plates." He didn't pause to get my reaction. "You're in for a cartload of woe, Inspector."

I relaxed. So that was it. He didn't think I had done anything, and he really wasn't trying to make it look like I had. He needed my help; otherwise we wouldn't be in plain sight in the Koryo at dinnertime. I nodded, partly because I finally figured out what he wanted, partly because I needed a second to think. "You've omitted a few details."

Kang laughed. "Well, I must be losing my touch. I guess I'm not getting through to you. So let me try again. The body was about 250 meters from your observation post. It was wearing the uniform of a senior colonel. Someone had cut his throat."

"Only he wasn't a senior colonel." My stomach sent up another warning lurch, and my mind started racing. How would Kang know where my observation post was? I had picked it out that morning; even my chief inspector didn't know the precise place.

Kang rubbed his eyes. "I'm tired. You're not listening. And if you don't listen, you'll just get in deeper."

"No, I heard you. But there was no body, no car in any ditch when I drove back. And the car I saw was moving so fast, if it had blown a tire it would have gone airborne and smashed more than the left front window."

"You done?"

"No. Was there a radio scanner in the car?"

"Strange question." I could see I had caught him off guard. "How did you know?"

"I was put on camera duty. I don't know whose job that is, but it's not mine. I'm supposed to look after the safety of the good citizens of the capital, their foreign guests, and their fanny packs. Thirty kilometers down the road isn't my jurisdiction. Dead bodies on the side of said road aren't my problem. Especially if the bodies are wearing phony uniforms. Especially if the bodies are planted there after I go by."

"That's twice you jumped to a conclusion." He looked past me, watching something in the lobby. "One more point. There was another body. On a hill near the road. A young boy. His throat had been cut, too."

I exhaled. He was watching me again, but not carefully, not minutely. He wasn't interested at this point to see if I twitched. Even so, he waited a few seconds before continuing, it was part of his rhythm. "The farmer claims he was checking the field at dawn and saw your car pulling away. He says he read your plates."

I could have sat and pretended to consider this. That's what he wanted, so I didn't do it. "There was no farmer in no field, Kang. I was watching. That's what we do almost all the time, we watch. That's my job, and believe it or not, I know how to do it. What do you want from me?"

"Better." Kang raised his head again. "Another beer?"

"I repeat, what do you want from me? I can't work for you. We only work with the Investigations Department through liaison. A beer at the Koryo doesn't count as proper channels."

"You and I share a problem, Inspector."

"That would be Colonel Kim." A little light went on in Kang's eyes, and went off just as quickly. I never thought I'd see it, that light. Now he realized I knew Kim's real rank. I might as well go the rest of the way. "Let me guess. The Military Security Command is investigating your department. They're trying to use me to get at you." This was just speculation. All Pak had told me was that Military Security wanted a picture of the car, though it was clear he was plenty worried even with that. I had filled in the rest, about Kang being the target, while I was driving over to the hotel. Kang could only have been in the room for one reason, and it wasn't to second the motion. He needed to find out what was happening, and he needed to know urgently. "If Military Security wants you, you must be in a lot of trouble."

Kang folded his hands and rested them on the table. "Anyone"—he smiled—"involved with Military Security is in a lot of trouble." He finished his beer, then put the glass to his cheek. "Difficult job, catching a speeding car at dawn on film."

"You didn't want that picture. Kim did." I waited for that little light to flash again, but he must have disconnected it. I figured the conversation was over. "Thanks for the beer, Kang. I've got to clean my apartment."

"Inspector." Kang pushed something across the table. "Don't forget this."

It was my pin.

# 9

*"That was the first time you met Kang?" The Irishman was studying the birds on the cloth as if he'd never noticed them before.*

*"No, I met him in Pak's office, remember?"*

*"Yeah, yeah. I meant, that was the first time you spoke to him at any length."*

"Is it a problem for you, paying attention? We can end this right here, if that's what you want."

"I'm surprised you're so polite. I thought you'd be, how to put it, nastier."

"Is that an Irish compliment?"

"No. The one thing I remember from the briefings is that Koreans don't like foreigners. Don't get excited. It wasn't meant as a criticism, just a statement of fact. Like saying cow shit smells."

"What makes you think I like you?"

"Good, you don't, then. I hate it when the briefers are wrong."

"It's not that we don't like foreigners. It's not foreigners, it's ourselves we don't like. In our minds, we are small, quivering, bowing, submissive, beaten, cowering dogs. If we like foreigners, it can only be because we are afraid, or currying favor, or kissing their feet."

The Irishman grunted. "So why did I hear Koreans are tough?"

"Different parts of the anatomy, Richie. Different altogether. I once heard a foreigner, a very dumb Russian, complain that I was a tough son of a whore. It wasn't grudging praise. He was mad because I wouldn't take his suggestion. Normally, a suggestion from a Russian is like falling down a well, but this time it was a good one. I knew it. He knew I knew it, but I knew if I took his advice, he would have an edge, or he would think he had an edge. Same thing."

"What was the suggestion?"

"We were driving on an icy road. He told me to slow down."

"What happened?"

"It was his car. Russian cars don't steer well in the cold."

"What happens when Pak gives you advice?"

"He never did."

"Guidance, then."

"Ah. Very good, Richie. That's different. Advice is a question of will. I can take advice or leave it. The burden is on me. Guidance is all about re-lationships, circles overlapping."

*"Did Kang ever give you guidance?"*

*"No. He wasn't the type."*

*"What were you doing in Berlin?"*

*"What?"*

*"You said you were on a procurement trip in Berlin. You picked up that piano roll. But that's not why you were sent. Since when do police do procurement?"*

*"I don't work for you, Richie. I told you already, I'm not going to describe the phones or the cars or anything that doesn't pertain directly to our discussion. This is my session; I'll tell you what you need to know. That's how we do it."*

*"It won't work. You were in Berlin. If I don't ask why, I get dinged when they read the report."*

*"Alright, ask."*

*"What were you doing in Berlin?"*

*"None of your fucking business."*

*The Irishman smiled. "Well, now I am beginning to like you, Inspector. Why, I don't know, exactly. It gives me the feeling I'm falling down a well."*

# 10

The next morning wasn't so humid. It was still August, but the light was starting to change. The sun was losing its edge, and the morning shadows were softening so that even my neighborhood looked less ragged. Across the river, people in the tall new apartment houses were probably out on their balconies, scratching themselves and yawning, looking down on boulevards ten lanes wide. Very grand, but I found it depressing whenever I drove through that part of town. Nice buildings, but no sense of belonging to anything. No place for the old ladies to sit.

When I walked into my office, there was a note from Pak on my desk. He always arrived early, read the overnight logs, prepared the duty sheet, and then went for a stroll. The note said I was to call Kang as soon as I got in. At the bottom of the note Pak had scribbled three stars over a tree. It didn't mean anything to me. I figured Kang would keep while I made some tea, but then remembered our kettle had disappeared, so I went over to the Operations Building to borrow a cup of hot water. By the time I got back, Pak was waiting for me.

"Did you call Kang?"

"No. You didn't say it was urgent."

"Didn't you see the three stars?"

"Since when does three stars mean urgent?"

"Inspector, anytime the Investigations Department calls, it's urgent."

"What can be urgent? I just talked to him last night at the Koryo. You want to hear? Oh, and he gave me back my pin."

Pak looked at my shirt. "I'm glad it's back home again in your top drawer. Maybe you should wear it sometime." He motioned me to follow him to his office. "You had a good chat with Kang? Anything special he wanted to discuss?"

I went over what Kang had told me about the wrecked car and the bodies, including the boy. Pak drummed his fingers a couple of times on the desk, then stopped. It was a sign that something was bothering him. "Call him back. Let me know what he wants." I started to pick up Pak's phone, but he put his hand over mine. "Use yours. There's less static."

"Something the matter?"

"No. I had a dream last night."

"How many times do I have to tell you, dreams don't mean anything. All chemistry and biology and electrical impulses."

"It was about a tiger."

"What was the tiger doing?"

"Nothing. It was swishing its tail. Kind of a hypnotic look in his eyes. Just behind him was a house. Or what was left of it."

"Where were you?"

"I was in bed."

"No, I mean in the dream. Were you climbing a tree, or trying to run away but couldn't, with a hopeless feeling, stifling, like? Then you woke up and you sweated a little, maybe let your heart calm down as you looked at the ceiling?"

"The tiger wasn't doing anything. He wasn't chasing me. He never chases me. He doesn't have to. He just has to wait and swish his tail, in front of that ruined house. It's an omen. I had the same dream just before my son died."

"Tigers are symbols of strength and pride. Cats and crows are a problem. Pigs are good. That's what they say, anyway. Keep dreaming of tigers, as long as they aren't chasing you."

Pak shook his head. "Dreams don't mean anything, you say, and then you repeat old grandmothers' tales about cats and crows."

"Trying to be helpful, that's all."

"Try to be helpful by calling Kang from your office." He waved me out the door.

# 11

Kang wanted to meet me at the top of the Juche Tower. He said there wouldn't be anyone there at this time of the morning; the observation deck wasn't even open. "It'll be nice and cozy," he said, "just the two of us. We'll lock the elevator, and I can guarantee no one is going to climb 170 meters of stairs to find out what we are doing."

Pak was noncommittal when I told him where Kang wanted to meet. "That's his style, everything in plain sight. And you can't be any more in plain sight than at the top of that tower at nine o'clock in the morning."

"You think I shouldn't go?"

"I'm not wild about it." He tapped his teeth with a pencil. "But it doesn't really matter where you meet him. Every place is equally bad at this point. Let's just see what he has to say."

The drive over to the tower took twice as long as usual because the normal route was closed off for repairs, and they hadn't bothered to set up any signs. The next street over was blocked by a stalled trolley. I ended up on a flyover that took me the wrong direction, going toward an empty part of the city where there are a few stadiums and sports halls but nothing else. I looped around back into the center of town, took the old Japanese bridge downstream from the tower, and bumped along an alleyway between buildings to join the main road paralleling the river. When I pulled up, Kang was standing by the ground-floor entrance, under the base of the monument. I could tell from the way he glanced over at my car that he wasn't happy that I'd made him wait again.

As I walked over, he made a show of looking at his watch. "You ever turn up on time, Inspector?"

I tried to look ashamed—no eye contact, the muscles in my neck relaxed so my head sort of hung down. "Screw you," I thought to myself, but as long as I was looking at the ground, he couldn't read my thoughts. It was positively the last time I was showing any deference to this guy.

Kang nodded to a woman standing in the shadow of the low doorway behind him. "This is Miss Shin. She's been kind enough to put the elevator into service for us."

Miss Shin had a round face and playful eyes. Her hair was swept back into a single braid that was tied at the bottom with a band made of silver and gold thread. She wore loose-fitting leopard-spotted maroon pants and a white blouse with no collar—not exactly your everyday work outfit. The pin of the Leader rested over her heart, just above where her blouse swelled gently out. You pay more attention to some pins than to others.

"Let's get started." Kang went through the doorway and started down the long hall that led to the elevators. Miss Shin fell into step with me.

"You're not afraid of heights, Inspector?" she asked in a low, throaty voice.

"Don't worry, I've been to the top of this thing, many times. Whenever foreign police officials visit, I have to take them up here and then walk around the grounds to hear the tour." I looked over at her. "Funny, I've never seen you. Did you just start?"

"It takes plenty of people to keep this place in working order. When it opened twenty years ago, there was a small army. We've cut back since then, but still there's a lot to do. I've been here awhile. You've not seen me"—she winked—"but I've seen you."

None of us spoke in the elevator. Kang looked at his watch and then at Miss Shin. She gave a little shrug. I tried to figure out how well acquainted they were but gave up when I felt the pressure building in my ears. The motor whined for a moment just before we stopped moving and the doors opened. Miss Shin pressed a red button on the control panel. "Enjoy the view," she said.

Kang walked once around the observation deck alone, making sure it was clear. No one else could have been there, but like every intelligence type, he was a creature of habit. I stopped at the railing and looked out toward my neighborhood. East Pyongyang didn't look so run-down from this height. The breeze had picked up, which meant the day would remain as clear as it was now, giving the city a sense of life it lacked under cloudy skies. When they were built, many of the older buildings had been surfaced with shiny materials, either designs made of tile or glitter mixed in with the paint, so that when it was sunny they danced and sparkled. From the top of the tower, the light glinted off everything below, a window here, a building or a car roof there. I traced the road from my apartment to the chestnut trees where the old man fixed bicycles, but he didn't seem to be around.

Kang tapped me on the shoulder. "No sense in looking at the old part of the city. You want to see the future, it's there." He pointed across the river toward the big ceremonial square and the massive People's Study Hall on the opposite shore. "Funny, people say that Pyongyang resembles Washington. River down the middle, lots of parks and monuments, big tower in the center, not a lot happening. I don't think they have anything like Kim Il Sung Square, though."

"I thought you said we'd be alone."

Kang shrugged. "You mean Miss Shin? Don't worry about her, she's fine."

I turned back toward the view. "The shade from the foliage along the streets looks deeper in this sunlight. See those trees, just at the bend in the river, on that little hill?" Kang followed where I was pointing. "They're more than four hundred years old. They were planted by the royal gardener, who was executed a year later for treason. As if a gardener could have anything to do with politics!" I snorted. "Before he was executed, he asked to be buried beside the trees, so his body could feed them and, as they grew, he could demonstrate his loyalty to the king."

Kang looked skeptical. "What'd they do?"

"They chopped up his body and threw it into the river."

"Looks like the trees grew anyway."

"That's not the point."

"How far does your jurisdiction run, Inspector?" Kang waved his hand lazily toward the city across the way. "If someone chopped up a body and threw it in the river, let's say, from the base of that hill, would that be in your zone?"

"We don't really have geographic areas. We operate in three sections. Concentric circles in theory, though they aren't actually circles because of the way the streets run and how the city developed. We call them fortresses. Inner fortress—key buildings and neighborhoods where mostly upper ranks live. Middle fortress—the hotels, monuments, subway stops, and major roads. And outer fortress—everything else."

"You?"

"We don't talk a lot about our individual assignments, if you know what I mean, Kang." He leaned back against the railing and waited. I did some quick calculations. The Ministry didn't want us discussing details of our assignments with other security offices. Coordination was not banned, but it wasn't encouraged. No service could run an operation or a surveillance or even a simple patrol without worrying about stumbling over someone else's activity. On the other hand, if Kang was determined to find out what I did, he could do that with a couple of phone calls to the right places. He knew it, but he wanted me to tell him directly. Part of the stupid games the Investigations Department people played. "Middle," I said.

"That means you end up doing most of the city. But whatever you don't handle must have a red line around it, an inner fortress that is someone else's concern."

"Something like that."

Kang looked at me thoughtfully for a moment, then turned back to the view. "From this height, Inspector, the city makes perfect sense, wouldn't you say? It all fits together, tall buildings balancing traditional rooftops, rigid open squares balancing meandering parks, everything anchored visually and psychologically by this tower. Not like Beijing, with buildings springing up to no purpose and a jumbled skyline that can only create confusion and disorder in people's minds."

I wasn't about to interrupt. He wasn't talking about architecture. Kang moved around to the northern side of the tower. "But this place doesn't exist in a vacuum. From here what do we see? Fields lapping at the edge of the city, and beyond that, in the distance, mountains. Mountains. They last a long time, Inspector." He walked around to the southern side. "And there, in the distance, the glorious road south. Let's drive out there together some afternoon soon. Maybe we'll be able to find where they buried that boy's body."

Miss Shin had settled beside us, her eyes closed, a smile on her face as she enjoyed the breeze. The moment she heard Kang mention the body, she stopped smiling and drifted away.

"The corpse from the wrecked car was taken to the morgue last night. The boy's body was buried way back in the hills. His relatives never saw the body. They got an urn of ashes and a note from the hospital expressing regrets that the boy had been killed in an auto accident."

"And he wasn't?"

"I never knew a car crash that cut someone's throat. Did you?"

"Why are you telling me all of this?"

"You know some things I don't know. I know some things you don't know. Simple addition, Inspector."

"Not possible, Kang. What you know and what I know don't add up."

Kang turned to look upriver toward the trees I had shown him. "Too bad about that gardener." He walked into the elevator where Miss Shin was waiting, reached around her, and pressed the red button. "Come on, Inspector. Back to earth," he smiled. "Such as it is."

# 12

As soon as he heard my report on the conversation with Kang at the tower, Pak reached into his desk and pulled out a ticket. "Go home. Pack a bag, take the rest of the week off. You need to be out of the city for a while. Trust me. Maybe Kanggye isn't such a bad idea after all. Be at the train station tomorrow morning early, at 4:30. Give this to the stationmaster, name is Pak, not my cousin as far as I know. He'll see you are comfy, away from the cigarette smoke and confusion of the masses. Good luck. Don't keep in touch. I'll contact you if there is any need. Stay away from phones." He saw the look on my face. "This is for your own good. It isn't punishment, Inspector. I just don't want you anywhere near Kang for now. If Military Security is gunning for him, something is out of kilter. Everywhere Kang goes these days, that thug Kim won't be far behind. Better yet, hand in your resignation."

"Are you crazy?"

"No. Resignation will get you onto the sidelines. We'll say you were drinking again and I had to let you go."

"What's gotten into you? I'm not resigning. And I've stopped drinking. Pretty much. Everyone knows that."

"Fine, be stubborn. Here, at least take the ticket." He turned back to the papers on his desk, then glanced up at me, a look of concern passing over his face. "Can you wake up that early, Inspector? Whatever you do, don't miss the train."

# PART
# TWO

When we are apart,
The moon through the pines
Is never bright in Kanggye,
But a pale reflection on the lake that
Nightly grows, watered by my tears.

—Pak Hae Gun (1456–1497)

The stationmaster moved slowly for such a small man. He took the ticket, squinted at the number, looked at me, then looked back at the ticket. At that hour, there was not much light in the station, just shadings of darkness. Somewhere in the building a bulb was burning. Whatever feeble watts it emitted floated in and out of clouds of cigarette smoke until sinking onto peasants with weary faces and expressionless eyes. A few sat on wooden benches, but most squatted on the floor beside battered cardboard boxes. Each box was tied with ropes that had been mended and spliced a hundred times. It seemed impossible that any of them would survive another tug or twist.

"Pretty old ticket," he said, in a voice that just carried the distance between us.

"The number not lucky anymore?" I was guessing that it meant something to him, maybe from a list agreed on years ago. Pak wouldn't have called him; he wanted me to slip out of town, not blare the news over the phone.

"Numbers don't bring luck." The oversized hat the little man wore might have made him seem taller, but it tipped to one side, so he just looked off balance. He was tired—maybe he had been up all night— but mostly he was wary.

"Up to you," I said, and turned to go. He took a quick step and put his hand on my arm, gently, as if he didn't want to startle me.

"Don't turn around." He had lowered his voice even more, so I could barely catch his words. "Just walk to the corner, over to the right. Stand in the shadow. I'll be back."

He had my ticket, and I didn't want to let him keep it because I was beginning not to trust him. Maybe things had changed since he and Chief Inspector Pak had last met. Things change. People change. You never know.

"Go." His voice had a new tone, urgent, not the voice of this hushed waiting room. The peasants nearest on the floor turned to look and then turned away, not wanting to see, already forgetting.

I waited in the corner. It was so dark I couldn't read my watch. And other than coughing and a few snores, the only sound was the slow drip of water reverberating around the walls. Everything was muted, even the sense of time. The train must be delayed.

"Here is your ticket, Inspector." He was beside me. I hadn't heard a thing. I didn't like this muffled atmosphere. It was unhealthy. "You have a seat on the third car. Everyone will scramble when the train gets here, and it will get here soon enough. You'll hear it whistle as it pulls into the station. Saddest damn whistle; no reason to sound it so early in the morning, but the engineer says it's regulation, and I don't mind. We'll throw everyone off the third car, or most of them, anyway. There should be three passenger cars, two boxcars, and a caboose. I let army officers stay on your car, maybe a few cadre kids, and anyone who slips me five dollars. The view from the caboose is the best. You can see the countryside slipping away behind, makes you think you're actually going somewhere."

I had a ten-dollar bill ready to give him. He shook his head. "From you, nothing. I stamp your ticket, then I walk away. I don't even remember your face."

I felt the ticket put into my pocket, turned to ask how he knew to call me "Inspector," and found nothing but still, empty air.

# 2

The train should have been scrapped years ago. The small engine looked too tired to pull the collection of cars hitched behind. The first two coaches were brown, Korean made, but the third car was bigger, huskier, European. It had been bought secondhand, probably in the past year, and rolled all the way across Siberia. There were no lights along the platform; a single light was shining about thirty meters away, in the middle of the empty train yard where it was doing no one any good. Dawn was still an hour away, but already the darkness had thinned enough for me to distinguish some details on the third car. From the manufacturer's plate beside the door, I saw it was Czech. The instruction placards placed over the passageways at either end hadn't been changed to Korean, but it didn't make much difference. If they were meant to inform passengers that the dining car was five cars back and the first seating was at 6:00 P.M., no one needed to know. If they were safety instructions, they weren't any use, either. Trains rarely picked up any speed on these tracks. Even on minor grades, if you jumped off the rear car and started to walk, you could overtake the engine. Most derailments only resulted in a few bruises, unless the whole train tumbled off a bridge.

The train bumped once and then started slowly out of the station. Other than a rainstorm or two, the coach I was on must not have seen a washing since it left the Czech border. The original color was hidden under a thick coat of dust, and the windows had so much dirt baked on by the sun along the bottom ledge that they wouldn't open. There were small signs over every other window. Maybe they said USE ONLY IN EMERGENCY but I couldn't read Czech and didn't plan on taking lessons. I banged on the window next to the seat with my fists, trying to force it open.

An army colonel was slumped on the seat across the aisle, his hat over his eyes, boots untied, trying to sleep. "Enough," he said and pushed back his cap so he could see what was going on, "enough pounding. Leave it be, can't you? I've got to get some rest." He looked over at me with a bleary frown. "Once the sun is up, the air outside won't be any cooler. Why let in the noise from the engine?"

The young woman in the seat facing me shook her head. "Ignore him. He is always like this, contrary. I need some air, go ahead and open these filthy windows, if you can. I don't plan to suffocate on this train to nowhere. You don't smoke, I hope." She stopped and tilted her head slightly. "You're not mad at me, are you?"

"We haven't even met. Why should I be mad at you?"

"You look mad." She squinted at my face. "Maybe it's your eyebrows. Close together. People with wide foreheads and broad faces tend to be happy. Haven't you noticed? Lots of room to smile. But your forehead"— she shook her head—"with those eyebrows. You don't smile enough. When you get older, all your wrinkles will go the wrong direction."

She was in her late twenties, not very pretty, or maybe it was the way her hair was done in a permanent that made her head seem about to swallow her face. For this early in the morning, she had on plenty of makeup, more than most girls I knew wore any time of day. It looked like she was going to meet someone, or had just left.

I tried to find a comfortable position. It was too hot to sleep, and still too dark to see much scenery through the grime. I'd made sure to sit on the right side of the train, so that I could watch dawn find the hills.

"This side of the coach is going to roast, but there might be a view."

The girl had a habit of raising her voice at the end of each sentence, making every statement into a question. It was a sure sign she had spent time overseas. They didn't do that in China. She must have been in Europe, doing what I couldn't guess. "Are you going to open the window or not?" This, at least, was a real question.

From across the aisle, the colonel groaned and rubbed his eyes. "Open it or she'll go on like this all morning. And there'll be more about foreheads, I guarantee." He turned to look out his window, and as he did, the sun rose over the mountain tops. I watched the light touch each peak separately, and each, as it emerged, marched jagged and sawtoothed along the edge of the day, nothing like the smooth, caressed hilltops only a morning ago.

"It's already stifling in here. Open the window, and I'll give you some tea." The girl pointed at the small canvas bag that served as my suitcase. "You wouldn't seem to have any in there."

"I'm going to murder her if she doesn't shut up," the colonel muttered, but he looked hard at the jar of tea she'd removed from a plastic carry bag. With no warning, the train lurched and the jar flew from her hands, shattering on the floor at my feet. The colonel rested his head against the seat back and closed his eyes. "Someone please remind me why I even bother." He growled to himself, and the next moment, he was asleep.

The girl stared mournfully at the broken glass. "This is a bad beginning." She turned toward the window, almost in tears. "A journey ill begun finishes badly." It sounded like something she had read once but never had the chance to say out loud.

"Pretty gloomy for such a young person." I brushed away the tea that had splashed on my trousers. "And much too gloomy for so early in the day. We'll find some tea at the next station." The train lurched again and shuddered to a stop. From outside the car came shouts. Two railway police had a small boy by the collar, though because of the long shadows and the dirt on the windows, it was hard to tell how old he was. They dragged him to an embankment and gave him a shove.

With the train stopped and the sun climbing, the air in the car became even hotter. The windows on the colonel's side were still shut, but I finally managed to tug the one at my seat open just as the taller of the railway policemen shouted, "And don't let me catch you again, or I'll shoot." He turned to his companion. "Or I would if I had any ammunition." He waved to the locomotive, and the train inched forward. A trio of goats alongside the tracks looked up as we moved by. The smallest scampered away; the other two watched without interest, then turned back to a row of newly planted fruit trees, which they were slowly stripping bare of leaves.

The girl was starting to perspire. I could see her makeup was already suffering. She leaned toward me. "Go ahead," she said, "open the window on his side." She nodded toward the colonel. "Don't worry about waking him."

"You two know each other?"

She sat back and smoothed her dress. "We are acquainted, yes."

The colonel opened one eye. "I want that window shut. Even if this car reaches the boiling point, the window stays shut, understood?"

I stood up. "Makes no difference to me. Broil if you want to. I'm going to get some air." I opened the door to the platform between the cars. It was crowded with people, most of them dozing, a few hanging off the side. The one nearest me moved slightly so I could step around him. "This is reserved space." He turned his head, and his left eye looked past me, into the sky, while the other searched my face. "Moreover, it is illegal to ride between the cars of any train, at any time."

"Strictly forbidden." An older man beside him spoke into the hot wind. I stood silent; the others turned to me, one or two expectantly, the rest with blank faces.

I took out my notepad and flipped it open. "All right, I shall have to arrest each of us, once we get back into my jurisdiction." Just then the door to the car behind me opened, and the two railway police stepped through.

The first one, the one without any ammunition, glared at the group. "Not one of you has a ticket, and it is strictly forbidden . . ."

". . . to ride between the cars," the man with the roaming eye muttered, and his older companion finished, "of any train."

"I'd push you off here, but it's not worth my time." The second policeman, smaller, with a cap that went over his ears, meant to sound tough but only managed to be shrill.

The first one eyed me suspiciously, taking in my clothes and the pack of cigarettes in my shirt pocket. "Looks like we've got a comrade here, riding with the masses. You know the regulations, brother?"

I pulled three cigarettes from the pack, handed one to him, one to his small partner, and crumbled the third into the wind. He knew what it meant: You and the breeze, my friend, have equal standing as far as I'm concerned. He shook his head. "From Pyongyang, sure enough. Terrible wasteful, you people are. Not all that smart, either." He had the accent of someone from the tiny valleys buried among the mountains of Yanggang, close to the Chinese border. Whenever these people slipped into Pyongyang, it meant trouble. They were all crooks. The security patrols in the city complained that it was hard to deal with them because you couldn't understand their accent, and they always had long, complicated stories to tell about the loss of their travel permits, or why they were wearing so many watches.

"That's enough." The man with the bad eye addressed the policemen, whom he obviously knew and certainly didn't fear. He was much taller than he seemed at first. Tall and thin, with a crooked eye but a straight back. "You stand around, he'll crumble another, all to loss, and we'll none of us be better off." This was no peasant; he spoke with an elegant, learned cadence that had no connection with his worn appearance.

The conversation tailed off as we passed through the next station, a wilted place with a deserted platform. There was not even a signboard. You either knew where it was and got off because you had no choice, or you didn't bother. I could see the stationmaster slouched in a chair in his hut; he didn't even wave at the train as we crept by. The two policemen puffed on their cigarettes; the others went back to watching the countryside pass. I smoked part of a cigarette but tossed it away into a ditch running along the tracks and spent the rest of the journey chewing on a rice cake I'd bought at the Pyongyang station. I reached into my pocket and pulled out the piece of persimmon wood, smoothing it in time to the sound of the wheels clacking over the tracks. I didn't want to think about how long it had been since I'd had any tea.

## 3

*The Irishman reached over turned off the tape recorder. "All stop. I'm not paid to go on any train trips. I told you, we're supposed to be talking about Kang."*

*"Relax, Richie. I'm getting you there."*

*"I'm relaxed. You're the one whose fingers are drumming on the table."*

*"I didn't know the Irish were so observant."*

*"I hadn't heard Koreans were so transparent." He stood up from the couch and stretched. "Seems like a lot of people in your country talk quietly."*

*I didn't say anything.*

*"Any special reason? Fear, maybe? Must be a quiet place."*

*"I realize some cultures see a virtue in being boisterous. We don't. Public decorum has a lot to recommend it."*

*"Especially if you need to be invisible." The Irishman pointed to the wall. "See that clock? It says 2:40. Know why? After a while, they figure maybe you won't realize how much time has passed. They figure you won't be checking your watch. But I know you already did that, twice. Maybe you*

have an appointment, planning on meeting someone?" He waited, but I didn't respond, so he went on. "Psychologically, it's supposed to be a good time for this sort of meeting—2:40, I mean. Midway to nowhere. You ever awake at that time of the morning? Gives me the shakes." Moving to the clock, he reset it to 11:15. "That's better, huh? You might say it's not long until lunch, or about time to cuddle, depending on your a.m. or your p.m." He sat down again, this time at the other end of the couch. "Tell me about your chief inspector, Pak. I'm guessing he knows Kang better than you do."

"There's nothing to tell. Pak is dead." I felt the coffeepot. It wasn't even lukewarm. "Anyway, Pak is not your business."

"That so?" Lines creased his forehead, then went away. "Let's review, shall we? Kang is dead. Pak is dead. Everyone who touches you dies, is that it? Anyone else I should cross off my list?"

"Since when do you have a list?" I stood and wandered around the apartment. It was sterile; no one ever lived here. My little room back home had more character, though this one had the advantage of a lamp.

"Go ahead, get the urge to ramble out of your system. Feel better? Alright. Forget Pak." The Irishman fiddled for a moment with the tape recorder. He sighed and pounded his shoulder a few times. "Kim, give me something on Kim. You don't like him, I got that much. I take it he is still alive."

"A sad state of affairs, Richie, when men like Kim are left standing." I sat down again and poured myself half a cup of coffee. It looked cold. "Kim is a problem in search of a solution."

"Couldn't tell by me. So far, his only sin is a bad haircut."


# 4


The Inn of the Red Dragon in Kanggye was a two-story building that had given up the struggle with the weather. The roof sagged, its windows were cockeyed, and the exterior cement facing was chipped and cracking where it wasn't streaked with water stains. A few blocks east of the train station, the inn sat alone, across from the burned wreck of what used to be a clinic, according to a sign on the boarded-up door.

I had asked at the station whether there was an inn nearby. There were several, according to an old lady who leaned against the wall with a blanket spread in front of her, selling cigarettes stacked in two small pyramids—one Korean, one foreign—a circle of rice cakes, and a few pieces of fruit. A pile of party newspapers sat beside her; the one on top was old but in remarkably good shape, an edition for Kim Il Sung's sixtieth birthday, dated April 15, 1972. She also had four or five children's books in English, brightly colored, one of them with a duck in pants and a hat on the cover.

"Buy an apple," she said. "You look hungry."

"Grandmother, I need to wash my face and go to sleep. Do you know where a poor boy can put his head down?"

"You want a girl?"

"Grandmother, look at me," I said. "First you offer me an apple, then a woman."

"Yeah, biblical, ain't it." She smiled, and her eyes disappeared in the wrinkles. I must have looked surprised, because she suddenly stopped smiling. "Don't worry, this isn't Pyongyang. Bibles around here come as thick as flies. Decent paper. Some people use it to wrap fish."

"And you?"

"I can read, can't I?"

"An inn, Grandmother."

"I know. There's three. Five actually, nearby, but two's not for you. One of them, the White Azalea, is only for military, which you're not. Then there's the Lotus. Very elite, for fine gentlemen from Pyongyang and foreigners." She looked at me. "Not you. Anyway, just between us, it's a dump. The party lets them charge through the sky, and for what? The food stinks. The cook is crooked and only buys spoiled goods at a discount. They caught him once, but his uncle is someone important up there"—she pointed a finger into the air—"and he got let off with a warning." She laughed. "Big deal. A warning. They should have broiled his ass good." She paused and looked thoughtful. "You, you try the Red Dragon. Nothing fancy." She paused again. "I'm surprised you don't know much about Kanggye."

"Why would that be?"

"You look like one of General O Chang-yun's boys. Same eyes."

I shook my head. "Don't know any such man, but we've all got to have eyes, don't we, Grandma?"

As I walked up the hill to the inn, I tried to calculate the odds of the first person I met in this sorry city knowing my grandfather, General O, "Hero of the Struggle and Beating Heart of the Revolution," as they called him on the radio the day he died.

## 5

The clerk behind the desk at the Red Dragon did not move. I stood for a moment taking in the cluttered counter and the spare furniture against the walls, trying to decide if this place would keep me out of Kang's sights. The man finally stirred but kept his face in a book. He worked his lips a few times to check if they still functioned, and then his voiced slipped up over the top of the pages into the room. "You needing something, or just here to observe?"

This was not said sarcastically. It was with considerable boredom. He did not strike me as someone who was enjoying his job.

"I was thinking about a room."

"Grandma Pak sent you, no doubt. People don't show up here this time of day, unless she sends them." I waited, but he stayed behind his book.

"She recommended you, said it was better here, more suited to me. Funny thing for an old lady to say to someone she's just met." I looked around the room again. "But she definitely had a low opinion of everywhere else." The closer I studied it, the more I realized that the place was not as shabby as it seemed. It reminded me of Kang's carefully scuffed shoes, like a safe house I had been assigned to watch a few years ago in Pyongyang: barely used, so someone had to kick the dust around and muss up the woodwork to give the place a lived-in look.

"That's good. It means she likes you." The book came down, and the clerk was suddenly watching me closely.

"A room?" I decided to get to the point. That seemed to bring him around.

"Got one. Got one with a view. Overlooks a pine tree. Very evocative."

"Wonderful. I'll take it."

We stood eyeing each other. I broke first. "I believe it is customary at this point for you to tell me how much it is, for me to say that's too much, and then for you to give me a registration paper, check my ID card, and so on."

He shook his head. "Don't have any registration forms left."

I could see four or five of them on the desk. He followed my gaze, then picked up one of the forms and waved it over his head. "These? These? This paper is pathetic. It's not even good for the toilet. I wouldn't send a form like this in. It's an insult to the nation."

I leaned across the counter and looked directly into his eyes. "You always so patriotic about not keeping track of guests?"

He stared back. "If a record is what you want, that's fine by me. But if I have it and the special police or a couple of lunkheaded colonels from Military Security come asking, then I have to give them the form, don't I?"

"And what would you know about Military Security?" There was no sense in leaning into his face if he didn't react. I turned to a TV set sitting in the corner nearest the door. If you weren't paying attention, you could miss it when you first walked in, just like I had. It was new, big screen, a South Korean make with the name still on it. An oblong dish aerial perched on the top, nothing you'd need if all you could receive was the central TV channel, but something you'd want if you were looking for foreign broadcasts.

The clerk acted as if the TV were perfectly normal. "First, this is Kanggye, if you were wondering. The place is full of special sites which"—he shrugged his shoulders—"I have heard nothing about. This means it is full of military security. Second, I'm from Pyongyang myself. I know what I know." He saw me look back at the TV. "Go ahead," he said, "turn it on if you want. This time of the day we can't get much, but in the morning and at night we can pull in Chinese stations. The game shows are pretty funny, even if you don't understand the language. If that's capitalism, I say it doesn't look too difficult."

"Been here long?"

"Three years. I was in the Foreign Ministry. They asked for volunteers to move out when they took cuts. I raised my hand and was cheered gloriously at the train station the afternoon I left, along with a few hundred others. Here I sit. It's a life."

The book he was reading was in English. It was a paperback, the cover nearly coming off and some of the pages hanging loose. It looked like it had been read and reread plenty. "A gift from a foreigner long ago. Don't worry. It's legal. I'm supposed to keep up my English. No one to talk to, so I read this."

"Very literary town, is Kanggye," I said. "You read English novels; the old lady at the station reads the Bible. She's seems a tough bird, smarter than she lets on."

He shot me a speculative glance; then his diplomatic training kicked in, and the shutters came down over his eyes. "Your room is up the stairs, down the hall, on the left. Number 7. The door doesn't close all the way, nor the window. We lock the front door at 10:00 P.M. Be inside before that, or you sleep under the pine tree. No exceptions."

"You lock the front door? Even out here in the countryside?"

"Got to. The town is full of robbers and thieves."

I shook my head. "Don't they have any regular police in this town?"

The clerk smiled grimly. "Sure, that's why we lock the door."

# 6

Maybe it was the cool wind coming through the open window, or maybe the voices from downstairs, but I woke at 2:00 A.M.

"Plenty of rope." Suddenly the sleep fell away. It was Kang's voice. "I want him to have plenty of rope. Just let him roam."

"You're the boss." The desk clerk must have been asleep as well, because his voice had the irritated edge of someone who did not want to be awake.

"Say that one more time and I'll get you transferred. Far out into the countryside. Without books." Kang's voice didn't change pitch, and I was willing to bet that his face didn't betray any emotion. "And tell Grandma Pak to forget she ever saw him."

I sat up in bed.

"Don't worry about her."

"I worry about everyone." Finally, Kang's voice went up a notch, then fell back to normal. "That's my job. It's my calling. It makes me happy. If you haven't noticed, I have perfected worry to a fine art."

The front door slammed, and a car started up. It was an old Nissan, from the sound of it, badly in need of parts. So, Kang knew Grandma Pak. I wondered if she sent him to the Lotus. I wondered if he had filled out a registration form.

# 7

It was a bird in the pine tree that woke me at dawn, which came early. The bird warbled, waited a moment, then warbled some more. It could have been calling a mate, but mostly it seemed to be talking to itself. I was sure there would be no tea in the inn, and I wasn't sure where I was going to get anything to eat at this hour.

"You slept well?" The clerk stood behind the desk, reading the same book, with a cup of tea beside him when I came down the stairs. The test pattern filling the TV screen disappeared, replaced by a man and a woman waltzing across the floor, with the man counting in Chinese. He kept turning his face to the camera.

"It's a dance program. They teach people to dance, Western style." The clerk lowered the book for a fraction of a second. "You like to dance?"

"No, not something I've thought a lot about. I wouldn't mind some tea, though, and maybe a bite to eat."

"No one in this town dances." The clerk returned to his book. "Might be some food down the street." He didn't look up. I couldn't tell if he was really reading or just didn't want to make eye contact. It was barely light, and I still wasn't awake enough for an argument, but I like people to be friendly in the morning or it ruins my day, and this guy was pressing the limits. An invitation to dance didn't count as being friendly, not from him, anyway.

"Down left, down right, any place special, or do I just wander until I bump into something edible?"

"I'll draw you a map." He handed me a piece of paper. His face was puffy and his cheeks sagged, as if he hadn't slept much.

Out on the street, I held up the paper he had handed me. It was blank. I turned it over and saw two words: "Blue sky." I began walking back toward the railway station. "Blue sky" was Pak's emergency code. He had worked out a list one afternoon during a typhoon in the middle of a political storm when we had nothing else to do but watch the trees blow and keep out of trouble. "Just in case," Pak had said when he handed it to me. "In weather like this"—Pak always said "weather" when he was talking about politics—"we need a way to communicate, just us." There were five or six terms. "Blue sky" meant "Call the office, now." Not so difficult in Pyongyang, but I didn't know where to find a phone I could use without attracting attention in Kanggye. When he handed me the train ticket, Pak had told me to stay away from phones. Now he wanted me to get to one. And I knew Kang was around somewhere. He'd been at the inn last night, ordering around the clerk who had slipped me Pak's message. It didn't surprise me that Pak might have a way to get to hotel staff around the country; if the Ministry couldn't do it, no one could. But Kang worked for an external intelligence group. What was he doing walking around Kanggye as if it were his territory? And how did he know where I was?

"Buy an apple." It was Grandma Pak. The same collection of rice cakes, fruit, and cigarettes was spread in front of her. The book with the duck was gone, but the stack of newspapers was untouched. Nobody had bought the birthday edition.

"Good morning, Grandma. And thank you for sending me to that inn." She sat there as if she didn't know what I was talking about. Well, that's what Kang had said she was to do, forget. The blank look on her face was very convincing. "Remember me? I was here yesterday."

She shook her head. "Lots of people around. I don't spend time memorizing faces, you know."

If she was this tough now, I wondered what she'd been like before she got to be an old lady pushing foreign cigarettes. "Where can I find some tea? I haven't had a drop in days."

She picked out a small apple and two rice cakes. "Give one of these cakes to Comrade Dumbo in the station office." I had no idea what she meant. "The old man," she said, and then pointed at the sky. "Real blue today."

An old man with big ears sat behind the stationmaster's desk. He squinted at me, maybe from being in the sun too much, maybe from reading too many railway timetables without glasses. His mouth turned down at the corners, like Pak's, but he didn't look unhappy. I noticed that all his wrinkles went the right way. He had a cup of tea. "Next train isn't until tonight. The freight derailed just after midnight in the Number 6 tunnel. What a mess. Scrap all over the place, and it's black as pitch in there. You can bet they are stumbling over themselves trying to clean up. Nothing's moving up or down the line." He paused to take a sip from the cup, then wiped his mouth with the back of his hand. "You might as well relax."

"How about a rice cake?" I put both of them on the desk. There was no response. When I reached to take one of them back, he nodded toward the corner of the office.

"Railway phone, to the rail switchboard. Tell them you want to route it through central, it'll get you anywhere in the country. Even China, if you talk sweet to the operator." He stood up, put one rice cake in his pocket, and walked out of the office holding the other.

The ancient phone was heavy, the weight itself a sign that only solemn matters of high importance to the people should be squeezed through the five unevenly spaced holes in the mouthpiece. You can say anything you want into a modern phone, an unending rush of lightweight, pastel words that float across continents. Not this phone. I clicked the cradle several times to get an operator. A voice from far off came on. "Okay, okay, you can't be that important, just take it easy."

"Sorry, I didn't realize I was interrupting."

"You want to be connected somewhere, or do you want to chat? Who is this, anyway? It isn't the stationmaster."

"No, he told me I could use the phone to call Pyongyang."

"Lines to the Pyongyang rail switch are tied up. Always are at this time of day."

"I need central."

"This is a railway phone. I don't do central without authorization, and the stationmaster doesn't cut it."

"Grandma Pak says hello." It was all I could think of on the spur of the moment. The old lady sat at the train station all day; she watched who came and went. The hotel clerk knew her. Kang knew her. And she knew my grandfather. She certainly didn't look like any street agent I'd ever seen. She didn't act like one, either.

"Who says hello?"

"Grandmother Pak."

A brief silence. "I can give you central and you can ask the city girls to stop doing their nails long enough to connect you, or you can ask me to do it."

So, I was right, Grandma Pak wasn't just a street agent. Mentioning a street agent's name wouldn't get you the time of day from a switchboard operator, much less a phone call placed through a restricted line. Not even up here in the countryside. "I tell you what. I need Pyongyang." I gave the operator seven digits, slowly, then repeated them.

"That's a police number, and I heard you the first time."

"You've got a sweet voice, like a sparrow. Sometime we should go for a walk, or we could have dinner. But at the moment, I need that number."

"Delighted. Must be something they put in the Kanggye water that makes you so romantic, Inspector, but are you sure I'm your type?" It was Chief Inspector Pak at the other end.

I hadn't even heard the click of the connection. "What are you doing on the line?"

"Phone rings, I pick it up, though from now on I'll have my calls screened. Too many cranks around these days. How's the weather?"

"Nice."

"That's it?"

"About like Pyongyang, only cooler in the morning—" Then I remembered he had something for me. "No clouds. Just nice, bright blue sky."

"Splendid. Kang run into you?"

"Sort of. Wasn't I was supposed to stay away from him?"

"Don't worry."

"Did you tell him where I was? Can I know what is going on? Are you related to everyone in this city?"

"No, just lots of friends. Listen, Kanggye isn't your sort of town."

"Fine. Can I get some breakfast now?"

"Screw breakfast, Inspector. Get up to the border. See what you can find out."

"About what?"

"Catch the train for Manpo. All hell may break loose, so keep your head down."

"I thought you wanted me to resign."

"Forget it."

"What about Kang?"

The phone went dead for a moment; then the operator came on again. "You want me to reconnect?"

"No."

"What about that dinner?"

"Maybe later. Who do I ask for?"

"We don't give out names. Bad for security. Just say you need '55.' They'll patch you through to me, if I'm on duty. 'Bye."

The stationmaster came back into the room. "You done?"

"What time is the train to Manpo?"

"When it runs, it gets here between ten in the morning and five in the afternoon."

The door opened, and Kang walked in. "Going somewhere?"

"I thought you wanted me to have plenty of rope."

For that I got a bleak look. "You have trouble sleeping at night?"

"No, but your car is pretty noisy."

Kang strolled around the office, the way he had walked around the tower in Pyongyang the morning we met, looking for nothing, just force of habit. "Manpo is a boring little town." He glanced along the baseboard. "You might not like it."

"It's a border town. From what I read in our reports, it's filled with smugglers and smart people who think they have all the angles covered. They get hold of a new stereo for someone in Pyongyang, maybe some spare parts for a DVD player. If they make it past the checkpoints and finish the delivery, they get to coast for a couple of months. Nice." I was getting a bad feeling about being in the same room as Kang. I looked past him, searching for unusual movement out in the square that fronted the train station. It was filling with people, a few bent under A-frames loaded with vegetables, several army officers, the rest nondescript, thin, tattered, and tired.

Kang kept his eyes on me. "No security goons moving in, Inspector. Just a crowd going to Manpo in hopes of making money. Some will cross into China after the sun sets. A few won't come back."

"Not my business." What Kang said was right: There were no signs of a security squad moving through the crowd.

"True. It isn't your business. So try another city if you want."

"Look, I'm a little grumpy. Didn't sleep all that well, not much to eat, and tea is a commodity beyond my reach. I don't like trains a lot anymore, either. So you tell me, what is this all about?"

Kang nodded to the stationmaster, who backed out the door. "We have five minutes. Sit down and listen." Kang unbuttoned his jacket. He had a shoulder holster with a 9 mm Israeli pistol. He saw my eyes flick to the holster and then back to his face. "Manpo isn't the well-disciplined crowd of Pyongyang, Inspector. Kanggye's not so bad, but just step up the line, and no one is in charge. They don't like people they don't recognize nosing around. Sometimes those people disappear. Poof. Vanish. We never find them again. Personally, I've stopped caring. I lost two men last year." He reached for a train timetable on the desk and studied it for a moment. "So if that bothers you, I'd get back to Pyongyang as fast as my little legs could carry me."

I stood up, angry at Pak for sending me up here, angry at Kang for playing me like a fish on a line, angry at myself for not just sitting in my office, sipping tea and letting the days pass. "Why does everyone insult my legs? I've got news for you. These legs are going to walk outside to find me something to eat. Nice talking to you."

When I reached the door, Kang said in a low voice, barely above a whisper, "In back of the Manpo Inn, Friday, at sunset."

I kept walking. The stationmaster was dozing on a bench, under a poster screaming about the Kanggye Spirit. His hat had slipped off, and his head was resting against a greasy spot on the wall, the same place he had slept for years, decades maybe. Posters came and posters went; he didn't seem to pay attention as long as he could snore softly in the dusty light of a yet unspoiled day.

# 8

*"You have tape in that thing, or is it just for show?" I nodded toward the recorder.*

*"Not to worry about the machinery, my friend." The Irishman's eyes opened wide in mock surprise. "You get that feeling, too, that we're becoming friends, Inspector?"*

*"Time for a break."*

*"Up to you. So far, there's no energy drain on my part. I'm just sitting here. Not even any need to take notes yet. You're just getting warmed up, I assume." He smoothed the cloth on the table in front of him. The little*

birds weren't so cheerful anymore. A couple of them were drooping with fatigue. "You looked at your watch again. You sure you're not going to meet someone? No appointments? Let me know, we can hurry this along."

"Nowhere, nobody. Relax, Richie." I held up my watch. "It doesn't run, hasn't for a couple of months. Makes people nervous if you don't wear one, though."

"Well, then. Rest your pipes awhile. I'll tell you the time." He pointed to the clock on the wall. "Or we can not worry about it." He plumped the pillow behind him. "Comfortable couch, probably better than that chair you're on." He was at ease, not tired at all. This was what he was good at, listening, an open ear into which you could pour a lifetime of unspoken thoughts. I checked myself. No one listened like that; it was fantasy.

"What?" I was musing and missed his last remark.

"I said, I'm all ears, Inspector. I'm ready whenever you are."

"You like to listen, don't you, Richie."

"Most wonderful thing in the world, to hear other people talk."

"Maybe in your world."

"And in yours?"

"Listening is the anvil that forms the sword, the fire that melts the lead for the bullet. Listening is the time to recoup, to gather your wits, to plan your attack. If you listen to anyone carefully enough, you'll hear the slip that points to their vitals. It's the compass on the killing map. People talk, but no one wants to say anything, because someone might listen."

"My God, Inspector, I think you're serious."

"Listen carefully, Irishman, I might find a voice we never knew I had."

He looked sad, as if something in him had bent to its limit. I could see he was uneasy. He tried to shake it off, cleared his throat and ran a hand over his scalp, just to get an extra second. That wasn't enough, so he coughed and looked at the clock. Finally, he crossed his arms over his chest. "However you want to proceed, Inspector."

"Just pretend you didn't hear me say that. I'm not looking for sympathy."

"Don't worry." He nodded, and I knew he'd found himself again. "I'm not looking to give any. You said Pak told you to go to Manpo. Curious thing for him to do. Makes me wonder. Why would he send you right into Kang's arms?"

"Pak spent most of his days trying to keep me out of trouble, one way or another. It's always been easy for me to step over the line, I don't even know where it is half the time. The other half I don't care. Pak didn't want me transferred away. We were comfortable, a comfortable office, nice way to spend the days. Pak took his job seriously, and he looked out for me. That's just the way he was. I would have done the same for him." I paused. "I should have."

The Irishman lit a cigarette, looked at it with distaste, then put it out. "Should have. Another way of saying, 'Didn't.'" He tapped the tape recorder. "Ready? Nice and slow. Keep your voice level, would you?"

"Screw all machines, Richie. Have they got buttons on that thing for sarcasm, or irony, or the unspeakable? Do they make machines like that in the West? We don't. We still just use our voices to help out where words can't quite bridge the gap."

"Now you're really breaking my heart, Inspector. Can we get on with it?"

# PART
# THREE

A mountain road runs by
The stream where we rested.
Listening to the wind in the larch trees,
I wonder if summer
Still lingers in Manpo.

—Kim Yun Sook (1799–1835)


The station platform at Manpo at three in the morning is filled with people, but it is eerily quiet because none of them speak. When they move, they are no different than the fog drifting past the naked bulbs that flicker on the low wooden ceiling overhead. It was August, but colder here than in Kanggye, and I wasn't dressed for it. Later in the morning, maybe I could find a jacket; for now I needed a place to stay and something to eat. I had a few meal coupons with me, some dirty Chinese currency, and about a hundred wrinkled dollars, but at this hour there probably wouldn't be anything open.

I squeezed through the crowd and emerged onto the square in front of the station. I did not expect to find anything, and I didn't. The vendors were all gone. Out of the darkness I heard a voice behind me, low and close. "You want a girl?" In Pyongyang, I would have grabbed the voice by the throat and pushed it against the wall. One thing I didn't allow in my sector was pimping out in the open. I couldn't stop it in the clubs or the hotels, but I drew the line at the street, and after a couple of months nearly everyone got the word. Once in a while someone came in from out of town who didn't know the rules. They learned, or they sashayed into another section of the city. Here, though, I had no jurisdiction. I turned around slowly. The voice belonged to an old man. The sleeves of his shirt were too long for his arms, while his trousers were too short and the waist, too big, was cinched tightly with a rope belt. When he raised his hands, a gesture to show he meant no harm, I saw that both of his sleeves were torn at the elbows. He dropped his hands to his sides, then put his thumbs through his belt and smiled. I was amazed to see he had all his teeth. "Nice girls." He smiled again, not a leer, no hint of anything lascivious, just a friendly observation.

"Grandfather, I want a place to stay and something to eat."

He kept smiling. "So do we all, my friend. So do we all." He paused. When he turned slightly, I saw that despite the worn elbows, his shirt was crisp, freshly pressed, not a wrinkle on it, and on his chest was a badge, a small round portrait of Kim Il Sung. It was from maybe twenty-five or thirty years ago, the sort ranking cadres used to wear.

"How the mighty have fallen." He watched me closely, the unwavering smile no longer necessary, past time to fade. Most people smile quickly at a stranger and are done with it.

The air was getting unpleasant as the fog thickened. It passed through my mind that standing in the damp, holding a conversation with this old man, was not what I wanted at this hour of the morning, yet there was something hypnotic about him. He glanced down at the badge, then back at me. "The sun rises, the sun sets. It only seems brighter at noon," he said, and grunted softly. "Yet right now, it is very dark." After the barest breath of a moment, the smile left his lips and his face became a portrait of indifference. Too blank, too fast. I felt my stomach tighten. He looked past me. "Not much open at this hour, but I know a restaurant. A few Russian girls. A few Chinese girls. You'll have to buy them drinks. If you like, after that, there may be a place to stay."

"No, thanks. Too complicated. I'll just walk a little."

"I wouldn't advise that." He didn't look thin or old anymore. Something stern passed over him, as if he suddenly recalled a time when he was obeyed immediately and without question. "This isn't Pyongyang." Just as the last word was spoken, I felt the back of my head explode, the dim light behind the old man went red, and my knees buckled. The left one went first, so I knew that, as usual, I would wrench my back. As I slipped to the ground, I wondered if there was any tea where I was going, and then I was gone.

# 2

I knew I was in a bed. I was pretty sure not much time had passed. I didn't know my name, or why I smelled perfume. If I didn't open my eyes, I didn't have to deal with where I was, or why. But if I didn't open my eyes, the perfume might go away forever.

There was one lamp in the room. The bulb was dim under the yellowed shade, and the light didn't get very far. The perfume was a woman sitting on a chair tipped against the wall. She didn't look Korean, barely Asian. Her eyes were closed and she might have been asleep, but she was smoking. It was a Russian cigarette. She had long black hair and wore a white blouse with shiny blue buttons. The buttons annoyed me. So did the cigarette. The perfume still won. It was like sitting in a meadow looking at rows of mountains slumbering against the dawn. I groaned, remembering how I got here. Sunrise, waiting for a black car to come up from the south.

"Good, you're alive." The woman sat up in the chair and opened her eyes. They were Asian but reaching west. Even in the half shadows of the room, her eyes were vivid, brighter than the lamp beside the bed. For a moment I could see the steppes, Mongols on ponies sweeping through villages, blood and flames. Then I realized I didn't have a shirt on. I pulled the blanket up.

"Did the earth move for you, too?" I said to no one in particular.

"Hemingway," she said. One word, but she took her time saying it. Her voice was like what I remembered from breakfast in Budapest, honey on warm bread. "Nice. But don't flatter yourself. I only took off your shirt because when you fell, you fell into something not so sweet. It's bad for business if the bed smells like a sewer." I wondered if my head had been hit harder than I thought. One minute she looked Asian, then she didn't.

I noticed she had a cup of tea on the small table beside her. She watched me lick my lips. "Sorry, the hot plate is broken and I'm out of coal for the firebox until tomorrow morning. All I have is beer and black bread with jam."

"No honey? Maybe a drop of vodka?" Beer and jam. I shuddered, and it wasn't from the cold.

"Jam," she repeated irritably. I didn't say anything, so she shrugged. People do that, it doesn't mean much, but the way her shoulders moved, you paid attention. "Suit yourself." As she took a deep drag on the cigarette, she looked slowly around the room. It was her exercise, like taking a walk in the park. I could feel myself getting short of breath, waiting until she exhaled. She was in no hurry. Finally, when her eyes were back on me again, she made a perfect circle with her lips and the smoke came out, a little at a time. "My name is Elena. My father was Finnish. My mother Chinese. I wish I were in Finland, but I'm not. I'm in this stinking city." She was speaking Russian. She still smelled divine.

"First"—my head cleared a little as I focused on each object in the room, the bed, the chair, the small table, the lamp—"I'd appreciate getting back my shirt." I tucked the blanket under my chin. "I assume you are washing it."

She didn't move a muscle.

"Second, I love your perfume, but it's drowning in cigarette smoke."

She put on a pouty look, but somehow she didn't resemble a traffic lady. "You asked for a nonsmoking room, perhaps? Let me check your reservation."

I decided not to be distracted by her lips. "Third, who is grandpa, why did he drag me here, and what time is it?"

"Aren't you going to tell me your name?

"What for?"

"I told you mine." She leaned against the wall again, the cigarette dangling from her fingers. Her nails were painted a glossy red. She wasn't wearing shoes, but her skirt was so long I could only see the tips of her toes.

"Your blouse?"

She sighed. "Yes?"

"Is it Finnish?"

"Why, do you want me to take it off so you can see?" She barely hid the disdain in her voice.

"No, it's the buttons. They're blue."

"Yes, like the lake beside the town where I grew up."

"Blue like Lake Keitele," I said without a pause, and she nearly jumped off the chair. I realized I had scored a bull's-eye, totally by accident. I hadn't even aimed the shot. "Surprised?" I tried to smile, but it made my head hurt. "Don't worry, I haven't looked at your file. I had a conversation with a Finnish businessman a few years ago in a bar in Pyongyang. He was drunk and talked about Finland. Funny man. He said he wanted to be a police detective, but there was something wrong with his knee, so he became a salesman—machinery, cosmetics, something. I didn't ask, and he was vague. He showed me a little book of landscape paintings by Finnish artists he carried around so he wouldn't get homesick. One of the paintings was of a place called Lake Keitele. It was a beautiful blue, peaceful but ice cold all at once. I decided that someday I wanted to go there."

She had settled back in her chair. "Do you know much about Finland?"

"Not much besides vodka, blue buttons, and paintings of blue lakes. I've heard the forests are endless. In the summer, when the wind rustles the leaves, they say it sounds like a hundred distant waterfalls." I felt like pressing my luck. "Your father was from near Lake Keitele?"

"He was. He drowned himself in the lake on his seventy-fifth birthday."

Another bull's-eye, only this one I didn't want. I must have turned white. "Don't worry," she said. "He always told us that was what he was going to do, and so none of us were surprised. My sister wrote and said he just announced one day that he was tired of getting old, finished his coffee, and walked out the door. It was a pretty day, in summer. The lake must have been very blue."

The whole time she was talking I was searching my mind desperately for an exit line. "The bread might be good after all." It was all I could find. "Is the jam blueberry?"

"Supposedly from your Mount Paektu, very sweet. Your Russian isn't bad. Not many people can change the subject so smoothly in a foreign language."

She stood up. She was tall. I tried to imagine how her father, the taciturn Finn, had stumbled into China. Must have been in the northeast; no woman in southern China would give him such a daughter. After she closed the door, I threw off the blanket, which I knew was a mistake as soon as I'd done it. My back screamed. I'd wrenched it. Every time I was hit on the head, I fell off balance to the left. Pak complained that I was the only one in the unit who needed an extra three days to recover after getting knocked out. The dizziness would clear—it always did—but the back would linger. That meant limping through Manpo, even though it was plain this was not a town where you wanted to be marked as a wounded animal.

I shuffled to the window. The sky showed no sign of dawn, so I guessed I'd only been here a few hours. I was on the third floor. In the moonlight I could see we were in an old wooden building. The last time it had been painted it had been white. I didn't hear the door open behind me, which was a surprise because in old buildings like this, the doors usually stick. It's easy to fix, but no one takes the time.

"You want me to close my eyes while you jump back into bed?" Elena had two pieces of black bread on a plate, a spoonful of jam next to each one. "Your shirt won't be dry for a while. Then it needs ironing. The girl who does that never gets here before eight o'clock."

It was cold, and a little hammer inside my head was pounding my brain. She put the plate on the bed, then moved to her chair. She didn't look at me, she hadn't done anything wrong, but I suddenly didn't like her or the accommodations. "You don't have to sit and watch me. I won't run anywhere without my shirt."

"This is my room. I've nowhere to go. Believe me, watching you is not paradise. When I'm alone, I can imagine I'm somewhere else. With you here, I cannot forget I'm in this godforsaken land."

"It's not so bad." My headache was getting worse, which made me determined to contradict whatever she said. "Pyongyang is peaceful. The parks and the trees give the place a sleepy feeling, especially in the summer. You can hear the trolley bells clang in the morning, and the river sparkles on sunny days. From the top of the Juche Tower, you can see the whole city stretched out like a miniature village in a museum."

"God, what are you, a travel advertisement? Do you know what you are saying? Have you ever been anywhere real?"

"Real?" I forgot my headache. "Real?" I walked back to the bed, my back shrieking at me with every step. It was all I could do not to drag my leg, but I wasn't going to give her the satisfaction. To hell with her eyes.

"Yes, where there are real restaurants, real buildings, real people."

"So. We're not real?" Getting into bed was torture. How could I lift my legs over the side without moaning like an ox? "If that's how we impress you, I must apologize. How rude of us, not to seem human to someone like you." I saw her body stiffen. Good. I pressed the attack. "We're real, every one of us. Don't forget it. And, yes, I have been overseas. Some things are good, some things aren't, same as here. Nothing is perfect. This godforsaken country, as you call it, is where I live. This is my home. The little room I have is where I go at night to find shelter from the storms of the day. Maybe a Finn would think it too cramped, not well furnished, lacking blond wood and bright furniture. But I like it fine." My voice was rising a little at the end as I dropped back on the pillow. It was a good thing I was so angry; it was just enough to cover over the pain that nearly strangled me as I remembered, too late, that I was supposed to lie on my side.

"Now you're mad at me. Why do Koreans get angry so quickly?"

"We don't. We just don't hide our feelings." I closed my eyes. "You may not always know what a Korean thinks, but you damn well know what he feels. If anything, we're melancholy more than angry. Listen to our songs. Always longing for something."

"The Russians are like that. Melancholy."

"Any country that produced Stalin has reason to be melancholy."

"And your country doesn't?"

"I just told you, we are melancholy, but it's in our blood, nothing to do with leaders. It goes way back. Maybe it's the mountains. If you can't look off toward the horizon, if there's always a mountain in front of you, you start to brood."

"The Swiss have lots of mountains."

"I know, I've been there. If you ask me, they're cold, not melancholy. To be melancholy, you have to have blood flowing in your veins. Have you ever heard them yodel? Depresses the hell out of me. It's an unnatural sound."

She sighed. "Why don't we just stop talking. It's too difficult, finding something we agree on. The silence will do you good."

I opened my eyes and looked at those blue buttons. "Surely you can find another bed." It was a mean thing to say and I said it in a nasty tone, something I find is easy when I'm tired and in pain from having been hit on the head needlessly.

Her face betrayed no emotion, but the voice changed, much less honey to it, and it wasn't just because she had switched to the Mandarin she learned at home from her mother. "As I told you, I wish I were in Finland, but I'm not, I'm here. What I did not tell you was that I despise this place. I despise this country. And I despise you. This room"—she looked around it as if surveying a battlefield—"this room is all I have. So you can eat the bread or you can choke on it." She finished off in a language I didn't recognize. She switched back to Russian. "That was Finnish. It's the language of endless forests and lakes so blue you feel it is impossible to drown in them." She smiled grimly. "And what I just said is, 'I couldn't care less.' Only it wasn't that polite. Good night, Inspector." She lit another cigarette and blew the smoke very carefully in my direction.

I started to wonder how everyone knew to call me "Inspector," but then I closed my eyes again and went to sleep.

# 3

*"Why do Koreans get mad so quickly." Richie laughed. "A good question."*

*"Not coming from an Irishman, it's not," I said softly.*

*"There's that low voice of yours again, Inspector. Come on, we're alone, you can roar at me if you want. Let off a little steam."*

*"I'll tell you a story, Richie. Take it for what it's worth. One day I was driving down a road in the countryside, and on the slope of a hill, sitting on a rock, was an old woman. In front of her was a small girl. The girl stood with her head bowed, sobbing. Finally, she turned and walked into an empty field, as if she wanted to disappear into the earth itself. Why, Richie?"*

*"Why what?"*

*"Why would anyone want to make a child so unhappy? Why would anyone who had already lived their life want to grind a child into the dirt? What possible reason, do you think?"*

*The Irishman hunched forward, his hands on his knees. "That happens sometimes."*

*"No, not like this. This wasn't a scolding. This wasn't a lesson. This was destruction, an A-bomb on a dollhouse. That child had nowhere to go, no sun left to shine, no birds to sing, desolation and sorrow in front of her as far as her eyes could see. She had collapsed, you could see it. I cannot imagine she could ever be made whole. Richie, listen to me. That girl had nothing left to hold her together, no tomorrow, no hope. She wasn't really crying. Tears are for the living. She walked into that field like she was already dead."*

*"Inspector." The color had drained from his face. "Children are like that. They collapse, then they bounce back."*

*"You didn't answer my question, Richie. Why would the old woman want to destroy that girl?"*

*"How can I know? I wasn't there."*

*"You see? You can't believe it would be done for no reason. And you know what is worse? You can't possibly understand. So don't talk to me about anger."*

# 4

When I woke, the sun was streaming through the window. The curtains were long gone, but the rods remained, as if waiting for the return of better days. The plate with the bread was on the floor. There was no sign of the girl, her perfume, or my shirt. I needed to find the Manpo Inn. I needed to buy a jacket, and I needed some tea. I limped to the window again. Judging by the sound of a train whistle and the rumble of a locomotive, I was not far from a rail yard. It seemed very close. Off to the right stretched a line of hills. The river was nearby; I could smell it on the morning breeze. Probably that was where I needed to start. Though start what, I didn't know. With luck, Pak would get a message to me explaining why I was here with a throbbing head and an aching back, instead of in Pyongyang. In Pyongyang, I knew, things didn't always make sense, but at least there I was not inclined to care.

I dozed off again, and this time when I woke, my shirt was folded on the chair. There was a note in the pocket, written in Russian. "Perhaps we will meet again, Inspector." It wasn't signed, but it looked like it could be her handwriting, and the hint of perfume was enough to make me fold the paper and put it back in the pocket.

Downstairs, the clerk looked at me suspiciously. "Checking out?"

"I didn't realize I had checked in, but I might need a room for tonight."

"Got none."

"The place is empty."

"Yeah, so?" I saw him open a drawer behind the counter with his right hand, while his left hand tapped a pencil on the magazine he had been reading.

"Nothing. This isn't up to my standards, anyway. Not even close. Bread crumbs on the floor. Attracts roaches."

"Well," he said, "it's not the Ritz."

"What would you know about the Ritz, my friend?"

"What's it to you? You Pyongyang people think you are the only ones that know about the big, wide world and the rest of us are just yokels? Time for you to leave. I've got work to do."

"Friendly town. Who says I'm from Pyongyang, anyway?"

He started thumbing through the magazine. "Door is behind you. Beyond that, the street. Watch where you walk, the jeeps are murder."

"Just one thing." I figured if he wanted to get rid of me so badly, maybe he would answer a simple question. "A restaurant."

He didn't even look up. "Too early. Plenty of vendors. They take cash, foreign currency, none of those lousy food coupons."

"One more thing, where is the Manpo Inn?"

He looked quickly in the drawer, which was still open, then shut the magazine and examined his fingers. When I didn't move, he glanced behind me. "Like I said, the door."

As I walked out into the street, I turned briefly back to see if the clerk was using the phone. He wasn't. The magazine again had his full attention. The sign over the door said NEW MANPO INN.

At this time of year, there were another fifteen hours until sunset, when I was supposed to meet Kang. It was likely he was already here. Driving would have been quicker than the train, even over bad roads. Hell, for all I knew, Kang had ironed my shirt. I wondered if Elena worked for him.

The streets were already filled with traffic, mostly small trucks. All of them were heading toward an area some distance away, on the other side of the train station. It was a peculiar layout, making the town seem split in two. The Inn was in a run-down section, the usual ramshackle buildings on narrow dirt streets that dissolved into narrower alleys. On the main road there were a few tall trees, a building that had the air of a local party office, and further on, a large shed with a rusted metal roof that sagged badly in the middle and looked as if it would collapse but probably wouldn't. In the other direction, about two hundred meters this side of the train station was a one-storey wooden building. It stood pretty much alone, almost aloof. There were no windows along the front, just a blank wall right on the street, with four wooden steps that stuck out into the traffic. The building must have been there a long time, even before the road was built, maybe before the Japanese took over, but not longer than the hills, which it faced on the back. Beyond the old building was a cleared area, where a market had been set up, and a few more trees.

Walking toward the new section, I could see it was laid out carefully, though not by someone who had studied urban planning. Every detail followed a single imperative. It was meant to be brutally practical, and it was. Five narrow roads, all packed dirt, fed into a traffic circle. The roads served lines of warehouses and several other low buildings I couldn't identify from where I stood. Only one way, a new two-lane paved highway, led out. To get to the highway, the trucks had to stop at a guard station in the middle of the circle. There was already a line of trucks waiting. As each stopped, the drivers stepped out for a document check and a cargo inspection. It didn't look like a cursory check, either. Every driver disappeared into a guardhouse for several minutes. No effort was made to move those trucks to the side; they sat blocking traffic until their drivers reemerged. None of the trucks were waved through. That meant the bribes were all paid inside, recorded, credited, and enforced with a tidy discipline that made the whole thing run like clockwork.

There were no uniforms in sight at the checkpoint; the guards, big men with broad shoulders, all wore civilian clothes. No one slouched. The guard station wasn't the normal shack. Two stories, solidly built, it had large tinted windows all around so whoever was inside could see 360 degrees and a blue tile roof with radio antennae on the top. A line of saplings stood on either side of the walkway leading up to the front door. Someone thought this operation was going to be in business for a long time.

Two women walked past me on the opposite side of the road. One wore a pale green long-sleeved blouse with a lace collar and white pants that ended just above high-heeled brown leather boots. The other was dressed more simply, a white silk blouse with black pants tied at the bottom with ribbons. Around her neck she wore a scarf, dark blue with vivid red flowers linked by a golden chain. Her boots were soft leather. Their clothing was not what you'd see in Pyongyang—not on the people I pass on the street, anyway—but more than what they wore, what attracted my attention was how they moved. People in Pyongyang walk intently, pumping their legs and swinging their arms to put their energy into getting somewhere. These women walked with a nonchalance I had never seen, bent back slightly at the waist so their hips seemed to be leading them. They walked without effort. Their shoulders barely moved; their long legs swung so slowly that you could imagine the scenery was being rolled past them. I stood and watched the other pedestrians. No sneakers, no plastic boots, no canvas shoes. Only leather. There were no children, no girls holding hands, no boys chasing each other into the street. Then it occurred to me. No one was born here. No one called this place home.

A jeep roared by, a military jeep heading for the guard post. It passed so close I could see the driver's eyes in the mirror. There was no license plate on the back. The passenger in the front was holding a Chinese-built radio scanner. I needed to talk to Pak.

When the jeep was about ten meters beyond me, its windshield shattered in a burst of gunfire, a fat burst, sort of lazy, as if whoever had been waiting to pull the trigger was not in a hurry and not worried about getting away. The jeep swerved, barely missed a work gang on the side of the road, and hit a good-sized larch tree at high speed. The work gang didn't pause. Nobody moved in the jeep.

"Let's walk." Somebody grabbed my arm. I knew it was Kang, though he had on an old brown cap and dark glasses. "You should have stayed in bed." He slowed when he saw I was limping.

"Where are we going?"

"Just a nice stroll to the train station."

"Thanks, but I'm not getting on any trains for a while."

"You want tea or don't you?"

"What's with the jeep?"

"Accident, too fast, poor visibility, slippery road."

"Gunfire."

"Really? Not in Manpo!"

"Friends of yours?"

"My friends don't drive jeeps. They also don't use Chinese scanners. The Czech models are much better."

We turned the corner just as the jeep's gas tank caught fire. I turned to go back, but Kang kept hold of my arm. "Forget it, they're all dead. No loss, believe me."

The heat from the explosion and the stench were stifling. "Pretty cruel thing to say, when their bodies are still—"

"Warm, yes, they are that. Don't fret, Inspector. If it were you in there, they wouldn't give it a second thought."

"This is completely crazy, Kang."

"No, it's Manpo." He quickened his pace slightly. "Thanks for coming up here, incidentally."

"What?"

"I said, thanks for coming up here."

"I thought you advised me to go back to Pyongyang. 'Get your little legs back to the capital,' you said."

"Wrong. I asked you here."

"You did? I thought I was here because Pak ordered me. He didn't say why. Just told me to get here."

"You always do what he says?" I couldn't tell if that was a jibe or just a question. "You're here because I asked Pak, and he asked you." This made no sense. Pak wouldn't do favors for Kang. Though I still wondered if Pak had told him where I was in Kanggye.

Kang took off his hat and dark glasses. "Damned silly, but the hat always throws them off. That's Pak's idea." He glanced at me. "Confused?"

I didn't answer. I was trying to figure out the next step.

"Pak doesn't work for me." Kang slowed momentarily to keep pace with my limp but then sped up again. He wanted to get off the street. "He doesn't work for me, but we do favors for each other from time to time. He likes to keep his distance, and he tries hard to keep me away from his inspectors. That's why he sent you out of town. Usually succeeds."

"But this time . . ."

"This time he owed me a big favor."

"That's me."

"Very good. I needed someone I could trust."

"That's not me. You've got the wrong boy, Kang."

"I'm betting otherwise, Inspector. You and I are going to establish a mutual assistance pact. Nothing elaborate, just something quick and dirty. To do that, we're going to have to trust each other."

"I need to call Pak."

"Sorry, can't be done. Pak told you to stay away from phones. Anyway, there isn't a phone in Manpo I trust, not even my own."

"Let me clear up something, Kang. I don't work for you. And I don't work with you. I'm a poor, dumb inspector with Unit 826 of the People's Security Ministry."

"In that case, tell me why are you three hundred kilometers out of your jurisdiction, with no authority, on the border with no lifeline, no cover story, and already with three tails on you?"

"I'm here because Pak told me to get out of town after he heard what you and I talked about. What tails?" I resisted the urge to look behind me. Three tails? Couldn't be. Who had that sort of manpower to throw at a nobody police inspector? I stopped and leaned against a building for support when I realized the answer a second later. Military Security, that's who had the manpower, and they always worked in three-man teams.

"You all right?" Kang looked around. "Let's keep moving. And don't worry, the tails fell off when the jeep blew up. Probably looking to scavenge their friends' boots. After our chat on top of the tower, I asked Pak if I could borrow you for a few days."

"So he sent me out of town."

Kang smiled. "He told me to get lost. You rode partway with the enchanting Miss Chang and her friend the grumpy colonel."

"Friends of yours?"

Kang pulled slightly at my elbow, enough so I winced. "Going to have to do something about that back. You could use a good sauna, but there isn't one in this town, not one I'd recommend, anyway. After you got to Kanggye, I called Pak again and renewed my request."

"That's when he told me to go to Manpo?"

"True."

"But you told him to tell me."

"True."

"But I can't call Pak to check this."

"Trust, my dear Inspector. I knew you would catch on eventually."

We crossed back over the dividing line, passed the train station, and then Kang stopped at the narrow wooden building. Close up, I could see where there had once been small round windows on the front. These had been removed, not covered but removed completely, and filled with round plugs cut from the trunks of old trees. The front door was solid, five thick oak planks fitted together, with a big new lock.

We went in and sat at a tiny wooden table, crammed near three other tiny tables, each one more polished than the next and all of them made from a type of wood I couldn't place. Unless they had trees around Manpo I'd never seen, the wood was from somewhere far away. It wasn't from Siberia; China, maybe, though I never worked too much with Chinese wood. There was a vase with flowers on every table. A girl came out from a back room. Before she closed the door behind her, I could see the room was flooded with sunlight that entered through a bank of windows looking out at the hills. Another door led to the outside. It was open, and a breeze came in, fresh, as if it were from someplace other than this town. The girl had a pretty face, and she almost smiled when she saw Kang.

Kang's eyes scanned the walls, then the molding along the floor. The girl watched him. She didn't nod at him so much as let her head drop a fraction, as if she had spotted something under a table and then decided it was unimportant.

"Coffee for me." Kang turned to her, and this time she did smile. "And tea for my friend."

# 5

"Trust," said Kang. "A wonderful thing, in short supply. You trust me. I trust you."

"And then you put a knife in my ribs."

Kang stared at me. Amusement might have passed over his face, only it moved too fast for me to be sure. "Knives are not my style, Inspector. In any case, at the moment we are in this lovely tearoom." He stood up and began examining the flowers at each table. There weren't many, but it was a nice touch. Kang did not seem moved by the artistry of the scene. Very deliberately, he lifted each vase, peered at its base, and then felt around the edges. When he put down a vase, he arranged the flowers again.

The girl came in with the tea and a cup of coffee. She glanced at me, then at Kang, then walked a few steps to the rear of the room where she had a book waiting on the counter. She pulled her hair back into a bun to keep it out of her eyes, took a sip of tea, and propped the book open, resting it against a bowl filled with polished stones. All of this was part of a routine; I could tell she did it every morning. I can't read a word of French, but I know it when I see it. The title along the book's spine was in French.

"Nice place," I said, and nodded toward the girl. "Very cultured."

Kang gave me a level gaze. "My daughter. My eldest daughter." The teacup was halfway to my mouth. I put it down slowly, but even so it rattled slightly when it reached the table.

Kang's face lit up. "Surprised?"

"That you should have such a nice-looking daughter?"

"Or that she is here and not in the capital?" Kang drank his coffee in three swallows and smacked his lips. "Strong, good and strong. Made the way it should be."

"Not a lot of coffee around," I said carefully.

"You'd be amazed, Inspector. This is a border town. Lots of things here will amaze you. Actually, this isn't really Manpo. That's down the road a bit. It's crooked in its own way, but nothing like this. This is a new town, Sinmanpo. Lots of activity."

"Never heard of it."

"It doesn't exist, officially. There's no such place in the administrative records. No official police presence. Everyone wants some of the action, especially the army. Every security agency is watching every other agency to make sure no one gets too far in front. As far as your ministry is concerned, this place might as well be on the moon. The regional police know better than to venture over here, even when they drive up for their regular patrols through Manpo. That's why the girls in the leather boots are so bold. They don't worry about police."

"And at the train station?"

"People don't look at each other. It's neutral ground."

"Nice place to live, I suppose, as long as you stay out of jeeps." I didn't know if Kang would tell me why his daughter was here. If it was a family matter, it was none of my business. If it was a political problem, then it was his business and I didn't want to know.

"She asked to come here."

"Here?" I felt a twinge in my back and thought of the old man at the train station.

Kang ran his finger around the rim of his coffee cup. "She said life in the capital was dull and too political. Three years ago, when they asked for volunteers to move out, she put in her name. She didn't ask my advice, but I told her not to do it. She said it was for her to decide, and anyway, she added dryly, it was the Fatherland's wish. You know the funny thing?"

"You're golden."

Kang folded his well-manicured hands. "I think I like you, Inspector. Yes, it got into my file that even though I am a ranking cadre,

I volunteered my daughter to leave the comforts of Pyongyang for the hardship of the border. Of course, my enemies say it was my way of insulting . . ."

"You mean Colonel Kim?"

"Among others. He has to stand in line, though he'd like to think he's at the front and gets the first shot at me."

"You see her often, your daughter?"

"No. Once, maybe twice a year. Actually, she seems to be doing well." He paused. "You don't know how to get your hands on some books in French, do you?"

"Pleasant place," I looked around the room. "The flowers are a nice touch."

Kang nodded. "Those are my idea. I told her flowers make it like a mountain cottage. Especially those tiny purple ones. People relax around purple, don't ask me why."

"What about the tables?"

"Figured you'd ask. They are made out of wood from old Chinese chests. Who knows how old. Someone said Ming," Kang shrugged, "but I doubt it."

"You said you needed my help. Alright, how?"

"I'm not sure." He said it simply, like it was a completely natural answer to my question.

"You drag me all the way up here, and you're not sure? Are you crazy? I was knocked out last night, my back is killing me, and I nearly got machine-gunned a few minutes ago. If I hadn't been limping along, I wouldn't be here now."

"I was going to apologize for last night. But if it saved your life today, I'll keep the sentiment for another time."

"You knocked me on the head? You are crazy."

"No, not me. You were arguing in front of the station, and it was attracting attention. Another minute or so, a security monkey would have come up and started asking questions. I had to get you to the Manpo Inn.

"The sign out front says it's the New Manpo Inn."

"That so? I'll make a note of it. The thing is, you weren't taking the old man's hint." Kang absently rearranged the flowers in the vase. "So one of my people had to improvise. We didn't exactly have time to plan this whole thing down to the rat's whiskers, you know. I told you in Kanggye, I've lost people up here. That means I'm shorthanded. I needed someone with no profile to fill in. You're smart. I've checked. In case you haven't realized by now, I've been watching you, Inspector. For quite a while."

A jeep hurried past, and there was angry shouting outside. Kang leapt up from the table. "Time to go."

"My tea." I pointed to my cup, still full.

"Never mind, lots of it around." Kang grabbed my arm and pulled me toward the door with one hand, unbuttoning his shoulder holster with the other. As we stepped out into the street, there was a single pistol shot from the direction of the Manpo Inn. Kang paused a moment, then buttoned his holster again. "I've got an errand to run. You poke around, get the feel of the place, figure out an escape route if it comes to that."

"Comes to what?"

"You saw what happened to that jeep. We're okay for now, but they saw you with me, so they need to figure out who you might be. You didn't register at the hotel, did you?"

"I was carried in unconscious, if you'll recall."

"Alright, keep that profile. Low, not unconscious. Don't attract any extra attention. Tell people you're from Wonsan or some damned place on the east coast. If they ask, which they won't, say you're here to meet a shipment of seafood bound for Chinese stomachs. Happens all the time. Friday is fish day, when the trucks go across the border next, so that gives you some excuse for loitering."

It didn't sound very convincing to me. "Why would anyone ship fish from here, when there's a good road up the coast?"

Kang put his arm around my shoulder. "In the space of forty-five minutes, you've heard gunfire twice. That tell you anything? And just so you know, the road up the coast is bad in most places. Don't you people ever get out of the capital?"

"Okay, I deal in fish."

"Good." He stepped back and looked at my clothes. "Not flashy enough for Wonsan. You look like every hack from the capital, but it'll have to do." He frowned. "Improvisation."

"I'm smuggling fish, not starring in a movie."

"You're staying alive, if you can. This is Manpo, remember? What are you getting in return for the fish?"

My back whimpered. I didn't want to get knocked out anymore. I'd be laid up for a week, swallowing warm beer, eating black bread with blueberry jam, and looking at blue buttons on that white blouse. Maybe I'd learn the words of a Finnish song or tap into a regular source of Finnish vodka, but it still didn't seem worth the trouble.

"I don't know, what do I get?" But I was talking to myself. Kang was gone. The door of the teahouse locked behind me with the grim heavy sound of steel wrapping itself in steel. All of a sudden, I couldn't think of the name of a single fish. Well, trout, maybe, but who knows if that really qualifies as seafood.

# 6

I walked from the tearoom toward the train station and back up the street where the jeep had crashed. It was gone, and the larch tree had been chopped down. Three thugs with flat faces and small eyes were standing around. They were dressed as laborers, which was laughable. They had the unmistakable air of a Military Security squad, but I didn't bother them, and they didn't bother me. The long-legged girls had vanished.

I looked closely at everyone else, mostly to be sure I wasn't being followed. Kang had said I could expect to be tailed simply because I'd been seen with him. Well, that was my fault. Pak had sent me out of Pyongyang to get me away from Kang. Now I was having tea with the man. Well, almost having tea. I should have told him to get lost. Not that it would have done any good. I had the feeling that Kang was never lost.

No one asked me if I was smuggling fish, which was a good thing. I'd never been to Wonsan, though once at the office I'd read in a magazine about a vacation beach near there. Everybody in the picture was smiling and looked to be having a swell time, even allowing for the fact that everyone always has big smiles in the magazines at the office. It was an old magazine, from the 1960s, when everyone was poor but still had hope.

We had hope then, too. My grandfather and I planned to open a furniture shop. The leadership wasn't sure it wanted an old hero of the revolution toiling that way—no one uses the word "toil" anymore, but we did then. He was stubborn, and they finally decided they couldn't stop him so they might as well say it was alright.

We went north into the mountains toward the Chinese border to find a supply of lumber, good old trees, chestnut, elm, maybe some maple, though my grandfather said he didn't like maple. In 1937, one of his friends had been hanged from a maple tree by the Japanese army. He hated the Japanese—all the more, he said, because they'd turned beautiful trees into gallows.

After a few days wandering around, we could see there weren't many trees we could use. There was scrub pine all over, useless for furniture, even bad furniture. When we climbed to the back reaches of the Kangnam Range, my grandfather howled with disgust. None of these forests had recovered from decades of heartache and slaughter. The Japanese had exploited them—cut a lot down for spite, the old man said, though I thought he might be exaggerating. During the 1950s, what remained was blasted by armies marching back and forth, fighting in places none of them even knew existed and never wanted to see again. Anything left was picked over during the hard years that followed.

Grandfather said we'd have to go farther afield to find the right wood, so he requested permission for us to cross the Soviet border at Khasan far in the northeast and catch the train to Siberia. At first they only granted a passport for him, with a note attached that I would have to stay. My grandfather read the note over dinner. The next morning he got up early, pulled on his old uniform, and walked down the street before I was even dressed. I went into the woodshed and took down two or three tools, just to hold them, though this was forbidden. In the afternoon, while I was putting things back, I heard him singing as he climbed the hill to our house.

At that time, his tools hung from pegs on the whitewashed walls, the saws on one line nearest the floor, the measuring tools on a middle row, and the scraping tools along the top. I was so short that I had to stand on a box to reach the highest row. Everything had to be in order when he got home, but as I reached to put a small plane in its place, the box tipped and I crashed to the floor. Grandfather appeared at the door. "Are you alright?" he asked. I ran over and put my arms around his legs. He stroked my head for a moment, then pushed me away. "That plane has just had a bad shock. Put it back where it belongs. Tomorrow before dawn, you'll have to come in and ask forgiveness as it wakes, lest it get crooked on us." He walked partway out the door, then turned and reached in his pocket. "Here, don't drop this." It was my passport.

After sitting on the train for days looking out the window at the same scene, rivers and forests and meadows morning through night, we stopped at a station in the middle of nowhere. I never saw so many trees, before or since: miles of white birch forests, rivers of tall pine spilling down hillsides, aspens along stream beds, poplar trees with their leaves fluttering in the wind growing in mysterious circles around bog fields of berries, stands of maple that I knew would explode in color in a few months, tall elms that gave shade so dense it was like walking into the night at noon. What caught my attention most of all was the groups of dead trees. Always in groups. Trunks stripped of bark, broken, leaning, branches stiff and leafless. Never a single one standing by itself. I finally asked my grandfather. "Trees are not like people." His lips tightened, and his cheeks lost their color. "They're more civilized. People lose someone, what do they do? Nothing, they just keep going. Some people lose everything, everything. They lose everything, they keep going. Not trees. Trees don't do that. They live together, they don't move away, they know each other, they feel the wind and the rain at the same time, they can't bear it when one of them dies. So the whole group just stops living." He paused while the train went past a patch of open ground with an abandoned log cabin. "Don't listen to anyone who tells you about loyalty to an idea. You're alone," he said. "Without your family, you're alone."

One afternoon, we stumbled into a prison camp. There were no fences, no barbed wire, but the air changed as soon as we stepped into the clearing. A moment later, three guards appeared in front of us, submachine guns unslung. Each guard had a dog, snarling and pulling on a thick leather leash. The guards told us to get the hell out or they'd put the dogs on us. My grandfather was in his late sixties then, but still a fighter. He stared straight at the head guard, a young fellow with a sharp face and Tartar eyes, and told him in perfect Russian, softly so the two other guards had to strain to hear, that if the dogs got off their leashes, we'd make soup of them. The three guards laughed, but they backed off. That night my grandfather didn't say much, and he was subdued for the rest of the journey. It was only at dinner weeks later, after we finally got home, that he cleared his throat, put down his rice bowl, and told me that I was near the point where I'd have to make a choice in my life. "You can't shape people," he said, "just like you can't shape wood. You've got to find the heart and work from there. There's no such thing as scrap, not wood, not people."

# 7

In the summer, Manpo stayed light until late, but near eight o'clock the shadows from the mountains fell across the streets, then the sun dropped out of the sky and it was cold. I still hadn't bought a jacket, and most of the stalls near the train station had been taken down for the night. I could trade some of my fish for a fleece-lined coat in the morning.

The few stalls still open were selling food by candlelight. When I showed the woman in front of one of them my ration coupons, she snorted. "I may not be young, and I know I'm not pretty, but believe me, I'm not crazy. Food costs money, friend. Chinese is nice. Russian will do. Dollars make the best meal of all."

"What do you have?" The stall behind her was covered down the sides with thin canvas and plastic sheeting. I couldn't place the odors coming from inside. Nothing I ever ate in Pyongyang smelled so bad.

"You just let me worry about that. If you're hungry, with five dollars you'll eat fine. Maybe the best meal you ever had."

"Five dollars?" I could eat for a week, maybe two, at home on that much money.

"You're not from here, are you?" Her eyes narrowed in suspicion. "In fact, I've never seen you before. No one flashes food coupons, unless they're new. Real new."

"I'm from Wonsan." I tried to smile like the people in the magazine at the office.

"Far from home."

"Yes, business, money."

"Sorry, I'm closed."

"Since when? It's too early to close."

"How would you know? What district are you from in Wonsan?"

I could see she was looking past me. Out of the corner of my eye, I caught a glimpse of two of the thugs who had been standing around where the jeep had been shot up. Maybe she thought I was Military Security, with them. They had picked up the scent of something out of the ordinary. One of them moved up close behind me. He had been drinking. I hoped he wasn't a mean drunk.

"Can I get some more potatoes?" It was Kang's voice, drifting out of the tent. The man was everywhere. The woman ducked inside, and I followed. Kang bobbed his head slightly and looked away. He didn't want to know me, not now. Not with a drunken Military Security type outside, sniffing the air.

"Last time I was here," Kang said with some irritation, "you had seafood. Tonight all you have is goat, and it must have died of old age."

"Sit on it, comrade," the old lady stirred the pot over an open wood fire. "Ask our friend here what happened to the seafood delivery that never arrived last week. He's from Wonsan, though he doesn't look like he knows anything about fish."

"I'm waiting for a shipment," I said, sitting down next to Kang at the overturned wooden crate that served as a table. "Of fish. Maybe I can let you have some."

"What kind of fish?" Kang asked.

"What's it to you?" I snarled. "Big fish, little fish. Who the hell cares. It swims, I make a profit, someone eats dinner. Everyone's happy."

"I knew he wasn't from Wonsan," muttered the old lady. "Big fish, little fish. What an idiot."

# 8

The party in the room next door was raucous. I don't mind other people being happy, but at that hour they should keep it to themselves. I didn't figure the Manpo Inn was a place where they smiled on parties in the rooms, but I was wrong. When I complained to the clerk downstairs, he looked at me blankly.

"You know," I said. "Sleep. What people do at night."

"Yeah, so, pleasant dreams, comrade. Do you mind?" He had a VCR in the back room, and there was a tape in it. Most of the people were blond. I couldn't tell by their clothes where they were from because they weren't wearing any.

"How about another room?"

"All full. People want to party, not my business. Not yours, either, for that matter."

"My idea is to get some sleep. That's why I'm paying for your crummy room. Either tell the party to pipe down or move me."

"I've got a third choice for you."

"Is that so?"

"Yeah. There's the door." He pointed.

"It's two in the morning."

"Dawn comes early in these parts."

"You wouldn't want me to complain to the local People's Committee, would you?"

He leaned across the desk, so close I could see the stains on his shirt from dinner. "Be my guest. They're in 305."

"That's next door to me."

"Correct."

"How about some tea?"

"Maybe the Finnish girl can get you some when she's done for the night." I didn't like the way he leered. "Look," I said, "accept my congratulations, you're as nasty as they come."

"Couple of baskets of fish, you might be able to get a quieter room." I must have looked surprised. "The way I hear it, you push fish across the border. A basket more or less . . ." He waited for me to say something, then frowned. "Up to you, I guess it's true. Wonsan people are pretty tight. Must be from having such a fat life, living by the beach and all."

"A while ago you said I was from Pyongyang."

"Yeah, well, I gave it some thought. Something about you isn't right, not smart enough to be from Pyongyang."

I decided this was meant as a compliment. "The truck doesn't get here until tomorrow. I need the room tonight."

"No problem. I'll know when it gets here. And it won't get across the border until a basket shows up at my back door. If this works out, maybe we can do regular business. Lots of fish in the sea, they say." He reached into a drawer and came up with a key. "Five-oh-one. We just painted it for an important visitor. Gets some use but never for more than an hour at a time. Your Finnish friend thinks it's a dump, but she uses it just the same." His leer was cut short by a shrieking coming from the video. "You think that party next to you is loud, you got no idea!" He turned, went into the back room, and closed the door behind him.

An amazing idea, fish as currency. Then again, why not? Maybe a little difficult to carry around. I pulled a few Chinese notes out of my pocket. At least you could eat fish. Even several more baskets of imaginary fish were not going to solve my basic problem. Last week I was minding my own business. Today I had the feeling I was slowly getting sucked into a deadly game between Kang and Colonel Kim. It had to be something more than a personal feud. Kim thought a picture of a car coming from the direction of South Korea could be used against Kang, but why? Military Security was a sledgehammer; it wouldn't be deployed for something minor. True, intelligence and security organs were always rubbing each other the wrong way. I once had a knife fight in my sector between two drunken agents. Neither would tell me where he worked, and both had identification papers that were laughable. When we reported this up the line, we got a phone call back with clear instructions to let them go. No explanation.

Kang's problems might be linked to an interagency grudge, but I doubted it could be the whole story. Pak wouldn't put me in the middle of something like that. Pak's words about "all hell breaking loose" went beyond bureaucratic tussles, and Pak had a good sense of the tides in the capital. More than that, he had good sources, including the Minister, who would feed him tidbits of information about things that were stirring in the Center, to get his reaction. Pak was discreet; he never said anything to me directly about these conversations. If there was something I needed to do my job, he had a way of telling me what I had to know—not a shred more. Kang said I was here to help. Do what? I didn't work for Kang, and I didn't have any orders from my office instructing me to help him; we had no arrangements even for liaison without strict approval. So why the hell was I limping around an outlaw town on the Chinese border, peddling baskets of nonexistent fish?

# 9

*The Irishman took a notebook from his pocket. He flipped through a few pages, stopped, flipped through several more. He found the page he wanted and bent its corner. "Finally, we're getting somewhere. Elena was in Manpo. At the Manpo Inn."*

*"I thought you wanted to know about Kang."*

*"Do you mind if I steer this car?" He looked at his watch and made a note.*

*"You going somewhere?"*

*"Some coincidence, you meeting Elena."*

"She a friend of yours?"

"Never met the lady. Not partial to her type."

"Meaning what?"

He looked closely at me. "Steady on, Inspector. I didn't ask before, but you don't mind if I call you that, do you?"

"You want another word out of me, try to keep to the subject—Kang."

He whistled softly. "Jumpy Jim, you need pills or something to calm you down. Alright, alright, leave Elena be for the moment. Let's talk about Kang. You said he has a daughter. She speaks French. Unusual?"

"Why should it be unusual? Lots of people speak French. Most of France does, so I'm told."

He turned off the recorder. "Jesus. Why don't you just point out for me the one or two subjects that you're not touchy about, and we'll stick to those. You have contradicted everything I've said tonight. Everything. Your people always like that?"

"My people? No, we mostly laugh from morning to night, joking around, you know, like life is a Caribbean island and we're waiting for the big white ship to come into port. Life's a lot of fun, that's what we always say to each other. That's what the old lady must have been telling that girl in the field."

The Irishman stared at the wall behind me. Finally, he broke the silence. "Kang's daughter. Why was she on the border? Trouble with her behavior, so they booted her out of Pyongyang? Family difficulties?"

I shook my head. "I was just beginning to think you knew something about Kang. Maybe I was too quick."

"Finally, a sign of self-doubt. This is good."

"I thought he was sailing alongside you, not working for your organization, exactly, but moving on a parallel course, just out of reach. Now I discover, when you suddenly lost track of him, you got worried. I'm wondering why."

"Kang is an interesting character."

"I thought so. Very complicated man. The sun bounced off him in a

*thousand directions. Like a diamond. Built up quite a list of enemies, as far
as I could tell."*

*"Nice image, Kang as a diamond. How many karats, would you say?"*

*"A diamond in a garbage pile, who cares what it might have fetched on
the world market."*

*The Irishman clicked his pen.*

# 10

I've seen the sun rise over the hills a thousand times, in different sea-
sons, in different weather, sometimes eager for the day, sometimes not.
Each time, I waited for that absolute moment of peace that comes the
instant the hills and the sky, the light and the quiet fuse into one. During one of my first trips abroad, when I was still in the Ministry's liaison office and traveling to Berlin to help set up a visit by the Minister,
I'd been ordered to Geneva to pick up instructions that I knew would
make no sense and could only complicate my assignment. The instructions never arrived, but it gave me an excuse to sit by the lake on a Sun-
day morning and watch day break over the Alps.

It surprised me that there was nothing peaceful about dawn creeping across those mountains. I'd seen pictures on calendars, but the pictures all lied; they were too pretty, too smooth, too much sparkle. The
peaks I saw clawed the sky, so that the dawn was wounded and the sunlight bled into the day. The Alps weren't a source of serenity. They
didn't calm your heart or even make you sad with memories. They
hulked over Geneva, defiant, threatening to tumble into the lake at its
upper end near a little town called Montreux, scattering the swans and
swamping the outdoor restaurants with their yellow umbrellas along the
shore. When I thought about it later on the train, I figured that must be
why the Swiss were so distant, always looking over their shoulders to make
sure those mountains were not about to crush them once and for all.

The hills around Manpo were not soothing, either. They were too close to China maybe, with the same pretensions of grandeur. But there was nothing defiant about them, and there was no danger they would molest the city. The hills were too tired; the city had no virtue to lose. So there was a separation: Manpo paid no attention to the hills anymore, and the hills disdained the squalid collection of buildings at their feet. Much as the Alps might glower at Geneva, at least it was Geneva they woke with. I couldn't imagine what they would have done if they had to watch over Manpo day in and day out until, pebble by pebble, they were ground down to foothills.

Kang wanted me to get a sense of Manpo, and I could only get that by walking around, not going anywhere special. The more I wandered aimlessly, the less interested any tails would be. Actually, if they were very good, they should become more curious the more I didn't seem to have a destination, but this far out of the capital, it was unlikely there would be anyone who was much good or curious about anything beyond breaking for dinner. All the good people wanted to serve in Pyongyang. Border cities ended up mostly as security service junkyards—unless a flying squad was sent on a special assignment.

I set out from the Manpo Inn before daybreak and wandered over to the teahouse Kang's daughter ran, on the off chance it would be open. It wasn't, not even a sign of life. No breakfast, but at least I felt rested. Room 501, which I'd bought with the promise of a bushel of phony Wonsan fish, hadn't been painted recently, unless "recent" had another meaning on the border, but at least it had been quiet. There was a soft knock on the door around four in the morning, but I hadn't ordered room service and wasn't curious who was tiptoeing around at that hour. When I left the inn, the clerk was standing behind the front desk. He asked if I'd slept well, but I could see his heart wasn't in the leer he tried to push across his face. It occurred to me that I hadn't filled out any registration forms here, either. In this town, it didn't matter who you were. Besides, all the documentation would be false, and everyone knew it.

Halfway out of town, the dark called it quits and it was day. That suited me fine. I had a feeling I was being followed, and daylight makes it hard to tail someone on a deserted dirt road leading up to the mountains. Once the climb got steep, I stopped worrying about the tail. If boredom was a problem for these guys, physical exertion was going to be one, too. None of them would want to stick with me all the way up a mountain, and they wouldn't have had time to set up another team, partway up the trail. More than the tail, I was worried about my feet. I knew that if I didn't watch each step, I'd stumble and wrench my back—again.

The road leveled off, and as it did, a view opened up of a dead-end valley. At its mouth, there were two buildings, a guard post, and a black Mercedes, real clean, starting to reflect the few rays of sun that perched on the top of the hills before tumbling onto the scene below. Smoke was coming from a chimney in the building that was still in the shadows. A lamp was on in one of the upstairs windows; then someone clicked it off. The other building was half in the sun but looked deserted. The buildings were about three hundred meters away, though because of the angle and the clear air at that hour, they looked closer. I could see the guard pretty well. He was leaning against a tree, sipping tea, a dog curled up at his feet—a violation of every rule I'd ever learned about sentry duty. Up the valley the sun glinted off something metallic, first only at one spot, then at another, and another. Probably machine-gun posts, judging from how regularly they were spaced. There was a double fence line. None of this impressed the dog, which was fast asleep.

I felt a tap on my shoulder and turned to see who it was. We'd been trained never to make that mistake; I made it anyway. The next thing I knew, I was on the ground looking up at the tree tops, my cheek aching. Luckily, because the whole thing happened so fast, I hadn't tensed: My back was fine. I relaxed on the pine needles and, for a moment, enjoyed the trees and blue sky.

Then the sky was blotted out by a face leaning over me. It was one of the Military Security thugs I'd seen the night before, loitering outside the goat lady's tent. I couldn't believe someone that big and ugly could have moved so quietly. In the darkness, I hadn't gotten a good look at him, but now he had my full attention. There was no doubt he was Korean, but neither could anyone miss that in his veins flowed blood from ancestors who never belonged here. The hawklike features, the sharp nose on a long, lean face, flashing eyes set deep in his head. Allowing for generations of marriage with the locals, this was the face of a long-ago Arab horseman, come far from home and trapped here by fateful orders he could not disobey.

I'd seen a face like this once before. On the road near our house, a traveling barber had set up shop. Same nose, same deep-set eyes. I'd stared, not just because he looked different, but because he had a different air; he moved like someone who wasn't comfortable surrounded by the fields and the hills. "Don't gawk at strangers," my grandfather said. Then he lowered his voice. "That one"—he nodded his head toward the barber—"beware of his kind." Centuries ago, he told me, when their empire stretched halfway around the earth, the Mongols had sent Arab princesses and their retainers to the Korean court. They stayed, or most of them, and mixed with the population.

Yes, but at that time the court was in the southern part of the country, I said; how could there be any descendants around where we lived, far to the north? My grandfather laughed and snapped his belt. "Do you think they didn't spend the night up here on the way south to Chungchong?" Abruptly, he turned serious again. Foreign blood, he warned, was a stain; it would never go away. "Anyone named Chong might be one of them. Watch for people named Chong." He spoke so gravely it gave me chills. "Watch their eyes real close."

In this case, I had no choice. His nose was almost touching mine, and I could smell the breakfast on his breath. "Surprised to see me?" He didn't expect an answer.

I started to get up, but he put a huge hand on my shoulder and pushed me back onto the ground. "No, if you stand, that might catch the attention of the guard down there. If he got off a lucky shot, it could kill you. Bad way to start the day."

I rubbed my cheek. "And this was a good way?"

He considered that for a moment. "Where you from?"

"Who wants to know?"

He growled. "Don't tempt me. If you disappeared in these hills, no one would care."

"You're not going to kill me. You'd have done it by now if those were your orders."

He grunted and stood up, apparently not worried about the guard down below. "I'm going to ask you some questions. If I like the answers, you can limp back to the inn, gather your things, and go back to where you came from. If I don't—" He opened his coat, and I saw he had a knife that had an odd blade. "It's used to gut goats." He let his coat fall back.

My cheek was going numb, and my eye was starting to swell. I was getting tired of this sort of thing. Pak had sent me out of Pyongyang, he said, to keep me safe. Getting hit on the head and punched in the face all in the same lousy town wasn't my idea of safe. What the hell was Pak thinking, telling me to steer clear of Kang and then pushing me into his path? If he knew something big was going on, why didn't he just tell me? Maybe I should have resigned, like he wanted. I looked up into the ugly face. No, I didn't want to resign, I wanted to get this guy's foot off my chest.

"I'm only going to ask each question once. Before I do, and to save us some time, I'll tell you I've checked in Wonsan."

If my cheek hadn't hurt so bad I might have laughed in his face. What was he going to check in Wonsan? I hadn't filled out any registration papers at the inn; there were no documents to trace. If he'd called the Wonsan State Security Department, they'd have had a good giggle and then gone back to sleep. They were incredibly lazy. I knew this for a fact because we needed their help once and when we called to explain our problem, there was nothing but a long silence on the other end of the phone.

"You checked. Good for you. If you know the answers, why are you asking me?"

"Name."

"Ho Tam."

Ho Tam had been a ranking party member years ago, a smart man with the normal number of enemies; he died in a hospital overseas. Ho Tam's father and my grandfather had known each other. We made a piece of furniture for Ho's family, and they liked it very much. At the time, Ho had been a college student. He was home when we delivered the piece: a blanket chest made of chestnut that I'd smoothed and polished for days before my grandfather nodded in satisfaction.

When Ho heard I'd helped build the chest, he took me outside into the courtyard. It was May, and the blossoms on the apple tree were new, brilliantly white. Ho was fairly short, so it didn't feel like an adult was talking to me, more like a brother. "Your grandfather is a great man. Still we need him, and we will need you, too, before all of this is over." I thanked him, though I found it odd he should speak to me in that way.

Later, when I told my grandfather, he became angrier than I had ever seen him. "Have you learned nothing from me, in all of these years?" he shouted. "When someone takes you aside and says even three honest words to you, haven't you learned not to tell anyone else, not even me?" His face was white with rage. "You'll get yourself killed, you'll get anyone stupid enough to trust you sent to the camps, and why? Because you don't pay attention, you don't see. Can my grandson be such a fool?"

"I'm not a fool."

"Then don't act like one. I lost my son to this. Don't let me lose the rest of the family as well."

"This. What is this?"

He grabbed me by my shoulders and shook me. "Look around you. Do you think this is what we wanted, that for this we fought the Japanese, for this I sent your father to die on a lousy winter morning? For Christ's sake, look around you!"

I froze. I couldn't breathe. I'd never heard him speak like that. Not once, never once. For weeks afterward we barely said anything to each other. Years later, when I was assigned to a guard detail for a visiting Romanian official, Ho, who by then had become Foreign Minister, came up to me during a quiet moment. "That chest is in my house. It still gleams." Just then he was called away, and we never met again.

"So, Comrade Ho, you graduated from the Wonsan Fishery College, did you?"

I had no idea if there was such a place, but he probably checked at least that much, so I stuck to the truth. "Never heard of it. Whoever told you I knew anything about fishing?"

"Word has it you peddle fish."

"As far as I'm concerned, they jump into the truck. I don't know how they get there."

"You're lying."

"Fine, someone loads them on, so shoot me."

He pulled his coat back, and the knife blade glinted in the morning sun. "Don't have to."

"Look, I'm just a middleman. I make a little, I spend a little, I make sure everyone is happy. Are you happy, Comrade Chong?" This was the second crate of fish I didn't have that I was giving away. From the funny look on his face, I thought for a moment I'd made a mistake. Maybe his name wasn't Chong. Then he pitched forward and collapsed across my legs. I pushed him away and scrambled clear. The guard in the valley was still sipping tea. The dog looked up for a moment, then put its head back down on its paws.

From behind a tree next to the road, I saw something move. Kang stepped out. "Not easy throwing a rock uphill like that. Luckily, he has a big, stupid head."

"Good morning. Taking a stroll, are we?" I glanced down at the lump on the ground. There was no movement.

Kang stood off a few feet. "His name is Chong. If he twitches, I'll shoot him."

"Here?"

"As good a place as any."

I looked back down. "He's not twitching. I'm not even sure he's breathing."

"Good."

"In fact, I think he might be dead."

"Better."

I knelt down and rolled Chong over. No fish for him.

Kang moved a step closer, no longer tensed to reach for his pistol. "Must have hit his head on something harder than his thick skull." He glanced down the valley, toward the guard. "We'll leave him here. Let's go."

"Leave him? Here? And then what?"

"Someone will find him, if something furry doesn't nibble on him first."

"I know this is Manpo, but don't the police like to be informed about unexplained deaths?"

"Inspector, please, they don't even have a filing cabinet. Anyway, it's not unexplained. He tripped on his shoelaces and fell on a rock. Often fatal."

"He was following me. Someone will know that. And the guard in the valley must have seen the two of us up here. There will be inquiries."

Kang was getting impatient. "Don't worry about the guard. He didn't see anything."

"You think you're going to pay him off?"

"I don't have to. He works for me." I couldn't tell if he meant to tell me or if it had slipped out—though I didn't think Kang was the type who let things slip.

"That guard? What is the Investigations Department doing with agents in the hills of Manpo sipping tea?"

"I didn't say he was an agent. Now, can we go?"

"Whose compound is that?"

"No one you'd be interested in."

"Suddenly, I'm very interested."

All at once, Kang looked tired. "Pak warned me you could be an awful pain in the ass."

"You want me to peddle some fish on that compound?"

This brought a thoughtful look. "Pak also said you were smart. That's an idea I hadn't considered. You'll need to be in there by this evening."

"Why?"

"I don't know." Kang stared down the trail. "No, really, I don't know. My information is that whatever is going on down there gets done tomorrow at dawn."

"Does this have anything to do with what Pak told me?"

"That depends. What did Pak tell you?" It wasn't a friendly inquiry.

"You want my help. That's what you said. But you have told me exactly nothing about what you want me to do. Or more important, why. I have developed a rule over the years. I stick to it, all the time. Never take a step, unless I can see at least that far in front. You don't want to tell me some secrets, okay, I don't want to know. But if you don't tell me something more than what you've given me so far, this is as far as I go."

Kang looked around. "Nice place for a conversation, I guess. But first, tell me what Pak said."

"All he said was, the ground was moving."

"That's it?"

I thought a moment. "He also said all hell might be about to break out."

"Not might. Will, and soon." I could see Kang was debating with himself about what more to say. "This has been coming for a while. Months. We first picked it up in February, in Japan. After our initial reports, we were told to stop paying attention, it wasn't our business."

"So you paid closer attention."

"What I don't know can hurt me. Basically, we dug around and realized there has been a decision to fix relations with Japan, finally."

"And that's bad?"

"No, nothing wrong with that, if you can stand smiling at the Japs in order to get a few billion dollars in blood money from them. But there is a hitch. The Japanese want some old problems"—Kang hesitated, then finished the thought—"solved."

"What has this got to do with that compound down there?"

"Nothing, directly. Except that's a Military Security compound, and Military Security has been unleashed to help solve those old problems."

"And they think you're part of the problem standing in the way of those billions?"

"I need to keep them off my neck for at least another week. Knowing what is going on down there might help."

"You're plenty interested in Military Security, aren't you? Is that what you needed from me when we were at the tower, some sense of the location of Military Security offices? I thought the Investigations Department had pretty good sources of information."

"On the outside, Inspector, not at home. Pyongyang is a foreign country to me. Ask me about Beijing, ask me about Moscow, even ask me about Budapest." He smiled. "In Budapest, I know pretty much what goes on, and where. But Pyongyang?" He shook his head.

"Won't it spook them if Chong's body is found on the road overlooking their buildings?"

"I doubt it. Anyway, stop worrying about Chong's carcass. It won't be here long. There will be some lumber trucks by in an hour or so. They drive fast and have bad brakes. It's a miracle no one has been hit on this road before."

"I thought it was bad shoelaces."

Kang was moving fast down the road. "So he fell in front of a truck."

"Why was Chong following me?" I started off after Kang, wondering how he could move so quickly downhill without falling over.

"He was stupid, but he had a sixth sense. Maybe you don't smell enough like someone who deals in fish. Maybe you look like a friend he once had from Wonsan. Who cares? We've got work to do, and only twelve hours left to do it."

I glanced down in the valley again. The guard was gone. The so-called guard dog had his nose in the teacup. It didn't look like it was going to be a problem to saunter in the gate. It was a cinch that the dog was working for Kang, too.

# 11

The clerk at the inn was cranky. "You know how to fix a video machine?" Through the door behind him, I could see videotape all over the floor. "Damn Chinese pirates." He kicked at some of the tape that was wound around his foot. "Everything they build breaks."

"Cost a lot?"

"What do you care what it cost?" His eyes narrowed, and he swayed from side to side like a rat snake pretending it was a cobra. "You owe me a basket of fish. And they better never have been swimming in Chinese waters."

"How would you like a new video machine?"

He looked at me coolly. "You stick to fish, alright? I'll do the electronics."

I shrugged. "Up to you. You know anyone else interested in some fish? I have an extra truckload coming, and if I don't move them, they go bad. Probably smell up the whole inn."

"Hey, you're not bringing them in here. The rule is, no animals in the rooms."

"No goats?"

He sneered. "Not even for you. You Wonsan people are disgusting."

"Too bad about your tape." I started toward the stairs.

"Wait a minute. What if I knew a certain person interested in some fish?" He paused. "Or a truck."

Kang had told me that if I mentioned the extra truck, the clerk would go right for it. "Truck? I don't know. It's new, Japanese. Refrigerated. Why would I want to sell it?"

"Because you'll never get rich with those stinking fish, but that truck is probably worth something."

"And if it disappeared, someone wouldn't be too happy, now would they?"

"Happens all the time, you know. Driver stops for a drink, or a trip to Finland." He smiled in his irritating way. "Leaves the keys in the truck. Comes out half an hour later, no truck. Driver is happy. Truck is happy. One big happy scene."

"Nice. Happy is good. But a new, sparkling white refrigerator truck is a work of beauty. Anyway, it belongs to Pyongyang, not to me. There'd be hell to pay once they saw it was gone from the gasoline reports."

The clerk was getting hungrier and hungrier. The more I described the truck, the more he decided he wanted a part of it. Even mentioning Pyongyang didn't scare him.

"Pyongyang is full of stuffed shirts and dopes."

I looked up on the wall at the two pictures, father and son, staring down. The clerk gave a nervous laugh. "This is a small country, but the Center is far away. In Manpo, we look at Pyongyang like the moon. All you need to know is what phase it's in."

"You're talking trouble, old friend," I said quietly.

"Don't lower your voice in here, pal. Someone might think we're not having a normal conversation. Listen, this place is filled with police, agents, investigators, counterintelligence goons, Chinese, South Korean, Taiwan, Russian. Last year we heard there was a pair of Japanese trying to set up an operation. Come to think of it, they said they were moving fish." He looked at me real hard, then half smiled. "Maybe I should ask you for some papers or something, after all."

"Maybe you should. Good way to lose a refrigerator truck. New tires. Not that retread crap." If the clerk was talking to me about counterintelligence agents and Russian operatives, he knew plenty. I might as well see how much more he had. Maybe he had some information on that Military Security site. I wasn't going to bust in there based on the little I knew about it. The dog didn't look to be a problem, but the machine-gun posts were another story. "What do you know about that compound in the hills, the one with the new Mercedes parked in front?"

The clerk was practically drooling at the thought of a new, white, Japanese truck. He stopped in midthought when he heard my question. "No idea what you are talking about."

"White Japanese truck, refrigeration brand-new, good tires. A battery in it as strong as a bull's—"

"Alright. Be at the river at sunset. Down by the bridge. There's a little restaurant off to the side, behind some trees. Run by an old Chinese man and his son-in-law. Just hang around outside."

"What have they got to do with it?"

"You want information, you show up there."

This did not smell right. I didn't even know why I had told Kang I'd help him out. Now I was going to be down at the river as the light was fading, probably in a deserted spot, to meet people who might or might not turn out to be helpful. "If I don't like the looks of it, I'm leaving. No truck. And no fish for you, either."

The clerk yawned and then shook his head. "I'm getting the feeling you don't have any fish, anyway."

"What makes you think I have the truck?"

"People have noticed you, pal. I wouldn't go out on walks in the hills at dawn anymore, that's what I wouldn't do." He moved toward his room. "Pirates," he muttered and kicked at a tangle of tape. Then he turned back to me. "Oh, this came for you."

It was a telex, from Wonsan. It was short. "Good fishing weather, lots of blue sky."

Even the Ministry couldn't locate me so quickly in a place like Manpo. So how did Pak know where I was, unless he and Kang were talking? And how was I going to call him? The clerk thought a moment and then handed me a name card he retrieved from the drawer behind the counter. "I'll bet Grandma Pak could get me another video," he said thoughtfully, as he shuffled into his room and shut the door.

I almost wasn't surprised that the old woman's reach extended all the way up here, to the border. Though if the clerk knew her, maybe he knew Kang, too. In which case, the two Chinese at the river might be helpful after all. I decided I needed to sit and think where it was quiet—no jeeps, no logging trucks with bad brakes. Kang had killed a Military Security operative; maybe it was an accident, but Colonel Kim wouldn't care. Military Security had orders to get Kang; now they had the perfect excuse to shoot him on sight. My stomach growled. A cup of tea was waiting for me, somewhere. Maybe it was time to crawl to the train station and get a ticket back home. Except Military Security would be looking for me. Surely by now they had a lead on who I was. Kim would have picked up something, noticed I was gone from Pyongyang, and put out a search bulletin. Someone would have read it and matched me with the man limping beside Kang a few days ago. Once they knew I was in the area, they would have doubled the surveillance. Maybe that's why Chong followed me up the hill, though it was hard to understand what he was doing operating by himself, without the rest of his team. They wouldn't all be as dumb as Chong. For sure, Kim wasn't dumb. Mean as a snake, but not dumb.

When I got back to my room, there was a note under the door, in Russian. It said: "A fresh jar of blueberry jam arrived today. Perhaps we could go for a picnic. Lena."

Lena. That must be the name she used with friends. Pretty name. A picnic was just what I wanted. Maybe on an old pavilion overlooking a meadow up in the hills, by a stream somewhere, where it was quiet except for the birds and the wind in the treetops. No fish. No trucks. Just Lena.

I looked again at the small card the clerk had given me. Funny name card, blank, no name on it. The back of it was more interesting. There was a portion of a train timetable cut out and pasted on. It listed a train to Kanggye, but that was crossed out; beneath it, underlined, was a train Hyesan-Musan-Najin-Harbin. Except I knew there weren't trains anymore to Harbin. This was an old schedule. The date, in small print along the bottom, was "Year 11 of the Reign of Showa"—1936, the year my grandfather joined the anti-Japanese guerrillas, based not far from Manpo.

I held the card up to the light and thumbed the edges and bent it in the middle to see if there was an extra layer. This wasn't a message from Pak; we'd agreed on codes that had to do with weather reports, not travel itineraries. Pak had gotten through to me; the telex from Wonsan was from him. So who was this card from? Najin was all the way up the coast, near the border with Russia. Why would I want to go up there? And Harbin. Harbin was out of the question. I didn't have a passport with me, I didn't have Ministry orders allowing me out of the country, and I wasn't carrying enough money to bribe the guards. I put the card on the table next to the bed and lay down to think.

# 12

The sky was clouding up rapidly, the tops of the hills shrouded in a gray mist; there was a thunderclap that echoed around the mountains with a deep rumble, and then it started to pour. It sounded like a freight train in a tunnel. The rain came in torrents, making it impossible to see anything, not even the trees in the yard. No picnic today. The window leaked as the rain blew against it. On top of everything else, this lousy town couldn't build a tight window frame. In winter, the cold air must pour into the room. My head still ached from the morning, and I needed to sleep.

The rain beating on the window reminded me of the first dinner I'd eaten in Budapest, in a quiet, frayed restaurant where I'd taken shelter from the darkness and the driving wind. The waiter had frowned when I spoke Russian to him, but when he saw I was alone, he softened slightly and assured me I was most welcome. He guided me to a table by the window, where the raindrops drummed against the old leaded panes. In the candlelight, I watched a couple across the room. The woman cut her food elegantly; he drank some wine and murmured a few words. She looked up slowly, their eyes locked, and then they laughed as if they hadn't a care in the world.

# 13

The sun coming through the window woke me, just after 5:00 P.M. The storm had passed, and the trees outside were sparkling. Manpo was still ugly, but the hills had softened in the early evening light. The road down to the river was not crowded. I was late for my meeting, but if they wanted a new truck, they'd wait a few minutes, whoever they were.

What they knew about the compound in the hills, and what else they might want for the information, was anyone's guess. I could throw in another basket of fish if necessary. Hell, I could throw in two baskets. Twice I checked but could not spot anyone following me. Either the Military Security squad was eating dinner, or they had improved their technique after what happened to Chong.

A few empty Chinese trucks bounced past, racing to get back across the river before dark. Along the road, there were patches of vegetables—plots the farmers tended on their own, so they worked late there, or sat and smoked if they wanted, leaning against fences they put up to keep out passersby. I stopped to ask the farmer nearest the road for directions to the Chinese restaurant. He didn't respond. When I asked again, this time in a less pleasant tone, another farmer ambled over. "No sense getting angry. He can't hear a word you're saying."

"What's his problem?"

"No problem, he just can't hear. More of a blessing, I'd say. Easier to be content if you don't have to listen to a lot of nonsense in meetings." He paused and searched my face. "Your first time in Manpo?"

"Does it make a difference?"

"No difference. Just asked. Hard to be from here and not know where that restaurant is."

"So you know where it is?" I realized I'd made a bad mistake. This might be a farmer, or it might be someone else. For sure, he kept an eye on the road, made it his business to talk to people. For all I knew his friend had perfect hearing. And there was no doubt they'd marked me.

"Over the next hill, the road meets a dirt path along the river. There's a guard post, mostly young kids. Just ignore them and look for the steps."

"Thanks. And thanks to your friend." As I turned to go, the deaf farmer gave me a smirk.

The sun was setting and still there was plenty of road in front of me. I didn't really want to be at the river when it was dark. The truck traffic was down to one or two, carrying laborers standing in the back, enjoying the breeze. A few waved to me, as if being in the same place at the same time, even here, created a temporary bond. I waved back.

The third truck that passed me going toward the river pulled over, and two men in the back motioned for me to hurry. "Get on if you're going to Old Liu's or you'll miss dinner." I climbed up into the truck bed, just as the driver accelerated. Kang was sitting in the corner, smoking. He nodded, motioned for me to sit beside him, then looked up at the sky. "Clear night. You planning to walk straight to hell?"

"I thought I was supposed to go to the river for a meeting. Incidentally, you never told me how I was supposed to get into that compound we saw this morning. You people must be very big on improvisation. In the Ministry, we like to plan things just a little. Especially when there are machine guns around."

"Swell. But there's a change of plans." The truck swerved, turned around, and headed back toward town. "You catch the next train to Pyongyang. Pak needs you at home. A body showed up at the Koryo. A foreigner."

"What about helping you?"

"I told you, change of plans."

"But my fish."

"Inspector, you've got no fish. And this truck has bald tires, not to mention a bad transmission."

"I suppose I'm not from Wonsan, either."

"Keep away from the border. You were never here."

"I need to pick up my bag."

Kang shifted his weight, and I saw my bag was under his leg. "The train leaves at two in the morning. More or less. When it stops at Kanggye, stay on. If anyone invites you off, do us both a favor and ignore them."

"What about my bill at the inn?"

"Never mind the inn."

"But the clerk."

"The clerk won't care."

"You know, he gave me—"

"Forget what he gave you. He's dead."

"When?"

Kang's lips tightened, and he shook his head slightly. "Don't ask me. Probably before they stuffed some filthy video in his mouth. At least I hope so. He gave you something?"

"Didn't you just say to forget what he gave me?"

"Don't be dense, Inspector. A name card, a piece of paper."

"You mean this?" I reached into my shirt pocket and pulled out the card with the old train schedule on it.

He took it from my hand. "You never saw this, or anything like it."

"The clerk passed it to me, but he didn't say who it was from."

"You gone deaf? You never saw this card. It wasn't for you."

"It was from Grandma Pak, wasn't it? I didn't connect it at the time, but the clerk mentioned her name."

"Back off, Inspector. Let it be."

"She works for you?"

"You don't let up, do you?"

"What's in Najin?"

"If I told you, I'd have to kill you."

I almost laughed, until I saw he had unbuttoned his coat.

The truck rattled up to the front of the railroad station. Kang handed me my bag. "Good luck. Don't worry, I wouldn't have killed you, I'm not deranged. A little too much to think about, that's all." As I took the bag, I noticed it was heavy. Kang sat back. "A jar of blueberry jam," he said.

# 14

The train to Pyongyang was late. Not like some places, where a late train means twenty minutes, even an hour on a bad day. This train didn't come that day, or the next. People drifted in and out of the station. A few set up housekeeping. There were no station police that I could see, no one checking papers, but everything stayed orderly enough. Jeeps squealed around the corner and passed by every hour, sometimes honking at a trader walking his bicycle, carrying an impossible load too slowly across the road. I kept away from the windows and back in the shadows as much as I could. At night there were no lights, but in the day shafts of sunlight played across the floor. The place smelled moldy, maybe because the roof leaked and the ceiling beams were rotting. There was probably a room reserved for officials, with more light and fewer puddles on the floor, but I didn't want to attract attention or have to answer any questions.

I found a dry spot against the wall, put the bag under my head, and tried to sleep. The jar of blueberry jam kept me awake. When I reached to move it aside, I realized what I should have known. There were some slices of black bread and a bottle of beer as well—and also a note: "Sorry about the picnic. Already I miss what might have been. Lena." Attached to the note was a blue button.

About two in the afternoon on the second day, the stationmaster shuffled past. I figured he might know something. "Any chance of a train, old friend?"

He stopped and looked down at me. "Always a chance, but they'll have to lift the hold first."

"What hold?"

"Whole line is shut tight, some official party traveling around the province, so they just stopped traffic. Nothing in. Nothing out. Nothing moving."

"And what do we do? Stay here forever?"

"No danger of that, is there. You may lose a couple of days, but sooner or later we always get a train. What's your rush, anyway? Where do you need to get that can't wait awhile?"

I thought it over for a minute. He took my hesitation for evasion. "You know where you're going? Or is it a secret? Let's see your ticket."

I patted my pockets, looking for the paper that Kang had given me at the last moment. "This will get you on the train," he had said. "It might even get you some fruit or dried fish." I asked if it would work for a cup of tea. Kang laughed as the truck pulled away. "Plenty of tea in China," he shouted, and waved his hand. Just before the truck disappeared around the corner, his head popped up again. "Books," he yelled, "in French."

# 15

"Your grandfather used to take the train all the time from here." I looked up suddenly. The stationmaster was peering at me intently. "You don't much resemble him. Except when you're not listening."

"Don't you have a station to supervise?"

"See, that's what I mean. When you talk to people, your face gets official, kind of hard, but when you're staring off, like remembering someone, then your face falls into place. It's the eyes, I suppose. You have his eyes."

What was this? Suddenly every old person I met thought I had my grandfather's eyes? "I don't know what you're talking about. How about you just tell me when a train is due?"

He laughed and put his hand on my shoulder. "Tough guy. I remember when you were little. Just after the war. Things were dirty and confused. People milling around what was left of this station, looking for relatives, military police barking orders, Chinese everywhere, and

I mean everywhere. There was one wouldn't leave my office. I told him he couldn't see the train schedules. Didn't matter how good an ally they was, the schedules belonged to us. We might not have much left, I said, but what we got is ours, and the schedule was not his business. He said troop trains were moving and transports and food, and if he didn't get the schedule, there would be a mess and I'd get shot."

Suddenly I was interested in this old man. He was telling a story I'd heard from my grandfather a dozen times over the years. "So," I said, "you pulled a big revolver from your belt and laid it on the table."

He was quiet a moment. "That table, your grandfather made it for me before the war."

"It was maple, with round legs, and golden oak trim inlaid along the top."

"That Chinaman put his boots on the table. I told him, 'Boots off the table, now, or your brains go on the floor.' "

"What did he do?" I knew, but I wanted to hear the old man tell it.

The stationmaster rubbed his eyes. He took off his hat and scratched his head, enjoying the memory. "The bastard told me to screw myself. Then he spat against the wall and left my office."

"My grandfather said that table had a secret drawer."

"It still does."

"You have that table? Here in the station?" I wanted to touch the wood, know what my grandfather had felt as he sawed and smoothed and found the heart.

"Why don't you come and see?" We crossed the main hall, stepping around people sleeping soundly on the floor, their packs of Chinese goods held in their arms like lovers. The stationmaster took out his key to unlock the door to his office, then stopped. The door was open. He gave me a puzzled look, stepped into the room, and groaned. There, on the table, was a fish, gasping to breathe, pinned by a knife meant to gut a goat. I pulled out the knife, and the fish flopped to the floor.

"My table . . ." The old man's voice was dull. "All these years . . .

I had that table all of these years, and now this." He looked at the knife in my hand, then at the fish. "Train's due at midnight, one o'clock more likely."

"Can I use the phone?" He stared at me dumbly. "The phone." I shook his shoulder, not too hard. "I need to make a call."

"Railroad connection, not for outside."

"I know, I know, but I can use it anyway."

He peered at me as if I were far away, or maybe he was. "That's a Military Security knife."

"They hanging around? You seen any of them?"

He glanced down at the fish. "Don't be here when I get back," was all he said, and then he was out the door.

As soon as I picked up the phone, I got an operator. It was the same one I'd had in Kanggye.

"You again," she said.

"Get me Pyongyang."

"How's the weather in Manpo?"

"About to storm. Look, this is urgent."

"Sure, I know. You guys are all alike. I thought we were going to have dinner."

"Yeah, a good meal. Bet you know some nice places, too."

The line was bad, but not so bad she couldn't catch my tone of voice.

"Funny thing," she said. "I can lose this connection real easy. Happens all the time. Oops. I hear static. That could mean a system failure. My orders are to disconnect and shut down. That way we don't cascade."

"You don't what?"

"I don't know. That was what they told us last Saturday. One girl had to admit she'd been talking to her boyfriend, a Colonel Yun in Haeju or something, and next thing you know, wham, a cascade. Is she ever in trouble."

I didn't say anything.

"You're not mad at me, are you?"

I coughed lightly.

"Listen, I'm sorry. There is really a lot of pressure around here. They scream at you when you lose a connection, as if this crummy equipment can ever work two calls in a row. It's Russian, you know what I mean? Built like those old Soviet ladies. Not like those Russian girls today, so pretty. I saw one on TV the other night. They seem to be doing okay these days, if you know what I mean."

I gave her a number.

"That same police line."

"I need to report a crime."

She whooped. "From Manpo? Man, I'd never get a free minute if people reported every crime in Manpo. Hang on, here we go."

There was a faint click, a moment of silence when I thought she had cut me off, then Pak's voice nice and calm on the other end.

"You're late, you're absent without leave, you're missing in action, where the hell are you, and why the hell are you still on the border?"

"More important, did you have any idea what is going on up here, before you packed me off? Military Security just sent me a message. I think it was a death threat."

"A what?"

"A fish with a goat knife stuck in its guts."

"Very subtle, those guys." It was silent for a moment, and I thought we'd been disconnected. Then Pak said, "Spare me the details right now. Put a full report on my desk when you get here. You can write it on the train. You'll have plenty of time, and nothing else to do."

"If we ever get a train. It's all locked up."

"Some Comrade Big or another." Pak was normally more discreet than this on the phone. "Anyway, it's not your concern. Your business is here. I have a dead body, a foreigner, a Finn from the looks of it. I'll tell you when I see you, and it better be soon." A series of clicks, a dead space, then a buzz.

The operator got back on the line. "That was a cascade."

"Somebody's boyfriend somewhere."

"You're not a colonel, are you?" There was a note of alarm in her voice.

I laughed. "Not even close."

"Dinner. Don't forget."

There was no sense replying because the phone started buzzing and then a new, tinny voice on the other end shouted that this was railway communications equipment, reserved for railway business, it was a breach of security to use it for personal business.

"We need a train," I barked.

A pause, then a suspicious "Who is this?"

"Never mind who this is, friend. Military Security says the train to Pyongyang better be here in three hours, or files start getting pulled."

The other end wasn't cowed. "The province is locked up top to bottom. No trains move without authorization. Those are my orders, so don't threaten me."

"Don't worry, friend, this isn't a threat. This is Senior Colonel Kim, Military Security, acting on direct and personal instructions of Colonel Yun, Haeju Field Headquarters. Get a train up here on the double, or I'll see you tomorrow—say, about midnight?"

Nobody in his right mind would follow an order like that.

Nobody did.

# PART FOUR

So long was I on the northern frontier,
Even my dog growls at my footsteps,
I had hoped to sing with friends beneath
The stars on my return, but some have died,
And two have moved to Pyongyang, much
the same thing.

—Hong Ki Bo (1665–1710)

As soon as I got off the train in Pyongyang, I called the office. They gave me a terse detail or two.

"That's it?" I wasn't in the mood for incomplete information anymore.

They squeezed out another sentence. Then, almost as an afterthought, "One more thing. Pak said if you called, he wants you over at the Koryo, eighth floor." There was a brief pause. "Where you been for the past few days?"

"No place good."

It wasn't far from the station to the hotel, and anyway I needed the exercise, so I walked. I considered getting a cup of tea in the hotel coffee shop but decided to do it on the way out. The elevator man was dozing in a chair. When I told him I wanted the eighth floor, he hesitated. "Ministry of People's Security." I showed him my ID. He frowned.

There was only one room with an open door on the eighth floor. Even from the hall, it was obvious that the place had not been properly secured or searched. There were no signs of the bits of tape that are supposed to be put on the door frame to show that a crime scene has been gone over, red tape for fingerprints, blue for the crime photographer. At one point, there used to be a piece of yellow if a guard was posted to restrict entry, but yellow tape is hard to get, so you don't see much of it anymore on door frames.

I knew what had happened; I'd been through it before. The place had been treated more like a museum than a murder scene, officials rotating glumly through, stopping here and there, a few rocking back and forth as they stood, glancing at their watches and wondering if it was near lunchtime. If there was a single real clue left in the room, it would be a miracle. Hotel security had wandered in—the piece of green tape on the hallway door was theirs—but they probably accomplished nothing useful beyond nervously gripping a chair for support, fretting about getting blamed, and wondering how to make a finding of "natural causes" compatible with a crushed skull.

# 2

"No good, Inspector. I'm not interested in police business. Maybe some other time."

"Patience." He closed his notebook. "You owe me a thanks. I told you the color of the railway phone."

"You also gave me a police telephone number, which I can't use. Do I believe you about Kang killing that Middle Eastern fellow?"

"He wasn't Middle Eastern, not for the last fifteen generations, anyway."

"People keep track?"

"Sometimes. I may have been paying more attention than normal because of the way he had his nose stuck in my face."

"Why should I care about this body at the hotel?"

*"If you want to know about Kang, that's the only way to do it."*

*"Kang must have decided he could trust you, if he told you anything about the Japan operation. Who did he first hear it from? Pak?"*

*"What makes you think Pak knew anything about Japan?"*

*The Irishman smiled. "I don't know anything about your sad country. That's why I'm investing in all of this tape." He pointed at the recorder. "I've been to Japan, though." He wiggled his eyebrows and laughed. "You thought I'd never been in the mysterious East, didn't you, Inspector?"*

*"You ever get to Pyongyang, Richie, call me. I'll take you to dinner, that's a promise."*

## 3

From my conversation with the office before coming over to the Koryo, I knew that hotel security had done at least one thing right: They'd called the liaison office in the People's Security Ministry as soon as the body was discovered. From there everything went wrong. There had been a moment of genuine panic at the Ministry when the first identification, based on a card in the blue polyester pants pocket, suggested the deceased was a Finnish citizen, and worse, an inspector for the International Atomic Energy Agency. Panic led to a call directly to the Foreign Ministry duty officer, breaking all rules. The chain of command was supposed to run through hotel security to the police, then to the party's security organization, from there to the party liaison in the Foreign Ministry, and only then to the Ministry's unfortunate duty officer, usually someone junior. That night, not only was the duty officer junior, but because it was a Saturday, it was his very first shift alone. He didn't bother to look in his instructions manual to see that he wasn't supposed to take a call about the murder of a foreigner from anyone but his own party liaison man. Even so, he was smart enough to realize that the death of an IAEA inspector would be a disaster.

Too bad he did the worst thing possible. He called a friend of his, a Captain Choi in the Military Security Command. Choi, smart and on his way up, checked his manual and alerted his duty officer, who called the police to ask why the hell the Foreign Ministry was involved in a state security investigation.

This caused seventy-two hours of complaints and accusations by various liaison officers, during which time the body was moved to the central morgue, well before any sort of crime scene report was written, much less filed. Just as things were calming down, the Military Police of the Pyongyang Military Garrison raised hell. It was one of those rare occasions when they were supposed to be alerted, but no one had their number—and even if they had, no one would have remembered to call.

Just as I walked through the front door of the room, Chief Inspector Pak emerged from the bathroom, wiping his hands on his shirt. "About time you showed up, Inspector."

"A pleasure, I'm sure. Do you want to hear about my trip and my conversations with Kang?"

"Screw your trip. Screw Kang. I have a dead foreigner in the morgue that no one can identify, cause of death unknown, time of death unknown, and a summons to see our friend Kim of Military Security this afternoon at three. Care to join me?"

"Pass. I've spent the past week dodging him, and I have reasons not to want to see him anytime soon. You were right. It's a good idea for me to keep as far away from him as possible."

"Luckily, someone is leaning on him over this case. I don't know who, yet, but as long as he is feeling some pain, he'll behave with us. I know his type. He's nervous, and he needs help. If this goes bad, he could end up walking to work in a coal mine."

I had developed a sour feeling about this case from the moment I heard how the notification had gone out of channels. The fact that there were no signs of an investigation had set off more warning bells.

Now I knew I was right. This was not an incident we wanted to touch. There was no way to win. Somebody's ox was going to be gored, and everyone else would try to make sure it was ours. Nothing was moving the right way. Simply getting things unsnarled to zero would take me a week, and by then there would be no trail left to follow.

"Why do we have to take this case? It's a foreigner, and we only deal with foreigners if there is a crime."

Pak raised an eyebrow. "Murder is usually defined as a crime. Criminal Code, Chapter 8, Section 1, Article 141, unless there are extenuating circumstances; also Article 142, fit of rage, or 143, self-defense."

"But we don't know where it happened, much less who's responsible and under what circumstances."

"That's what the investigation is for, Inspector."

"That assumes we can investigate. If another foreigner did it, and if it happened outside the capital, then we have no jurisdiction. We touch a case with dead outsiders, we'll get nothing but interference from the Foreign Ministry. On top of that, we'll get blamed for not solving it, and at this point, believe me, no one can solve it."

"You just stuck your nose in the door and you know all that?" As soon as Pak frowned, I knew where we were heading. I tried to put my mind somewhere else, somewhere peaceful, before he started the lecture. "Let me make something clear, Inspector: This is the capital city. It may not be a fine and fancy place, like Geneva or Prague, but it is the capital of our country, and it is the responsibility of our unit to keep it safe. At this moment, it is not safe. This isn't the border, Inspector, this is the capital, and I'm damned if I'll have dead bodies turning up, not anywhere, not on highways, not in hotel rooms. So, like it or not, we are going to find out what happened here. And we will do so quickly. And when I say 'we,' Inspector, I mean 'you' very specifically. I need a report by 2:45, something I can stuff down Kim's gullet."

As he pressed the elevator button, Pak turned and waved toward the room in a gesture of frustration. "Find me something, anything. That will give us a couple of days." The elevator door opened, and he said to no one in particular as he stepped in, "Too bad. Nice room, actually has a view."

# 4

I couldn't tell much about the view because the heavy curtains were shut, but as far as I could see, there was nothing special about the room. It had the normal dark entry hall, a small, slightly raised sitting parlor, and a bedroom. The carpet in the bedroom was worn in spots. There were two narrow beds, each covered by a shiny red silk quilt with a circle of flowers embroidered in the center. The short, square lamp on the table between the beds was new, as was the white phone that shared the space. A TV sat against the wall, facing a chair near the window. The bathroom had been renovated recently; it was one of those modular bathrooms with a low ceiling that makes you think you're in a fiberglass space ship. I never liked fiberglass. It doesn't grow anywhere.

When they were first installed, the bathrooms must have been considered modern and efficient, but they didn't wear very well, especially since hotel guests aren't all that careful. The shine rubbed off, and then the color went flat. They couldn't be painted, so the only thing to do was to replace the whole module. Usually the fixtures got broken in the process, so that meant replacing them as well. This one had a new sink—nothing fancy, but gleaming, like new sinks do. It didn't look like it had been used more than once or twice. The thin towels weren't new and didn't match, but they were clean, folded precisely, and hanging neatly from the towel bar. There was a phone over the toilet. Why anyone needed a phone in the bathroom, I never understood.

The sitting room had a couch that could hold two people if they were friendly, a couple of chairs, a standing lamp with an old silk shade, and a wooden table, badly stained pine, standing slightly askew. On the table was a glass vase with a bunch of wilted flowers. The shelves next to the closet in the entry hall were empty. So was the small brown refrigerator that sat in a nook between the armoire and a built-in chest of drawers. I opened every drawer. Each one squeaked as I pulled it out. Nothing a little soap on the runner couldn't fix.

"The foreigner was on the floor, in the sitting room. It looked like he had tripped on the light cord, but no one could hit his head so hard on such a small table and leave that vase standing."

I turned around to find the floor lady standing in the hall, a short, compact woman of about forty, in a plain brown dress with a white apron. I hadn't heard her footsteps because she had on socks but no shoes. "I found him. I went in to see if there was a bottle of water in the refrigerator, and there he was. I never seen a skull bashed in like that." She paused and then added, with a note of disapproval over what she seemed to think was a breakdown in procedure, "I didn't know anyone had checked into this room."

"My name is O." I bowed slightly to her and smiled. Most inspectors like to begin conversations with a witness on a menacing note—standard procedure, the way they teach it at training class—but I needed this woman on my side. She acknowledged my gesture with the slightest softening around her eyes, not yet a smile but something to build on.

"You a police inspector?" Without waiting for an answer, she continued, "Chief Inspector Pak scolded me, but what does he expect? If I had called him, I'd lose my job."

"Pak will be alright. Why don't you come in and sit down?"

"I can't sit in the rooms." She leaned against the open door. "I'm not even sure you can if you don't register."

I sat down on the couch in the sitting room, pulled the heavy curtain to one side, and looked out the window to make the point that the hotel's normal regulations didn't concern me. "Comfortable, tidy, nothing out of place. Tell me, why would you put flowers in a room you thought was empty?"

"They aren't our flowers. I don't bunch them up, and I don't have any vases like that one. We grow our own flowers out back, in the garden. Nothing purple, and if we did, I would never cut it so short. Anyway, that vase is all wrong. Too narrow a neck. Why put a bunch of flowers in something like that? Makes it look like they're in prison. The whole idea of flowers in the rooms is to make it seem like outdoors."

"Like a mountain meadow, or at least a cabin."

"Yes," she studied me to see if I was mocking her, which I wasn't. "At least like the hills after the rain."

"I'm not asking about the arrangement. I'm asking, if they aren't your flowers, who put them in the vase?"

"How do I know?"

I didn't like it when a witness answered my question with a question. It usually meant I had lost control. "Were they here when you found the body?"

"I couldn't say. I mean, it's awful dark in these rooms with the curtains closed."

"So, they weren't your flowers, you didn't put them in the vase, and you're not sure if they were here when you discovered the body or not. If they weren't already here, who would have put wilted flowers into a vase in a room with a murdered man?"

"Not me."

"Very good, not you. We've more or less established that. Then who?" She was edging into the room as we talked, and I could see she was looking for something, hoping I wouldn't notice. "Anything missing?"

"There isn't. No." She shook her head slightly, but her eyes were darting around.

I took out my notebook. "I'll need your name, for the record. And when I leave, I will have to instruct you to lock the door and let no one in here without my permission." Her eyes stopped darting and searched mine. "I mean that literally, no one. I'll get an MSS guard here as soon as I can, but for now, it's your responsibility."

"My name is Li, Li Yong Hui. I can't make any promises. The locks on these doors barely keep out the breeze, Inspector. And as we can see from your sitting on that couch, not too many people take orders from me."

I closed my notebook, then opened it again. It was meant to be a gesture of authority, tinged with annoyance. Pak could carry something like that off, but it usually only made me look indecisive. From the expression on the floor lady's face, I needed to practice it more. "I'm going to look around the room, make some notes. You can stand there in the doorway and watch or go about your business, Mrs. Li. In any case, this room is now the scene of a crime against the people, officially. That means the normal rules don't pertain. This room belongs to me until the crime is solved, and when you tell people they cannot enter, you are speaking for me, is that clear?" This was not even remotely true, but it might get me some extra cooperation from her, and it wouldn't bring her any harm. "Any information you have about the events or the scene is important to the solution of the crime, the apprehension of the criminals, and the dignity of the fatherland. You will be contacted by my office for a formal interrogation in a day or two. I trust we can work together."

She said nothing. Partly she was judging whether I was going to cause her extra grief, partly whether there was anything to gain from going along with my game. She nodded, not very convincingly I thought, and padded down the hall.

My second walk through the rooms took five minutes. There was still nothing to see. Everything had been bumped or jostled. The bedroom had been dusted and waxed in the three days since the body was moved out. I sat in the chair and turned on the TV with the remote. There was a children's cartoon on. A weak old king, a lovely princess, a handsome commoner sitting under a tree looking at the mountains. Even in a cartoon, mountains. I turned it off before the fire-breathing dragon appeared. There had to be a dragon, and he was going to threaten to barbecue the princess. Actually, he wanted something else, but they couldn't put that in a cartoon, not in this country, anyway.

The bathroom was spotless. The refrigerator was unplugged, and water from the melted ice had pooled on the bottom shelf. There was no water bottle, but there was a faint odor, as if something had been rotting. I looked in the sitting room again. No mess on the floor near the table. Skulls are not empty, and when they are crushed, they leak all manner of unpleasant things that don't clean up easily. There was no way the carpet had already been replaced, not in this hotel, not in this city. So what happened to the mess?

As I walked out the door, thinking about lunch, something nagged at me. I hadn't checked the closet. I went back and stuck my head inside. The entry hall light didn't work, which made the entry hall dark and the inside of the closet even darker. I didn't have a flashlight with me; even if I did, the battery wouldn't work. My eyes refused to adjust; there was no light, nothing to adjust to. I felt along the shelves that took up one side of the closet, but they were empty. I swept over the long shelf along the top. There wasn't anything, not even an extra blanket. Finally, I got down on my knees and traced my hand along the edges of the closet floor. In the far corner, my fingers found something small and round. I picked it up, walked into the hall, and turned it over in my hand. It was a button, blue like the sky, blue like a lake in a Finnish summer.

# 5

I was at my desk, typing an initial report, when Pak walked in. "You dispatched a guard to the Koryo?"

"I did. The room is a joke, but we might as well preserve what we can."

"On whose authority did you send the guard?"

"Mine. I do it all the time. It was standard procedure, last time I checked. If I ask for permission, we lose a day or two getting approval, by which time a guard is useless."

"I've pulled him."

"You what?"

"Captain Kim said a guard would only attract attention, and he wanted no attention. Also the Foreign Ministry said it would scare the foreign guests."

I yanked the form out of the typewriter. "Then there isn't any sense in starting a file, because there can't be any investigation."

Pak leaned against the edge of my desk. "You seem unhappy these days, Inspector. Nervous, jumpy."

"No, thanks, I'm against another vacation to the border." I sat back in my chair and focused on the molding between the ceiling and the wall. Our offices were in an old building, one of the first to rise from the shattered city after the war as a symbol of defiance and a statement of victory for people who had lost everything. Most of the trim had been stripped off over the years, victory not being all it was made out to be. A little remained, though, miraculously in my office. The molding had been carved by someone who had taken pride in his work, but the features had disappeared under layers and layers of paint. I often promised myself, on quiet afternoons, that I would find a ladder tall enough, climb up and take the molding down, sand off the paint, and restore it to its original glory. Sometimes I thought it was flowers or vines, but it might also be birds in flight. I had to hope it wasn't something foolish, like a line of workers waving tools.

Pak moved to the doorway. "I leave for Kim's lair in fifteen minutes. You can go partway. We'll stroll by the river. It's too nice to drive." That meant he hadn't received the month's gas ration yet, but he always hated to admit it to me.

# 6

Sitting at my desk the next morning, I sketched the layout of the hotel room on the back of an old memo. I don't read memos—especially those that come from the Ministry once a week—but they make good scrap paper. The body had been moved to the hotel from somewhere else and dumped next to the lamp table. Dumped, I was sure of it. I put the sketch to one side and reached in my pocket for the persimmon wood. After I ran my fingers over the smooth surface, my thoughts settled into place. Whoever did it wasn't trying to cover up the murder. They didn't even break a sweat setting it up like it was an accident. Hell, they didn't even go to the trouble of renting the room. All their energy was spent covering their tracks, and that they had done effectively. Not one of the hotel staff had seen anything, so they said, though that was hard to believe. The whole purpose of the staff, especially at a place like the Koryo, which is filled with foreigners, is to observe, to see. Making the beds is secondary. It is the ultimate negation of their purpose if a guest is murdered in the hotel or, even worse, a dead body is carried up—much less down—the elevator and none of them notice. Normally, if the staff has been instructed to say "didn't see anything," there is something indicating otherwise: a tightening of the shoulders, a glance held too long or not at all. I had sensed none of that in my first set of interviews with them. Some people can lie outright to me and get away with it. Not hotel staff.

I gave one last swirl to the persimmon; it was as smooth as it would get. I opened the drawer to my desk, tossed the piece in, and rummaged around for a chip that I hadn't worked on yet. There was some pine, but that was boring. Too easy, no character, nothing to help the concentration. Next to it was a piece of camphor wood. Not bad for winter when I had a cold, but otherwise it would make my fingers stink and my eyes water. Near the back of the drawer was an old piece of walnut. Tough and hard. Just what I needed for this case. Under the walnut was something I didn't expect, a torn, worn piece of sandpaper.

Sandpaper was hard to get, especially good sandpaper. Whenever I went overseas, or knew someone going on a trip, I tried to get another piece. Other people wanted tins of biscuits or televisions. I asked for sandpaper.

Once, when I was coming back from supporting a delegation to Eastern Europe, a border guard at the train station opened my suitcase and found four sheets of medium sandpaper, the sort you use when you can't find the grade you really want. The guard was young, and I could see he was trying to do his job. "What is this?" He was scowling. There was nothing in the regulations about sandpaper, but he was suspicious. No one had ever brought it in before, and exactly for that reason there must be something dangerous about it.

"It's sandpaper. I'm building wooden statues of the Leader, and to do it right, they have to be smooth, you know what I mean?" I winked. "Smooth as a baby's bottom." That flustered him. Referring to the Leader and a baby's bottom in the same breath was vaguely troubling. "You take away this sandpaper, the statues will be pretty ugly, and people will want to know why. They may question me. They may torture me. I'd have to tell them who confiscated the sandpaper." By now the guard was squirming, his face was flushed, and he was looking around for his squad leader, but his squad leader was probably off smoking behind a shed somewhere.

Anytime I wanted to build something, sandpaper was the bottleneck. Sawing and drilling a few holes didn't take much time, but then things sat around because I couldn't get any fine sandpaper. My grandfather used to argue that fine sandpaper was an invention of the devil. He believed, and said this with great conviction, that it was a question of concentration and patience. Any piece of wood could be made smooth and lustrous, he said. This only meant discovering what had been there all along; it had nothing to do with sanding. People who sanded wood without thinking were more apt to ruin than improve it. And people who used fine sandpaper were the worst, he insisted, because they wore down the wood instead of bringing it to life.

One day I found a book about inventions. It said that an American had invented sandpaper in the 1830s. "Who needed it!" my grandfather waved the idea away with an angry gesture. "My father's father prepared wood for furniture by smoothing it to a silken shine. He used a smoothing tool like a magic cloth, people used to say. There were no Americans around then, I can tell you that."

I wasn't going to argue, but I was interested in why he was so adamant. "Because we are always being portrayed as behind, beholden to others, backward and beggars." His face flushed when he spoke like this. "Not Americans, not Chinese, not Japanese—we've been making furniture for hundreds and hundreds of years. Beautiful furniture, when America was still covered with trees and peopled by savages who wore animal skin for clothing. What would they know about wood, about how to coax it, talk to it, romance it, sing to its spirit? Do they have any real carpenters there?" I didn't say anything, because when he was mad like this he treated me as if I were one of the enemy, someone who had gone abroad and come back tainted. "Well, do they, Mr. Korea-Not-Good-Enough-for-You-Anymore?" He was glad I was being assigned on travel out of the country—it meant I was trusted—but he worried I would decide not to be Korean anymore. "Sand!" He snorted. "Why would you use sand, anyway, on a piece of wood? Sand is fine for metal, maybe, but wood, wood, wood is like a beating heart."

"So now you're telling me that Koreans did not invent sandpaper because it is a bad idea."

"All I'm saying is that no one taught us how to smooth wood. We've known how to do it for a long time, longer than America has existed, and no American ever invented anything that I would want to use."

To please him, I said I would try the old way of smoothing wood.

"You wait," he said as he went into the back room and came out with the same simple scraping tool that I had dropped years ago. Heavy and unbalanced in my hand, it claimed its revenge by nicking the wood whenever my concentration drifted. When my grandfather took it from me, the damn thing assumed an intolerable grace, moving gently over rough spots with a soft "shhhusss." It sang so smoothly, he said, that the wood found its true shape and never wanted to be anything else.

Long after my grandfather died, I sanded wood in the evenings, alone in the back of the apartment house, as the stars came out. Constantly my fingers felt the wood; even in the dark I could tell if I was getting close to the heart. Concentrating on bringing the wood to life, listening for that song, my mind wandered until I was far away. My working alone like this annoyed our local security man, a tough veteran of the war. He limped from pieces of shrapnel still in his leg, dragging his left foot slightly behind him. Before he came around the corner of the apartment house, I knew it was him. He would stand silently watching me. Sometimes we would exchange a few words, but usually there was only the slight "shhhh-shhhh" of the sandpaper moving across the wood, not quite a song but tolerably close. Even on days when I was supposed to be in a study session, I was sanding, sometimes humming to myself. "Not healthy activity," said the paper they slipped under the door of my apartment. "Too solitary." Just to annoy them, when I finally did go to a study session, I told them that sandpaper had been invented by an American.

One night after work, I came back to the apartment and my stock of sandpaper was gone. Pak said it was my own fault for waving it under their noses. Then he told me he would help me build up a new stock. "Keep it in your office, but put it out of sight and don't invite other people to admire it. They won't care, believe me, and someone is liable to mention it to someone else."

The piece of sandpaper in my desk was worn but still had some life in it. I folded it carefully and put it in the third drawer of my filing cabinet, with the rest of my meager stock. Then I went back to my desk and stared at the sketch of the hotel room. I added the closet and drew a little button on the floor.

I was beginning to think that whoever had dumped the body had avoided the staff completely. No one was even trying to feed something tiny into the investigation, a crumb of a "clue" in an offhand answer that might have kept me chasing my tail for weeks. The whole staff saw "nothing," end and sum total of answer—except for Mrs. Li, the floor lady, who had been nervous but surprisingly forthcoming, even indignant at what had happened in a room that was her responsibility.

The flowers were a dead end. All that effort to get around the staff, and then leave a vase that didn't belong, on a cheap pine table that would have broken in two if someone had fallen against it hard enough to crush his skull. Anyway, pine tables don't crush skulls. The wood is too soft.

Pak yelled at me to come to his office. He was pacing, like a tiger. "Inspector, I don't care how our corpse got in the room, or how he met his end. Or even who led him to it. Right now, I need to know who he is. Was." Pak had been at a meeting the whole morning. I could tell he'd been sleeping through some of it. His eyes were puffy. I only hoped he hadn't been dozing during the part where he was supposed to be alert and keep us in the good graces of the vice minister in charge.

"Rough session?" Without meaning to, I was looking at the piece of walnut while working it in my right hand.

Pak stopped pacing and pointed at me. "You haven't broken that dirty habit yet? They're starting to bitch about it. Last month something almost got into your file. Someone called it 'antisocial.' I blocked it." He started pacing again. "Why the hell can't you just smoke, like everyone else?"

The vice minister in charge was named Yun. No one liked him, which he didn't mind. He was one of those people who felt safer surrounded by enemies. Maybe he thought it enhanced his standing with the Minister, though nothing would ever do that. The Minister was elderly, not quite one of the revolutionary veterans but old enough to have known them personally. He'd known my grandfather. They came from the same mountain village. When the war broke out, the Minister, who was then only a young army recruit and a country boy, was assigned to a head-quarters element. They were under constant air attack, moving practically every night, trying to keep some semblance of order and discipline. The Minister became a noncommissioned officer when all the others were killed. By war's end, because the casualty rate was so high, he was a colonel. He often said he didn't know the first thing about com-manding troops when he started and knew less when he finished, but he'd learned to yell convincingly into a field telephone so that whoever was at the other end stood at attention. When the war was over, he fig-ured he'd go back to the village and farm. He got home and there was nothing. The village had been pulverized. No one could figure out why. The bombs came out of nowhere; no one heard the planes arrive in the night sky, the survivors said.

A few people wanted to rebuild the village, but the forests were gone, the farmland had never been good for much, and the military de-cided to use the valley below for a special factory, so everyone in the surrounding hills was moved out. The Minister ended up in the capital. He never got in anyone's way, and he was reliable. He carried out his orders. He was invariably cheerful, even when he was drunk. He trusted his subordinates, treated them with kindness, and established a loyalty that served him well in the bad years. Everyone in the ministry, including Pak and me, worried that he would retire and that Vice Min-ister Yun would get his job.

"The vice minister thinks he's going to use this case to knock the old man out, I can sense it." Pak walked over to the window and stared absently into the courtyard. I moved so I could look out, too. One of the gate sentries had left his post and was leaning against the wall with his eyes closed, trying to draw the last of the morning's coolness from the concrete blocks. Pak stood for a moment with his back to me, then turned and made a wry face.

"The vice minister is sure we'll screw up this murder investigation. He asked if we needed help getting a camera that works. You know, in that bored tone of voice he uses before he sinks his fangs into someone."

"How much does he know? Who told him about the camera?"

"Not Kang. They hate each other. One of them isn't going to survive this." Pak gave me a funny look, then turned to stare out the window again. "So that leaves your favorite captain."

"You mean Colonel Kim? Does he know I was in Manpo?"

"He may have some sketchy report, but I doubt if he knows anything for sure. Just don't go to any fish restaurants with him."

"Humorous."

"What do we know about the corpse?" Pak rubbed at a spot on the window. "Can we get this washed, you think?"

"Nothing much. Dead. Caucasian. Male. Heavy blow to the temple crushed the right side of the skull. Never checked into the hotel. No papers. No identification. The name card in his pocket wasn't his, and the IAEA inspectors say they never met him."

"How hard can this be, Inspector?" Pak gave up on the window and moved over to his desk. "He didn't float down from the moon."

"Might have, for all we know at this point. It will take another day to run down the whereabouts of all foreigners in the country. Everyone in the city is accounted for."

"Autopsy report?"

"They won't do an autopsy."

"What are you talking about? By tomorrow morning, tonight even, the Ministry will be screaming at me, and then others will take it up, like a convention of jackals."

"At the hospital, they say their orders are not to start the autopsy until there is an identification."

"Sure, they want to know what set of knives to use."

I started to work the walnut again, then stopped myself and put it in my pocket. "Can't you get Kang to make a phone call?"

"This is our business, not Kang's. He won't touch it. Besides, the vice minister would like nothing better than to find Kang's fingerprints on what is supposed to be a criminal investigation, not an intelligence romp."

"What about the procurator's office? They are going to have to bring charges against someone, sooner or later."

"This is a foreigner. They don't want to know anything about it. They say it is foreign policy."

"I knew it. We're stuck working with the Foreign Ministry."

"The liaison guy, the short one with the ruddy face and the bad shoes, is coming here this afternoon after lunch. You want to sit in?"

"Maybe. No, on second thought I'd better get back to the hotel and shake the tree again."

"Just a minute. Let's play a game, Inspector. It's called Continents. I name a continent, you tell me if the corpse is from there."

"You already said he was a Finn. Anyway, all I've seen is the pictures, and they aren't very clear. The crime scene camera needs a new battery."

"I don't know if it's a Finn. That was just a hunch, fed by the card in his pocket. Apparently it was planted. But let's proceed. Africa?"

"No. Well, maybe yes. Could be South African. Could be an expat, I suppose."

"South America."

"Could be, but the clothes are wrong, from what little I could see."

"North America."

"Not likely. Wrong haircut."

"Europe."

"Probably."

"Russian?"

"*Nyet.*"

"Australia."

"Look, boss—"

"Humor me, Inspector. Australia."

"Yeah, sure, could be. But, I mean, he's white, too white, maybe. Not ruddy enough."

"Asia."

I thought for a second. "No."

"Lots of territory, a couple of billion people if you count India. Care to change your vote?"

I shook my head. "Not Asia. That doesn't narrow it much."

"Maybe yes, maybe no."

I stood for a moment, waiting to see if Pak was going to draw any conclusions from all of this. He sat calmly and quiet as a stone.

"Is the game over?" I moved toward the door. "If you need me, I'll be at the Koryo for a couple of hours."

Pak nodded. He looked pleased with himself, and I walked down the hall wondering what he knew that I didn't.

# 7

The floor lady at the Koryo was not happy to find me back in the room. She tugged at the sleeve of her dress. She refused to look me in the eye. It wasn't hard to see that by now she had been talked to by someone who had warned her that it was a bad idea to answer my questions. There was no sense in pressing her at this point. I told her that I'd call her later. She was relieved. "I'm busy this morning," she said. "A bus load of Romanian basketball players is arriving. Some friendship tournament. They are the worst. Tall, skinny, they all think because they have such long legs they are comedians. You should see what they do to the rooms. With luck, they'll go to twelve and above." She backed into the hall and slipped away like a shadow. Real quiet, well trained.

I went through the room again inch by inch. Pak had said his first priority was finding out the victim's identity, but that would only be a process of elimination. There were a limited number of foreigners in the country; each provincial unit would make an accounting based on the entry cards and then be told to do it again. Eventually, someone would come up one short, and that would be our man. Or rather, our corpse. My real problem was to figure out who did it, and we were drifting backward on that. So far, all we knew was that the body had been found in this room in the Koryo. Though we hadn't nailed it down as a fact, I was almost sure he was a Finn. At the very least, he was a European, but I pretty much ruled out southern Europe. He wasn't a Slav, either. According to the initial inventory report, all the clothes were from stores in Vienna. If that checked out, then it probably meant he worked for an international organization. Lots of nationalities did. So what made me think he was a Finn? A blue button. But I didn't even know it was his. None of his clothing had buttons like that. Maybe it belonged to his killer. Maybe the murderer was a Finn. But I didn't think so. I'd been through the hotel records. The room had seen scores of Koreans from Japan, a few Americans, and plenty of Chinese. Also newlyweds from Turkistan. There were no signs in the room of any of them, unless that button was part of a Turkistan wedding night custom. I doubted it.

The floor lady knocked softly on the door sill. "There's a call for you downstairs."

"You clean these rooms yourself?"

I could see her deciding whether this was the sort of question she could answer. It was. "Yes, each of us is responsible for an entire floor. Two actually. We used to work in pairs, but last year they cut the staff. We have to make a profit, they said. So I do all the cleaning myself here and on nine."

"The Turkistani couple, the honeymoon couple."

She rolled her eyes. "I don't talk about guests." I was into questions she'd been warned not to answer.

"When you clean, you clean the whole room?"

"Why not?"

"I ask, you answer. Try to remember that." I gave her what was meant to be a friendly look. "You're pretty busy. Two floors to clean. Easy to miss a spot."

She smiled tightly.

"Okay. So you never miss a spot. But if you did, where do you think it would be?"

"Believe me, this room was spotless three days ago. I came in twice to make sure." She paused and gave a little frown. "Anything in here since then came with . . ." She didn't finish the thought.

"I'll get that call now."


The phone was in the manager's office behind the reception desk. The manager was sitting on a wooden folding chair at a small table, sipping tea, not even pretending to go through his papers. His teacup was cracked down the side. I thought about asking him to leave, but it didn't matter. All the hotel phones were tapped anyway.

It was Kang's voice on the other end. "You free tonight?"

"Depends."

"I'll buy dinner."

"No goat meat."

"That doesn't leave much."

"You'll think of something. Fish, maybe."

"How's life at the Koryo these days, Inspector?"

"Fine." It was clear that he knew who talked to the floor lady. "Best hotel on the peninsula."

"Nine o'clock, if that's not too late. I'll swing by your office."

"You do that." I hung up.

The manager cleared his throat and gave me a sour smile when I turned toward him. "We're trying real hard to run a good hotel here." He paused. "This won't help."

The first law of capitalism, I thought. Corpses are bad for business. I tried to sound friendly and serious at the same time. "As soon as I get what I need and can clear out of here, I will. But if this isn't solved soon, you'll have a reputation, if you know what I mean. Bad for the honeymoon tours."

He thought a moment. "The eighth floor is hard to sell." I noticed his hands. They were folded. His knuckles were white, as if he were holding his fingers too tight.

"Thanks for the use of your phone." I got up and wrote down my number on a scrap of paper. "You probably won't remember anything. Don't strain yourself."

# 8

Kang showed up shortly past nine. He stopped in to see Pak for a few minutes. Then he came down to my office. "No dinner. Pak forbids it."

I put my feet on the desk. A headache was creeping up the back of my neck. "I knew it wouldn't happen. You're here. What do you want to say?"

"Remember our friend Chong?"

"The stone head?"

"His body disappeared. They don't even know he's dead. They've convinced themselves he's planning to skip into China, if he hasn't already. Kim is fit to be tied. He's put all of his people along the border on alert. He can't afford to have one of his men defect. Screws up the discipline."

"Bad for his reputation, too, I would think."

"We can hope. Meantime, he's distracted. He doesn't know you were up in Manpo."

"He must know by now."

"Then why have they issued a lookout for a guy from Wonsan, first name unknown, last name unknown?"

"What about the goat lady?"

"She won't help them much. All she knows is you were a little fuzzy about fish and flashed food coupons."

"That's what you came here about? Chong's corpse?" The headache had found itself a good home and was going to spend the night. I'd brought back a bottle of aspirin from Berlin but had used the last one a few weeks ago. Pak didn't have any; I checked.

"No. Your corpse. Kim's people talked to the Koryo staff."

"Thanks for nothing."

Kang started to say something, then stopped.

"What?"

"Not much. Only, Kim isn't mean, he's psycho. If he puts you on his list, there's not much I'll be able to do. He's watching me, waiting to move."

"So get out of the way."

"Not that easy."

"Why? One night, you just disappear."

"I can't, not yet."

"Well, whatever it is, it's your problem. Just keep it clear of me from now on, alright?"

"If it were just my problem, I wouldn't be here, Inspector. A word of advice." He paused.

"I'm listening."

Kang tore a page from that nice little notebook of his and wrote down one word. He pushed it across my desk and then walked into the hall. My headache heard the door slam. The word on the paper was what I expected. "Finn."

# 9

"Ethnicity is not an identification." The woman wore a white lab coat like armor plating. "No identification, no autopsy. I already told you that."

"His name is Gustav." I'd left my notebook in the office, which was a mistake. Taking notes makes it look like you're in charge; that's what they taught us in training class. Asking this iron lady for a piece of paper would just give her the advantage. I put my hands in my pockets and rocked back on my heels. Maybe she'd think I had total recall. Maybe she had an aspirin.

She sneered. "Gustav is a Swedish name. You lose, Inspector. I'm busy. Get me an ID, and it better be quick. The refrigeration is uneven at best in the summer, and these bodies don't keep too long. And find yourself a notebook, while you're at it. Good night."

"Wait a minute. I need to see the effects."

"They're bagged. You'll have to sign a form. And then I need to make a phone call." She looked at me coolly. "The bag is in that desk. When I get back with permission from Military Security, if I get permission, you can go through it." There was a phone on her desk, but I figured she knew that.

"I don't suppose you have a pot of tea."

"Tea is bad for you, Inspector. People drink entirely too much of it."

"Maybe some people do," I muttered as the door closed. As soon as I heard her footsteps receding down the corridor, I started going through the drawers. The bag was in the bottom one. Behind the first bag was a second, tagged CAR ACCIDENT/H1. On a hunch, I opened it and quickly rummaged through. It was from the body in the car Kang had told me about, the one with the smashed side window. The car might not have been there when I went by, but something bad had happened to someone.

There was plenty of blood on the clothing, which looked like the uniform of a Military Security colonel. It was new, good quality. Even for a colonel's uniform, it was well tailored. The stitching was neat and tight, the buttons were imported and fastened with strong thread; they were black, which was standard, but I looked twice in the dim light of the room just to make sure. There were two sets of keys in the trousers. I pocketed them both. There was a black leather wallet, real soft, obviously foreign, made out of some poor calf. It was most likely European, but it had never been stamped or embossed with a brand or country of origin. I ran my fingers along the inside edge to make sure. The wallet was practically empty. All identification had been stripped out. At one time, though, the wallet must have been bulging, because it was badly misshapen. An overstuffed wallet didn't match the trim look of the uniform. Sitting in a back pocket or even inside a coat, it must have ruined the tailored lines something awful. There was not much hope of finding what had been taken from the wallet; it could have been emptied by whoever killed him, maybe by a passing farmer, maybe by security people here in the morgue.

I went into the other bag, marked KORYO. The clothing was not of the same quality as the uniform, not even close, and wasn't as clean, but there was no blood on the clothes. No blood on the clothing, no mess on the carpet in the hotel. Maybe the guy had no brains. In the trouser cuffs I found some pine needles, which I pocketed. The labels on the clothes all said MADE IN AUSTRIA, but every one of them had been sewn in after the clothing was bought and worn. The thread was wrong and the stitching was off, though not by much. The wallet was new, nothing special, maybe a gift just before his trip, or purchased at an airport store en route. On the inside bottom edge were tiny gold embossed letters, MADE IN SPAIN. Like the other wallet, this one had also been stripped, though it didn't look like there had ever been much in it.

Most of the plastic sleeves for credit cards had never been opened. The wallet didn't show any signs of having sat in someone's back pocket during a long plane ride. It was in perfect shape. Maybe he carried it in his coat. So, where was the coat?

I heard footsteps down the hall, put both bags back in the drawer, and moved over to gaze at a chart of the human skeleton.

"The answer is no. I can't give you permission to see the bag."

"Too bad. Has the stuff at least been logged, so I can be sure it's all here when I come back with a procurator's order?"

A procurator's order would impress Military Security like pork fat impressed a hot frying pan, and even she knew that. She folded her arms. It didn't soften her overall appearance. "I'm a doctor, Inspector, not a clerk. I don't log things, I keep track of people's health. Or I do when I'm not being harassed. It's past midnight, I have patients who need help. And with what am I supposed to help them, Inspector? Procurator's orders? Find me some medicine. Especially aspirin for the children."

I gave an imitation bow. "Excuse my intrusion. Thanks for your time."

As I walked towards the door she called after me. "You walk so musically, Inspector."

"I do?" I turned and saw that her face had dropped its mask.

"Your keys, Inspector. They are jangling."

# 10

It was late enough when I left the morgue that I decided to take the duty car home with me. If I got it back early in the morning, Pak wouldn't care. My apartment was surprisingly cool when I stepped inside. There was nothing to eat, so I drank the rest of the vodka and tried to think of Finland, what it would be like to walk with Lena around a lake in the stillness of twilight. I fell asleep remembering her perfume, but all I dreamed about was bread and jam.

The sun was shining full in my window when I woke with a start, past 8:00 A.M. My headache was gone, but I could tell it hadn't wandered far. The woman next door was complaining loudly that their flowers would all be dead by noon if her husband didn't go downstairs for some water, because the tap in their apartment wasn't working again. I should have been at the office by now. I yawned. Pak would cover for me if someone else needed the car, but I knew he was going to make me feel guilty when he found out how little I'd learned at the morgue. "Never mind, Inspector," he'd say, and turn his chair to the window. "We have plenty of clues already, mountains of clues. Who could possibly need an autopsy in a case like this? Glad you went to the morgue. Good use of the office vehicle. That almost makes up for the fact that you didn't bother to sign for it."

I was already late; Pak was only going to be unpleasant; I might as well get some more sleep. If the man next door had gone downstairs to get the water like his wife asked, that might have been possible, but the two of them started arguing about one thing, and one thing led to another. At least I could get some tea at work.

Driving to the office, I yawned and went over what the doctor had said the night before. "Ethnicity is not an identification." It wasn't much of an excuse, but it was worth a try with Pak. As I pulled into the gate at our compound, I saw a military jeep in one of the parking spots. I decided it was the wrong moment to put in an appearance, backed out, and turned onto the road leading toward the place where I'd been on photo-watch, waiting for the black car. I didn't know what I'd find when I got there; maybe driving over the same route would show me something I didn't know I had seen. I rolled down both front windows. If I drove fast enough, maybe the breeze would blow away my headache, which was back.

The day was bright and getting hot, but you could tell autumn was coming on. The sky was higher, bluer, without the flatness of summer. Farmers stood in small groups on the side of the road, staring at the fields, as if willing themselves to begin the work of harvesting the corn. The countryside was ripe. Back from the road, farmhouses sat like dwellings lost in a Central American jungle. Roofs were overgrown with squash vines; a wall of corn towered over the pathways that wound between the buildings. Here and there, a few women squatted on the edge of the fields, enjoying the clarity of the August morning.

I was focused on a couple of goats strolling across the road from the opposite shoulder when, out of nowhere, an oxcart lumbered onto the highway. In a split second it emerged from a dirt path in the field to my right, where it had been hidden by the corn. I slammed on the brakes, barely missed the goats and the back of the cart, and then began a skid that, after a few anxious moments, put me in a ditch about ten meters down the road. The oxcart continued plodding across the highway and disappeared into the cornfield on the other side. Two men ran over to the car. One of them, the older of the two, put his head in the open passenger window. "You all right? This is a damned unlucky stretch of road. People drive like crazy. We lose an ox a month. In July we lost three. We can't afford that."

I shoved the door open, climbed out, and made a quick check of the car. If I could get it out of the ditch, it would get me back to the office. Pak would murder me over the repairs. He wouldn't let us drive a car that was banged up, said it undermined our dignity. Worse, when it went to the repair shop, they would check the log, and he would have to explain why I had the car overnight and hadn't signed it in. Hell, I hadn't even signed it out.

"You people have to drive so reckless?" The younger of the two men was angry. The older man put a restraining hand on his shoulder.

"What's your problem? Your ox is fine, my car is wounded, and I think I strained my back. I'd say your side came out on top." I didn't want any trouble. If a co-op farm manager wrote a letter of complaint to the Ministry, it would be referred to a discipline committee and I would find myself in endless meetings. I would also have to help with the harvest. This would entail days, maybe weeks, of bending under a hot sun.

The older man tightened his grip on the younger man's shoulder, then let his hand drop free. "We had an accident a couple of weeks ago. Car came flying across the road and killed his nephew."

"Cars don't fly." I had a sudden feeling that the ox I almost hit had not put me in a ditch but rather on the road to a solution. "What did you say about last month?"

"Three oxen hit by crazy drivers. Never seen anything like it."

"How come? More traffic?"

"Only in the morning. We like to move the carts across the road early. That way the ox gets to browse for a few hours before we get to work. For a long time, there was no problem, never any traffic that early. A couple or three years ago, a car came out of nowhere and killed an ox, must have been about six in the morning. It was a Thursday. Local security man came around and told us to keep away from the road every other Thursday morning."

"He tell you why?"

"I don't care. I'm not curious. Twice a month I sleep late, that's all."

"So, what happened last month? Couldn't sleep?"

"It was a Monday. Not me, one of the other men, it was his turn to move the carts. Ox stepped into the road. Wham. Dead ox, and the driver of the car almost killed."

"Did you see the driver?"

"No, I told you, it wasn't my day to move the carts. I was somewhere else."

"Alright, you were somewhere else. What about the other two accidents?"

"Following week, we stayed off the road on Monday, figured Tuesday was alright. It was my day for the cart. Same thing. About six in the morning. Ox stepped in the road. This time the driver tried to stop, sort of like you did. Only he was going faster than you were. He lost control. The car spun around and the back end hit the ox. Killed the beast, but it saved the driver."

"What did he look like?"

"Small guy, skinny, mad as hell."

"Was he in any sort of uniform?"

"Nah."

"The car?"

"Back end was caved in. Too bad, nice car."

"Black?"

"Yup. Clean as you'd want to see, except for the gore all over the back."

"Didn't anyone from Pyongyang come out to question you?"

"Funny thing, no one did. I kept thinking the party committee would chew us out, even though it wasn't our fault. They always blame us."

"You sure no one came to see you?"

The older man crossed his eyes and looked at the sky. "Well, no one except the local security man."

"And?"

"He told us he was sorry about the ox."

"And?"

"He gave us a little money to keep quiet. Wasn't much."

"Wasn't much. Alright. Third time. Must have been a Wednesday or a Friday."

"Wednesday. The youngster here had the lead. I was just walking alongside." The older man nodded at the younger one. "He looked both ways, didn't see anything, though there was a little mist. The ox got halfway across when it stopped. Must have felt the vibrations on the road. Wouldn't move. Sure enough, there was a car, almost stopped this time, but almost wasn't good enough for the ox. Not much damage to the car, though the driver howled that he'd have us all shot."

"Skinny guy again?"

"No, this one was military of some sort. Muscular, short hair. Gray uniform, nothing like I've seen before. Banged his fist into the top of the car, he was so mad."

"Still no investigation?"

"Not a thing. And no compensation for the three oxen, either. Just some hush money. Not very much. How are we supposed to explain losing three animals?"

"But last week it was worse—it wasn't an ox, was it, it was a child. You know what happened?"

Both men stood quietly, as if an invisible hand had pulled a string attached to their jaws.

"Okay, let me tell you what happened." I let my imagination spin out a reasonable scenario, based on what I knew. I liked to hear myself say these things out loud. When I just had a conversation in my head, it was always brilliant, but when it got fashioned into words, my ears could spot the weak points and tell my brain to take a walk. "The car took off after its side window, the driver's side window, was shot out. The driver, wounded or dead, lost control. The car was going at high speed, hit a bump on this lousy highway, blew a tire, spun around, and landed in a ditch. Almost where I am now. Your nephew, who saw it all happen from that hill over there, was naturally curious and came to investigate. He saw someone going through the driver's wallet. He turned to go, but the person, more likely two men, saw him, ran him down, and killed him. They told you later he'd been hit by the car, but they never let you see his body. All you got was an urn of ashes, which was buried the same night." It sounded plausible, not brilliant but plausible, though I made up the fact about the car landing on its left side and omitted that the boy's throat had been cut.

The two of them stared at me. The younger one trembled until I thought he would fall over. The older one shook his head slowly. "We don't want trouble."

"Well, trouble is what you've got, and you'll have even worse if you tell anyone, anyone at all, what I just said to you." I let that sink in. "Now help me get this car out of the ditch." Neither of them moved. "I'll put it another way for you. I'm your only hope of finding out who killed that boy, believe me. Or don't. If I were you, I wouldn't believe me. If I were you, I'd get to a phone and call the local security man, Li Min Sung. He and I were in the army together. We stayed in touch." I could see from the face of the younger man that this made an impression. The locals liked Li; they trusted him. He had been around here a long time and was always fair with them, didn't give them a lot of trouble over minor regulations. If Li and I were friends, then maybe they could trust me, too. "Tell him Inspector O says hello."

The older one spit on his hands. "Let's get this car back on the road."

# 11

"Where are you?" Pak was irritated.

"I'm calling from a street phone."

"You're supposed to be in here. People are looking for you."

"I gathered as much. Someone parked in my parking space, so I figured I'd take a ride."

Pak's voice donned the cloak it wore when he wanted me to listen closely. "A couple of muscular types were here about a guy named Chong. You know anyone named Chong?"

"Just a minute. Let me think." I let a decent interval pass. "No. What are the odds? You go through your whole life and never meet a Chong. Isn't that an Arab name?" I glanced out onto the street to see if anyone had stopped to watch. No one.

"Who's talking about Arabs? They wanted to know where you've been the past week. I told them you were jumpy so I gave you time off to rest. You felt rested when you came back to work, didn't you?"

"Rested isn't the word for it."

"One more thing. They said your brother is joining the case. He'll be here tomorrow to get briefed by you."

"Forget it."

There was a long silence. "Inspector, we weren't asked for our opinion. We don't get a vote. Your brother has been assigned to monitor this case. Do I make myself clear?"

"I told you. Forget it. And I meant it. I'm not working near him. Five years ago, we reached an agreement. We're not brothers anymore. We don't meet. We don't speak. We live on different planets. I'm sticking to the agreement. If he's on the case, you'll have to take me off."

"Family matters cannot interfere—"

"Look, Pak, it's not your business, it's not the Ministry's business, it's not the party's business. This is between me and my former brother. He's dirtying my grandfather's name. I won't have it. Can I say it again for you? I won't have it. Let's drop it, alright?"

Pak must have thought I was crazy, talking like that on the phone. Most of the time our line wasn't monitored—too many other targets and not enough personnel—but we both knew that this case had probably put us on the Military Security Red List, meaning the office phones were near the top of some roving team's weekly priorities. I was banking on it. What I'd said would get to my brother. I wanted him to hear it directly from me, even if it wasn't face-to-face. And I wanted the transcript to get circulated in places where it would put a question mark after his name. Not a big one, but a nagging doubt. It wouldn't destroy him, but he would be in limbo for a while. People wouldn't return his phone calls; invitations would dry up. That would make him mad, maybe ruin his appetite for a few days as he tried to figure out why people were avoiding him. He might even lose some sleep, wondering if his name was on the short, black list of those who had unknowingly said the wrong thing, made the wrong decision, had their heads up when they should have been down.

Pak was talking again, but the connection went bad and I missed the first part of what he said. ". . . so let's not get off track over private feuds."

"This isn't a private feud. It's moral. It's philosophical. It's about lofty ideals and people who are so eager to serve the revolution that they step on friends, family, even little children." I paused at that thought, but I didn't want to follow it through. "My brother doesn't know the first thing about murder investigations, only about murder, and he doesn't care. Someone has transferred him onto the case to get to me. Guess what? It won't work."

I heard Pak clear his throat. "Just get in here. We'll have a cup of tea and see what the tea leaves say."

"I have a better idea. How about you push me on the swings?" I didn't have the heart to tell him what I'd learned at the morgue, that tea was unhealthy in large doses.

"Then you have to push me down the slide."

Pak was sitting under the willow tree near the swing set when I got there. "No one around at the moment. You realize, not meeting in the office is going to get the listeners annoyed. They hate dead time."

"Yeah, well, I'll make it up to them. I'll read aloud from a book of poetry some afternoon. Meantime, we've got a problem."

Pak laughed out loud. "A problem." He laughed again, a long, rolling laugh, so that pretty soon I joined in. The two of us, sitting by a rusty swing set, laughing. A few people walked by, but no one stopped.

"Good, we both feel better now." I grinned. "You want to know what the problem is?"

Pak put on his sunglasses. "Sure. I don't have enough problems. I need another one to round out my hand."

"The corpse is a Finn. He was moved to that eighth floor room from somewhere else. Someone doesn't want an autopsy. His being a Finn means something to that particular someone. Maybe that's why they messed with the labels in his clothes. And I'll bet you anything this is all connected to the kid whose throat was cut near that black Mercedes with the scanner. You know, the car that ended up in the ditch." I wasn't sure this was the time to tell Pak about my conversation with the two farmers on the side of the road.

"That's it? That's what you have?" Pak snorted. "You're just dumping stray facts on me. All beads, no string."

"Wrong image. Don't think of beads. Think of trees."

Pak groaned. "Here we go. Wood, I should have known."

"I'm not talking about wood, I'm talking about trees. You ever seen tree roots? They go everywhere. No pattern. Same thing with branches, when you think of it. But they all work together. One thing about you, Pak, you always look at facts as mechanical. Each one has to fit in a certain place."

"I do that, don't I, Inspector? Try to see how things fit. That's how we solve cases. It's standard operating procedure. Proven, tested, gets results. Or after all of these years, do you have a better idea?"

"Facts are organic. They don't have to fit, they just have to work together. Think about it. A car doesn't go out of control at high speed, blow a tire, and then end up in that ditch without getting pretty banged up. I know that ditch. I saw it." I paused to see if Pak would react. If he did, the sunglasses hid it pretty well. "That car was planted there, same as the body in the hotel. What do you know about the eighth floor of the Koryo?"

"Meaning?"

"The hotel manager told me it was hard to rent on that floor. I'd guess that's where some of the central monitoring closets are. It may even be a floor that Military Security has taken over. Can't we check that?"

"Maybe. Maybe not. But why would they plant a body there? And whose body is it?"

I ignored the second question. "Maybe whoever did it was part of an out-of-town unit. What if it wasn't planned but was a big mistake, a screwup by someone who didn't check what he didn't know? Those rooms on the eighth floor are never rented unless the hotel is full. It hasn't been for weeks. It's slack. The manager is worried that if word gets out about a dead body in his hotel, it will ruin the Koryo's reputation and he'll lose business. That's why he told me about the eighth floor. He wanted to tell me the murder didn't happen in his hotel. Only he couldn't say it directly."

"So we need an autopsy, something that might show the victim was dead before being moved to the room."

"Kim is going to block it every way he can; the warrior woman at the morgue made that abundantly clear. But she let me go through the effects bags, on the sly. The Finn's trouser cuffs had pine needles in them. I took some. That gives us a place to begin."

"Good, you start with the pine trees on the west coast, I'll start on the east coast, and we'll work toward the center." Pak's head brushed the low-hanging willow branches as he stood up. "You done with this organic approach to crime solving? I've got paperwork up to here."

"They were short, fresh needles, not dry. Don't ask me what that means yet. I don't know. Also, I got two sets of keys from the Mercedes crash. Why two sets? The wallet of the driver had been stripped."

"So what's the connection? What does two sets of keys get us?"

"Do you want to know how those facts fit? Or how they work together?"

"I don't give a damn."

"Maybe they get us some more information on the cars that are part of this."

"Maybe. But people lose keys. Maybe this driver needed to carry a spare. Don't give me a maybe." Pak gave one of the swings a push. "I'm supposed to go to the Minister and say, 'Maybe we've solved the case. There were two sets of keys. I know because one of my best men stole them from the morgue.' Give me a fact, would you! And I don't want to hear about roots."

"We know the guy's a Finn."

"You keep saying that. What's this thing with you and Finns, anyway?" Pak wasn't mad at me; he was just behind in figuring out what was going on. At this point in a case, when we still had only loose facts and not much else, he tended to get cross.

"One more thing." I owed it to Pak to tell him what I knew, or thought I knew. "I had to talk to a couple of farmers."

Pak took his sunglasses off, very slowly, the way he does when he senses bad news. "Meaning?"

"One of them was the uncle of the boy who was killed. Long story. Anyway, they're on our side. I told them to call Li Min Sung if they wanted to check up on me." I smiled, without much conviction. "We need a little help from somewhere."

Pak nodded. "Good, now we have the floor lady at the Koryo and a couple of farmers working for us. And on the other side, Kim and his band of snakes." There was a pause. "You want to tell me about Chong?" Before I could open my mouth, Pak held up his hand. "Never mind. That's all I needed to know, and I don't want to know any more." He shook his finger at me. "I'll make a couple of phone calls. Can you please stay out of trouble for three or four hours until I get us some protection? The Minister likes you, but then, he doesn't have to put up with your wood chips. If I can get through to him, he'll throw up a shield for us, though how much good it will do against Military Security is anybody's guess."

"I could start checking pine trees in the city, if you want." Pak didn't respond. I could see he was thinking of something else. "No, forget it. I'm not working with my former brother. I'm not going to talk to him. The only reason he's on the case is to lead us over a cliff, I'm warning you."

# PART FIVE

I dreamed of a plain, flat to the horizon,
As if the mountains had crumbled
To dust around us; we were mad
With sorrow, and howled at the moon to
Bring back the soft rolling hills
That had echoed with our laughter.

—Pyon Kil Sun (1122–1145)

My brother had lost weight since I last saw him. He didn't look all that good. His face was empty, flat. Even when we were little, in the midst of the war when other children were thin and frail, his cheeks had been full. Mine would be dull and chapped in winter; his cheeks turned ruddy with the cold. People would stare, wondering where he got the extra food. But he didn't eat extra, sometimes he even gave me a little of his portion. He just looked fuller than anyone else. When he got older, he got round, especially his face. At first, when he was moving up the ranks of the party and he was pleased with himself, it showed in his face: round and smooth, unmarked by all of those he rolled over. Later the roundness went to fat and then, with age, to a menacing, distorted mask.

He was sitting in the beer hall in the Koryo, at the same table where I'd met Kang, tightening his fingers around a bottle of beer. He was annoyed because I was late, and he knew I was late on purpose. It annoyed him that I did most things on purpose. Then he spotted my reflection in the front window. He took a sip of beer, and I saw his body tense up.

I walked over to the table and sat down without saying a word. We stared at each other. "This wasn't my idea," I said finally. "I told you five years ago I would never talk to you again, and as far as I am concerned, I'm not talking to you."

He rolled the beer bottle between his hands. I thought he might grab it by the neck and shove it into my face, but then he relaxed. "Let up, just for a minute, why don't you?" he said. "We turned out different, that's all. I believe in what I do. You don't believe in anything. I've been assigned to this case, over my objections. You don't like it. But we both have our orders."

"No, you're wrong. We're not working together on this. Not on anything, ever, not even in hell."

He glared at me, and I glared back. I deliberately took the piece of wood from my pocket and began working it over and over in the fingers of first one hand, then the other. Before I drove over, I'd retrieved the piece of persimmon from my out-box. I wanted to have it with me for our meeting. My brother wouldn't know the difference between persimmon wood and balsa wood. But it wasn't for him. It was for me.

My brother was one of those people who was annoyed when I held a piece of wood in my hand. He said it was a character fault, and he didn't have sympathy for people with faults. "If you're doing that to get on my nerves, forget it." He watched as I put the wood on the table, daring him to sweep it onto the floor.

"It's persimmon," I said. "Very hard. Your friends in the Central Committee wouldn't like it. They need something softer, more pliable."

Before my brother could say anything, the player piano started up: my piano roll with the Beatles on it. He grimaced. "Music like that is poison. Why do they play that garbage? No wonder the kids today are so unreliable."

"Unreliable." I let the word sit between us, oozing like a sore. "Go ahead, give me the rest of the speech, about the socialist renegades who are undermining the revolution, diluting the Leader's ideas, turning back the clock."

He went dead white. "You may be a blood relative"—he was hissing softly, like a lizard pinned by a rock—"but you'd better be careful. You can still be brought to justice, along with the rest of them."

"A purge? Are you going to launch a one-man purge?"

"Don't tempt fate. Things are happening. All this garbage will be swept away, along with everyone who has fostered it. I'm through protecting you." His narrow, mean eyes were never his best feature, and they got uglier when he started talking like this.

I leaned across the table, so I could stare into his ugly eyes. "Get your orders changed. I'm only going to warn you once. Get them changed, and get out of my way on this case."

"My brother, the police inspector, threatening me, a Central Committee department vice director?" He didn't budge or back away. "The Heartbeat of the Revolution won't be able to save you much longer, don't you know that, you fool?"

Pure rage must have flashed across my face almost before I felt it myself, because I saw him recoil. My voice was hoarse; I didn't recognize it when I spoke. "Get out of my sight. If you ever speak that way about Grandfather again, I will kill you." I sat back and took a deep breath. "With my bare hands, I'll rip your stinking heart from your chest."

He sipped his beer, a show of unconcern, but the glass was shaking when he put it down. Then he slid off the bench, stood up stiffly, and walked out the door. The doorman started to tip his hat but stepped back when he saw the expression on my brother's face. The waitress at the bar, trying to make herself invisible, stood still as a deer when it smells trouble. She had heard the whole thing. When she noticed I was watching her, she started wiping the bar with a rag, on the same spot, over and over again.

# 2

For the next two days, the weather turned back toward summer, hot, humid, the air stifling under a heavy gray sky. It felt like a typhoon was coming, but there were no warnings on the radio for the farmers to make preparations. I went into the office each morning, followed at a distance by people who didn't care if I noticed. Pak was gone most of the time, either in meetings at the Ministry or some other place, where he wouldn't say. He didn't do much more than mutter good morning, didn't call me into his office, didn't ask to review any files, just kept to himself. I could see he wasn't sleeping much, but then, neither was I.

During the day, I went over my notes on the case, called a few people who swore they knew nothing about the feud between Kang's department and Military Security, and made a few more sketches for the bookshelf I would never build. Pak still hadn't replaced our kettle, so the first morning I walked over to the Operations Building for a cup of hot water. They told me to get lost; their plumbing was out of order for the next week, and they didn't have any water at all. I was about to suggest we combine our resources, my water with their hot plate, when one of them said hot plates didn't grow on trees, and if I wanted to use theirs, why didn't I chip in? To hell with them, I thought, and retreated to my office. One afternoon I went over to the Koryo, just to look around the eighth floor and to check the back entrances. I didn't learn a thing.

Whenever I went out, it was obvious I was being watched. The pattern was the same. In the mornings, they let me see them. For the rest of the day, if I went out they hung back, played peek-a-boo, but never tried to disappear completely. At night when I opened the door to my apartment, I could tell it had been visited. Nothing rough, a few things moved a little to the side, just so I would know they'd been there. They weren't looking for anything in particular, and I had a feeling they weren't about to plant anything.

On Saturday, the third day, Pak came into my office smiling. "We're going to have a visitor. A senior detective from the Finnish National Police Agency. His name is Pikkusaari. Something like that." He waited for my reaction, because he figured I would say no. I didn't say anything. "Wonderful, you are finally struck dumb. I'll tell you, the decision caused a lot of screeching over the past forty-eight hours. The vice minister nearly had a stroke, complained it was a terrible insult to us. That was definitely the wrong thing to say." He smiled radiantly. "The man has finally made a big mistake. I hope it's fatal. The leadership wants to show we have nothing to hide on this, so when the Finns made the usual request for information, someone at the top decided to invite them over." He went to my window and gazed into the empty street. "This Pikkusaari guy is supposed to get our fullest cooperation. That means"—Pak turned around and pointed at the files on my desk—"you tell him about the pine needles and maybe about the new labels in the clothing, but not about the Mercedes or the dead boy."

"The boy? What does he have to do with the Koryo case? And who told the Finns the corpse was one of theirs, when we really don't know that for a fact, not yet, anyway? It's what Kang says, that's all. And what am I supposed to do if this Pikkusaari finds out about the boy and the Mercedes on his own? No one is going to want a foreigner to get a whiff of whatever is going on between Military Security and Kang's department. In fact, if he does find out, someone around here will be accused of aiding the enemy, leaking sensitive information, something bloodcurdling."

"Don't worry, this Pikkusaari won't discover anything he's not supposed to. And you know why? Because you're going to be with him every minute he's here. He'll only be around for three days, arrives on the Tuesday flight and leaves next Saturday morning. Who knows, maybe he'll help positively identify the corpse. Maybe he'll even be able to supply something that will help us solve the case, miracle of miracles. The main thing is, he gets as much cooperation as he needs." Pak cleared his throat with one of his nervous coughs. "I don't know who told the Finns it was one of theirs. Could be whoever it was that killed him."

He looked at me, and I looked up at the ceiling trim. "You ever wonder about that trim molding? I mean, what's under all that paint?"

"No, Inspector, I have not. You want a guess?"

"Sure."

"Whatever is under all that paint has nothing to do with Finland."

"Okay," I said, "this guy gets as much cooperation as he needs, and he only needs so much." Pak nodded. I dug around in my pocket for a decent scrap of paper and started making notes. "Does he have permission to leave Pyongyang?"

Pak was never hard to read, and I could see the expression on his face shift like the gears on a truck from worry to suspicion and finally settle on resignation. "Why? What are you already planning?"

"Nothing. But if he identifies the corpse, that may lead us out of the city, maybe even to where they have those pine trees."

"Which is where?"

"They're a type of mountain pine, short trees, grow out of rocks on the sides of hills."

"How do you know this?" I could see he was trying to imagine what rules I had broken while he was busy fending off the vice minister.

"I had to do something for the past two days. So I did some research."

"Inspector O." Pak rarely called me by name; when he did it meant something like an official pronouncement was coming. "We're going to solve this case, despite the land mines being sown in our path. But we've got to do it in lockstep. And in this case, I choose the step, the pace, the direction. That means no bright ideas. No independent research. Can I be any clearer?"

"What about the boy?"

"Don't harass me about that boy, I'm warning you. We'll find out who did that, too. And eventually"—he stopped to let the word penetrate—"eventually, we may do some things your way. Hell, we'll probably end up doing most everything your way. Eventually. But for right now, you have to go along with me."

"This isn't about my brother, is it?"

"No, it isn't about that damned brother of yours, and maybe you don't know it but you nearly got us both sent to a camp somewhere in the mountains because of the fool way you handled that. The waitress at the Koryo nearly wet her pants, she was so scared at what she heard you say to him. For a grown man, you act like an idiot sometimes, you know that?" By the time he finished he was breathing through his nose, trying to get control again. Something was eating him; Pak never got this angry.

He didn't know my brother, not like I did. Still, he was right. We had other problems. I'd deal with my brother later.

"Trust me, chief, I follow your lead with this visitor." Pak hated to be called "chief." I did it to distract him. "Do I get an expense account? I've got to take him to dinner, just to be polite. He's the guest. I'm the host. I can't ask him for money, to pay for gas or my meals. It's embarrassing. We are a hospitable people. They're always saying that on the TV. Where's he staying?"

"I wanted him in the Ministry guest house, but the vice minister put up a fuss, so he'll be in the Koryo. That's good and bad. He should know enough to watch what he says in his room. If he doesn't, please give him a little talking to. I still don't know how Kim and his people fit in this. You may be right, there might be a connection between the eighth floor and Military Security, but you haven't given me any proof yet, and I haven't been able to find out anything. My sources stare into space whenever I raise the question. In the meantime, I don't want to let Kim know if we find any of his droppings."

"The trees grow around Hyangsan." I was studying a map spread out across my desk. "People think they're stunted because they grow out of rocks on the slopes of the mountains, but they're not stunted. They're full grown. Just small. That's why the needles are so little."

Pak looked at the map. "If the Finn was at Hyangsan, then this case is not what I thought it was. Where else do those trees grow?"

"They used to be in Chagang, some village on a mountaintop, but I think they were all cut down twenty-five years ago by farmers trying to clear land that no one else wanted."

"You an expert on mountain villages all of a sudden?"

"No, I made a phone call to the forestry department at the university. Don't worry, I didn't tell them who I was. They think I am organizing a botany tour. They said they were growing more of these trees and would try to plant them around the country starting next year, but right now the last ones in the wild are around Hyangsan."

"So how did our corpse get them in his cuffs?"

"Maybe he was staying at the Hyangsan Hotel and was hiking around. Maybe someone hid his body up there after he was killed. But at some point in all of this I'm betting he was at Hyangsan. Or at least his pants were."

"Won't the records at the hotel show who he was?" Pak knew if it were that easy I would have done it by now. He was just thinking out loud.

"No records. The last four weeks' worth disappeared. The hotel manager says someone came and announced they needed to take them away for an audit. He thought it was part of the new economic directive, until the central audit people showed up and asked to see his records. Believe it or not, they keep some of the records on a computer now, and whoever took the paper copies didn't think to look there. But the computer stuff is only partial, because the machines crash whenever the power fails, and that wipes out the memory. Our technician says he read in a manual there is a way to get at the memory if you have the right equipment." I suddenly realized how laughable that sounded. "Which means there is no way we'll ever get at the memory."

Pak was lost in thought. "I'm too old for this. We used to work just with paper, remember? And those paper files were real good . . ." His voice trailed off, "Damned good." He shook his head and started out of the office. "I'm going to get lunch. You think about how you're going to deal with your new Finnish partner. Give me a daily plan or something. I'll need to justify extra gas if you go to Hyangsan. And you'll need rooms and meals. Tell your new friend Pikkusaari to stick with the tea. The coffee they serve up there isn't so good."

# 3

*"What do you know about Kang's operations in Finland?" The Irishman turned off the tape recorder. He asked it quietly, but he didn't pretend he wasn't interested. I had been expecting the question.*

*"Nothing. He never said anything. And I never asked."*

*"Pak didn't talk about it?"*

*"How would Pak know about overseas operations?"*

*"Pak was a smart man. He knew Kang pretty well. People talk to each other, even in your country."*

*"How would you know whether people talk to each other in my country, Richie? Do us a favor, it's getting late. Stick to what you know."*

*"You haven't a clue what I know, Inspector. Could be I already have the whole story and I'm just using you to check a few facts. Could also be I don't care about the story and I'm just playing a game with you. For someone who isn't holding anything and is sitting at my table, you are one hell of a card player."*

*"Here's a card I'm holding. Finland. There's where you first got interested in Kang, isn't it? He must have been using it as some sort of base. Quiet, out-of-the-way place, where people mind their own business. I'll bet*

you can go for long walks with no one else around. What did he do to catch your attention? Or did the Finns alert you?"

The Irishman stared at me. "You ask questions you don't want to ask, Inspector."

"You mean you don't know?"

"Good, that will do. I don't know. You satisfied?"

"The man's dead. You've got a file ready for the trash. But you're asking me to give you more details for it, and I don't do that unless I know why."

"I'm not going to tell you anything." He turned off the tape recorder. "And this is nothing. Kang was what we considered our reality check. Fabulous code name."

"He had a code name?"

"Just for us, internally, a convenience. We called him Goldilocks." He paused. "You with me?" I nodded, so he continued. "There's a lot of garbage circulating about your country, but you know that already. Crazy stories. Dinosaur sightings. Of course, we deserve some of the credit—our people set loose a few rumors that bounce around until they get picked up in slightly different form by the Italians or the Germans. They repackage them and eventually pass them to us. Then there's the stuff put out by your people to keep us chasing shadows, a little of it very good, a little of it hilarious. Most of the rest is just someone trying to make money on the side, and someone else reporting it in order to get credit for turning in more paper. Hard to keep track of it all. Eventually, we figured there had to be something to keep us on solid ground. Someone we could trust."

"Kang wouldn't work for you."

Richie shrugged. "You don't work for me, Inspector. But you're here, and I have a tape recorder running." He let that idea float across the room, then he went on. "I never met him, but from what I heard, your Mr. Kang had a good head and a perfect sense of reality. Not too hot, not too cold. Just right."

"So what do you do, now that he's gone?"

"He can't have been the only smart person in your country."

*I smiled.*

*The Irishman waited. He closed his eyes and lifted his chin again, like a tourist pretending not to notice the clouds had covered the sun. "Alright," he said finally. "We can let that go for now, Inspector. Let's take your advice and stick to what we know. Pikkusaari, for instance. What would we say, friendly sort? Dour? Someone who knew his way around?"*

*"I'd love to tell you, Richie, but I can't. I never met the man."*

# 4

On Tuesday morning I was out at the airport as the plane taxied in front of the terminal building. I watched each passenger walk down the stairs and fixed on a short brown-haired man, about sixty, as my Finnish policeman. There was supposed to be an interpreter from the Foreign Ministry, but he hadn't arrived, and I had to hope the Finn and I had enough Russian between us for the greetings, getting the bags past customs, and then some small talk on the drive to the hotel.

The brown-haired man turned out to be a German agro-specialist. There were no Finns on the plane. As I went in search of a phone, the Foreign Ministry liaison man came running up to me, his face perspiring even though it wasn't warm in the building.

"What happened to our Finn?" The liaison man and I had worked together before. It probably wasn't his fault, but something about him irritated me whenever I saw him. Maybe it was his smile. It sat on his face like a fly on a rotting peach.

His eyes went toward my lapel, searching for the pin that, after years of working with me, he knew wouldn't be there. Some people stare in silence for a moment when they can't find it, then pick up the conversation. The liaison man wasn't one of them. He would always look away furtively, as if it were the first time he had ever encountered such a thing, then start to stutter slightly before he got hold of himself again. "The F-F-Finn couldn't make the f-f-flight. Visa problem."

"You mean the consulate in Beijing screwed up? Someone's head is going to roll and it's not going to be mine."

The liaison man wiped his face with a blue silk handkerchief, the sort they sell by the box at the Beijing airport. "The authorization never arrived. We called the c-c-consulate to make sure they would issue the visa. They said it would be no problem, as soon as they got the f-f-forms." He paused a few seconds; it seemed to help him calm down. "The code clerk said there was a transmission at the right time, but nothing came through, so he thought it was just the normal equipment problems. Then he looked again and saw that the send-number was valid. We double-checked it against our records."

"It was blocked?"

The liaison man swallowed hard and lowered his voice. "I d-d-didn't say that."

"No, you didn't say that. So, what about the train? Get him his visa tomorrow, put him on the train at Beijing station. He'll show up here a few days late, cranky and tired, but it won't be anything we haven't faced before with other official visitors, thanks to your ministry." I could see the liaison man was forcing himself not to look at my lapel again. "Don't worry." I leaned over and whispered in his ear. "They don't put it in your file if you stand near me."

"R-r-real funny." He took a step back and, as he always did, started mentally running through excuses for breaking off our conversation.

I decided to help him out. "We done?"

He nodded and looked relieved but then hesitated. "When the Finn found out he'd flown all the way to Beijing and there was no visa waiting at our consulate, he was pretty upset. Han, the guy at the visa desk, told me he asked him to stay an extra day while things were straightened out, but the Finn grabbed his passport, said he had better things to do with his time, and stomped out the door. We called his hotel room to offer the train—sometimes we can come up with ideas on our own, you know. You cops aren't the only ones who can think."

"Swell. You can think. What happened?"

"He had already checked out. There's a Finnair flight from Beijing back to Helsinki at 2:00 P.M. He's probably at the airport right now, waiting to board."

At the edge of the crowd, near the front door to the terminal, I spotted a familiar profile. "We'll be in touch," I said to the liaison man, just as he dropped his hankie. When he knelt to pick it up, the pin fell off his lapel. "Not your day, pal," I said. "Welcome to the club."

Kang gestured for me to follow him outside. As I walked into the parking lot, he was climbing into an old, dusty blue car, the Nissan I'd heard start up outside my hotel in Kanggye. I got in the passenger's side. Kang glanced in the mirror, adjusting it so he could see what was behind us without having to make it obvious. "Airports are exciting places, don't you think, Inspector? You never know who you'll see. Or who will see you."

"You know who played this stupid game on the visa for the Finnish policeman?"

"I can't say for sure, but we do a little of this and a little of that in Beijing. A while ago we rented an apartment overlooking the back of the consulate. We haven't shared either this or that with Kim, incidentally. From the apartment window we can see everyone who enters and leaves the consulate. A full three-man Military Security team was there the other night, late."

"How late?"

"Two in the morning. The lighting isn't so good around there at that hour, and we don't have enough night scopes, but we could see one of them was carrying a small bag, probably tools. They let themselves in—which they aren't supposed to do—and thirty minutes later they came out again. I figure they jiggled a few wires on the commo equipment."

"Why didn't the Chinese guards stop them?"

"They had some sort of identification papers. Maybe the Chinese service is working with them. I don't trust the Chinese, not one of them." Kang turned on the engine. It coughed, just like it had at two in the morning in Kanggye. "No sense in hanging around here. Let's go back to the city."

"Wait, I've got my own car."

As I started to open the door, Kang accelerated past a minibus and out onto the road. "Leave it. Get a new one."

"Are you crazy? Pak will bounce me on my head if I leave that car here. I'm not even supposed to be driving it half the time."

We were speeding past the first set of nondescript concrete apartment buildings beyond the airport, and Kang showed no sign of turning around. "Don't worry about Pak. I told him you need a new car. It's banged up anyway. What did you do, drive into a ditch?" We braked suddenly, crossed over the center line, and slid off onto a dirt side road, past a traffic policeman who was standing at a checkpoint. The policeman looked blankly at Kang and then put his face back toward the main highway. Kang drove to a small stand of trees, pulled behind them, and turned off the engine. From the direction of the airport, two black Mercedeses sped past. The second slowed for a fraction at the checkpoint, but when the traffic policeman waved in the direction of town, the car accelerated again.

"I'm guessing you didn't want that Finnish detective here." I watched Kang slump down in his seat and pretend to relax once the two cars were out of sight.

Kang's lips toyed with smiling, then dropped the idea. "Well, I'm guessing neither did you." He drummed his fingers on the steering wheel. "It would have been one more person I'd have to keep safe from snakes. Anyway, the two of you might have stumbled onto something that doesn't concern your investigation. But, no, I didn't stop him. And I never tamper with Foreign Ministry communications."

I opened the door. "See you around, Kang. I've got to get back to my car and then tell Pak I don't have to babysit for the next three days."

"Sometimes you don't listen very well, Inspector." When Kang reached over to pull the door shut, I saw he was wearing his shoulder holster, which was a surprise. The number of people authorized to wear concealed weapons in the capital is limited, very, very limited. "Your car is not where you want to be right now. I don't think it would have been a big explosion when you turned the key. They wouldn't have wanted to injure a lot of foreigners. But you might have needed the cuffs on one of your pant legs brought up several centimeters, like maybe to your knee. And any passenger in the car would have had his eyebrows singed." He rolled down his window to let in some air. "Now they're going to have to figure out what to do with your car. I hope the tank wasn't full. Waste of gasoline. I'll bet they drain it."

It took a minute before I felt like speaking. "Thanks. I owe you. I thought you said you couldn't help me here in the capital."

"I can't help you on the case, but Finland is important to my operations. I can't afford to have the Finns mad at us and tightening up on regulations."

"So why didn't you want that Finnish detective here?" Kang's fingers were drumming the steering wheel again. "Don't tell me he works for you."

This time Kang smiled. "Okay, I won't tell you that. Next subject. We need to talk."

"I doubt it. If Pak wants to work with your department, that's his business. If you and I can work out a deal on our own, that's fine. Like I said, I owe you." I could feel my blood pressure rising, and from the way Kang glanced over at me, my voice must have been following suit. "But I draw the line, a thick black line, at working with my former brother. I'll save us some time. Don't bother raising the idea."

"Believe me, Inspector, I don't like your brother. We've tangled more than once. He and his comrade friends get in my way. When it's only a nuisance, I can ignore them, but every so often they threaten my people by compromising an operation. Your brother is right on the verge of doing that. He is still your elder brother, incidentally."

I meant to laugh cynically, but the sound got stuck in my throat. "So you think I'm going to talk to him again? Have a fraternal chat? You must be kidding."

"Inspector, there are several threads here. I'd say you are starting to realize they come together in an odd way. You might actually reach some conclusions before it is too late. Meantime, your brother is about to cause me serious trouble. If you think that by keeping him off your investigation you've accomplished something, you're wrong. But that's your problem. If you rile him up, he'll get in my way. That's my problem. See what I mean?"

"I scared the piss out of him."

"Bravo. Not good enough. We need him neutralized." Kang paused. "Don't worry, I'm not talking about anything physical."

"Too bad."

"Wow!" He sat back. "A pair of scorpions. Do me a favor, put it aside for now. Whether and why you dislike him is not my business. But I need him off my back, and I need you to help me figure out what will make him crawl back into his hole on his own."

"Rat poison."

Kang sat still for a moment, took a deep breath and exhaled, and then turned the key in the ignition. The engine sputtered once and came to life. "Pak said you were unreasonable on this, but I said you'd help. I guess not." He ignored the traffic policeman's salute as we passed, turned onto the highway with a squeal of the car's old tires, and drove with bored, silent concentration the rest of the way into town.

When we got to the bridge across the river from my apartment, Kang pulled over and reached into the backseat for a small package. All he said was, "I think this is for your picnic." Then he got out of the car and walked to the riverbank.

I wasn't sure what he meant. The package was bulky, wrapped in plain brown paper. Inside was a hand-knit sweater. There was no note, but there didn't have to be. Maybe there was still a trace of her perfume on it, or maybe I only imagined it. The sweater looked like it might be too big. But it was blue.

# 5

The next morning it was raining and windy. I rode my bicycle to the office. The traffic lady was not there, but my satisfaction at crossing the intersection aboveground was short-lived. An army truck spewing black smoke threw up a sheet of water as it passed me.

Pak looked up from his desk as I stood in his doorway. "You are puddling on my floor, Inspector. Go dry yourself off, and get some hot tea. They might still have some in the traffic unit." As I turned to start down the hall, he stopped me. "Where are you going?"

"You told me to get some tea."

"Forget the tea."

"So, you heard about the car."

"The car has been taken off our books. There isn't much left of it, anyway. The damage you did to the left fender by driving into that ditch has disappeared. Likewise the left fender, along with much of the left side of the car. I hope the gas tank wasn't full."

"You mean it exploded? Who turned the key?"

"No one, as far as I know. Must have been a stray radio signal. Very sloppy job." Pak looked back down at his desk and I thought I was dismissed, but he looked up again. He pursed his lips, which he only does when he is thinking about how to say something delicate. "Kang is an ally. We have very few. He has helped us. He asks for our help, we give it, no matter what, and not just grudgingly."

I nodded. No sense in fighting this again, especially when being noncommittal would suffice. "Tell Kang I'll give it some thought."

Pak closed his eyes and rubbed his temples. "You still need to go to Hyangsan looking for pine needles?"

"The pine needles aren't the key, but if they match what was in the cuffs, we can rule out a lot of territory. If I go up there today, even with the rain, I can stay in the hotel and make friends with the staff. Those records may be gone, but the staff's memory isn't wiped out by power failures."

"Unless they've been warned off, like the people at the Koryo."

"I told you we shouldn't take this case. Didn't I tell you no one could solve it?"

"I have great faith, Inspector, that you will solve it. And do you know why? Murder is bad enough, but having a foreigner murdered in the capital is worse, and not finding the murderer is worst of all. If this case isn't solved in a hurry, there will be pressure from the Foreign Ministry. They will yowl for days about how it is harming our relations with the Finns, and to stop their yowling, the Center will lean on our Minister, and the Minister will lean on me. And you do know who I will lean on, Inspector?"

"I can't do miracles."

Pak smiled. "As long as we understand each other."

"You left out one player in all of this. Kim. Kim doesn't care about yowling, and no one can lean on him or Military Security."

"So, you think he's already gotten to the staff at Hyangsan?"

"No, I don't think he has. When Military Security lands, they land hard, but as far as I can tell, they don't get ahead of the game very often."

"Don't be so sure, Inspector. They cultivate a reputation as plodders so they can turn up where you least expect them."

"And that's what I'm going to do. Turn up where they don't expect us. For sure, once Kim hears I'm up there, he'll gag the staff, but for now, he thinks we're fumbling around the Koryo. In fact, why don't you go over there today and tramp through the halls. Make it look like we're closing in on a suspect."

"Any other requests, Inspector?" The question was tinged with annoyance, but Pak was already reaching for his jacket.

I thought a moment. "Get us a new teakettle, would you? I don't care what color it is, as long as it boils water. In fact, get a real plain-looking one. Maybe no one will steal it."

Pak stopped and started searching his pockets. "Have you seen my notebook? I had it with me last night. I didn't leave it in your office, did I?" He frowned as we walked across the hall into my room. "It was nearly blank. Damn, I hate losing new notebooks." He frowned again. "There were two pages from my meeting with the Minister, and a few odds and ends from what you found at the morgue."

My stomach got a funny feeling. "Anything about the pine needles in the trouser cuffs? Or the two sets of keys?"

"No, the main thing was what that doctor told you. Ethnicity is not an identification. Something odd about it, so I wrote it down."

"Maybe your notebook is sitting in the same in-box as the Hyangsan Hotel's records."

Pak nodded. "Maybe. From now on, those scraps of paper you call notes stay on your person, even if it means bathing with your clothes on." He smiled absently out my window. "Those notes from the Minister's meeting will curl their hair. The vice minister was droning on, and I can't stay awake when he does that. So my notes had him saying something more provocative."

"You want me to take the train to Hyangsan, or can we get another car so soon? And do we trust the local guy up there?"

"Take my car, but stay out of ditches this time. The local guy's name is Song. His family is from Japan, actually. He speaks some Japanese.

That's why he's at Hyangsan, to handle visitors. I trust him this far"—Pak held his hands not too far apart—"but no farther. He means well, and he may be a little help. Use your judgment."

As he threw me a set of keys, Pak said matter-of-factly, "Don't turn to look, but there's a black Mercedes outside on the street that wasn't there a minute ago. Pretty blatant." He picked up my umbrella from where it was propped against the wall. "This thing leak?"

"I don't know. I found it the other day."

Pak nodded toward the window. "They must be awfully concerned to play us like this. I'll lead them around the city and then to the Koryo. You wait a few minutes to make sure they don't double back, then zip out of here. They won't have anyone else standing around outside in this weather. Keep in touch."

I walked over to my file cabinet and pulled an armload of old files off the top. My desk is close enough to the window so that anyone in the street could see me, if that was what they wanted to do. I dumped the files on my desk, sat back in my chair, and lit a cigarette. Except when I'm traveling, I rarely smoke, but I figured from the street it would look like I was settling in on a rainy morning. With luck, they'd pull away before I had to take more than a few puffs.

Below in the courtyard, Pak made a show of trying unsuccessfully to start his car, got out, and used the telephone at the guard post to call the duty driver. It didn't take long for an old jeep to pull up; Pak climbed in, and they drove away. From the corner of my eye, I could see that the Mercedes wasn't moving. The motor wasn't even running. They knew my car was in pieces, and it looked like Pak's was out of commission. I wasn't going anywhere in the rain, even if it was lightening up to a steady drizzle. So why were they sitting there? The driver and his partner were probably arguing about what to do, whether to follow Pak or stay and watch me. Unless one of them pulled rank, they were liable to sit and argue all morning. Just as I resigned myself to being a prisoner in my own office, the window on the driver's side opened and a cigarette, barely smoked, was thrown onto the street. The tires spun, then caught the wet pavement, and the big car shot away from the curb. Our guards craned their necks to watch for a moment, then pressed back under the small overhang in a futile attempt to avoid the downpour that had just begun.

# 6

I put off leaving until the weather improved, but it kept raining hard and the wind picked up, so I ended up going over my notes again and calling around to see who might know something about Military Security operations. They didn't seem to have much of a rhythm to anything they did, but I figured they must have some sort of regular procedures. Every organization has regular procedures, even lunks and thugs. I wanted to have some sense of the telltale signs if they started after me in earnest. Nobody would talk to me. As soon as they heard me mention Military Security, their voices went toneless and they suddenly had to go to some meeting or another. The phone rang just before dinner, as I stood at my window watching rain splash off the sidewalk. It was my brother.

"We need to meet." I wasn't used to hearing his voice over the phone. It was low and rough, as if it had been soaked in gravel.

"We already did." I resisted the urge to slam down the receiver. "Once a year is enough."

"Half an hour. At the Koryo."

"I'm busy." As usual, I was talking to myself. He had already hung up.

When I walked into the hotel's lobby, he was in the beer hall, slumped at the same table, fiddling with a matchbook. I strolled over but remained standing. "I'm here. What do you want?"

He didn't look up. "Sit, please, this is serious."

"Since when do you have anything serious to say?"

"Do us both a favor, cut the police inspector crap. Sit, just for five minutes. Hear me out."

I took off my coat, folded it carefully, and laid it on the bench. "Don't waste my time." I sat down.

"Things are happening."

I started to get up again. "We've had this conversation."

"Sit. Shut up, just listen for once. Things are happening, but you don't know what they are."

"And you do?"

"I have a good idea, a lot better than yours. Everything will move, compass points will change, brilliant stars will be plucked from the sky. Rearrangements. Rethinking."

"It won't be the first time. We'll survive."

He ripped a match from the pack and crushed its head between his nails. "No, this time is different." He swept the powder onto the floor.

"Okay, this time is different. That's life."

"No, that's not life." The waitress walked over and started to ask for our order. It was the same girl who had overheard us last time. When she saw it was my brother, she closed her mouth and backed away. "You are my younger brother. We are all that is left of the family. I looked out for you during the war, or have you forgotten?"

"The war is a blank, an empty room, no echoes, no shadows, no light, no dark. I don't remember, I don't dream, I don't dwell on it."

"You're a sad case, you know that? Some people still ache from the war, but you act as if it's nothing."

"Get to the point."

"The point is, you're going to have to trust me for the next couple of months."

"Meaning?"

"Stay out of my way. Get off this case, drop it, break a leg. Better yet, resign from the Ministry. I can have your files pulled, so yours won't be there when there's a review. I'll put them in a safe place until things calm down."

"Funny, Pak wanted me to resign, too."

"When did he say that?" My brother's voice became smooth, suspicious.

"That got your attention, I see. Never mind."

"So, you'll do it?"

"Then what?"

"These things are hard to predict."

"What makes you think I'm in your way?"

"You are."

"And if I stay where I am, continue my investigation?"

"I can't help you when the boom drops."

"You mean you won't."

"No, I mean I can't. I'll be fighting for survival. I have others to protect, programs, people." He paused. "Ideas."

"Ideas?"

"I've warned you. I've asked you. Trust me, just for now, just this once."

"You said 'ideas.' You mean class purity? Human perfection? The collective will?"

There was silence. He sat still enough to be a statue guarding the entrance to an old king's tomb, nothing but sadness in the air between us.

"For the first time in years," I said, "you interest me."

"Will you do as I ask, or not?"

"You know the answer."

His closed his eyes for a moment and put his hand to his forehead. It was a gesture he used to make a long time ago, during the war, to contain the despair that washed over us on cold nights. "Then at least delay the investigation. That's all. Put it in a pending file. Cremate the corpse, lose a couple pieces of evidence, have the room lady reassigned."

"How do you know about her?"

"I told you, this case is beyond what you imagine."

"Don't touch her."

He stood up abruptly. "It's not a choice. I don't give a damn about the case, just where it leads. If you don't let it go, you'll burn. They'll scatter your ashes over the river at dawn."

"And if I burn, so will you."

"Maybe, maybe not. But I can't risk it."

"Ah, now we get to the point. I should save your skin."

He looked at me quizzically, then sat down again. "I thought you were smarter than this. You still don't get it." With his fingers, he traced a single Chinese character on the polished wood of the table. It was the character for family. "If you get too close on this case, you'll give them what they need."

"Them?"

He lowered his eyes. "You heard me."

I stood without a word and walked through the hotel lobby, out the front door, down the drive to the empty street. I walked quickly, but it was already evening, and the darkness overtook me.

# 7

*"You don't have a brother, you do have a brother. Which?"*

*"Are you hard of hearing? I have no brother."*

*"Strange country. You have a relative, a brother, let's say, then he's not a relative anymore. Any other relatives you don't have who are trying to help you?"*

*"Careful, Richie. You are stepping into a minefield. Back off."*

*"Your grandfather was a hero. I respect that."*

*"Your family?"*

*"Big, three brothers and three sisters. My father had four brothers. My*

*mother has a sister. They all have families of their own, a pile of kids. When we get together in the summer, you can't hear yourself think." He watched my face closely. "I have children, two girls." He almost said something more, then checked himself.*

*"My grandfather used to say that my brother and I were close when we were growing up, that my brother protected me. I don't remember. He came back once from the orphans' school after a year or two. Spoke in a loud voice, said he loved the fatherland. Grandfather said it was a good thing to see loyalty in a young boy, but afterward I heard him tell a neighbor that it was damned unpleasant to be lectured by a kid, especially your own grandson."*

*"You ever think about getting married? Having a family?"*

*"Kang, Mr. Molloy. Kang is your topic A, topic B, and topic Z."*

*"You say he's dead."*

*"So he is, but even the dead have much to tell. Maybe that's why we worship them so. Wisdom from beyond."*

*"The sarcasm button just lit up on the tape recorder."*

*"Good, it works. Where were we?"*

*"Going to the mountains. In Hyangsan."*

# PART
# SIX

The road to Hyangsan led to the clouds,
Still I climbed, listening to waterfalls,
Breathing the scent
Of sacred pine trees.

—Kim Po Pyong (1154–1198)

When I went to bed in the Hyangsan Hotel, it was a rainy, sticky summer night. When I woke, it was autumn. Not just the promise of a changing season, but the change itself, whatever the calendar said. The air was crisp and the light so pure that the mountains in the distance were etched sharply against the sky. The underbellies of the clouds off to the east were burning gold, but the sun was still low and the flanks of the rugged hills that ran alongside the fast-moving stream coming down from the Myohyang Mountains were mostly in shadow. Small clouds nuzzled outcroppings along the hilltops, baby white puffs that looked like they had needed something solid to lean against during the night. They had overslept and been left behind. As I watched, they grew more transparent with each sunbeam that touched them. No struggle or sound of despair. They just disappeared.

I stood on my balcony to listen to the birds gathering on the lawn in front of the hotel. On the hills off to the left, where the sunlight hadn't yet found its way, more wispy clouds dumbly awaited their fate. They had settled so close to the ground that they appeared tethered to the gnarled dwarf pine trees growing out of the rocks. The hills were steep. It didn't look possible to climb up there, but that's the funny thing about Korean hills. They're either harder or easier than they appear.

I left the city right after the meeting with my brother. It had stopped raining by then, but it started up again as soon as I got on the highway. There wasn't much traffic, and I never did see a train. At one point, near Kujang, the highway crosses the river coming between steep hills. Then, around the next bend, the river broadens out onto a plain, as if whoever had planned its course had a sudden change of heart.

Leaning support piles are all that remain of a narrow bridge that once spanned the river. It was on this old bridge that my parents were killed. A lonely F-86 had dropped out of the morning sky and made a single strafing run on a small convey of trucks halfway across. The convoy was to have moved at night and been snug against the hills by daybreak, but something held them up and they were hurrying over the river in first light. Fighter planes weren't supposed to be out that early. I never got mad when I thought about it. It wasn't murder. It was death by a fluke, a senseless confluence of the winds of chance.

My father was the only son, and my grandfather never really recovered. He blamed himself until the day he died, though he was miles away at the time, not even in contact with the units in the area. My mother was a nurse and had volunteered to work at the front. Most of the time she and my father were widely separated on the battlefield, but that morning they were together.

I thought about pulling over after crossing the span that now carries the highway across the river, to look at the remains of the old bridge for a while and think about things. By then the rain had stopped again, but the air was wet and my shirt was sticking to my back. The clouds had dropped to the ground, or maybe the road was starting the climb into the hills. The mist got heavier. In another moment, there was no place to pull over, or more likely I wasn't searching that hard. The highway curved around another hill, and the river was suddenly out of sight.

There was a knock at my door, and before I could say anything, a floor lady entered, with a short, wiry workman close behind. "The latch on your balcony window is broken, and it might storm this afternoon." The floor lady pointed to the top of the glass door leading to the balcony. "If it blows open, we'll have water damage, and that costs money."

"You always fix things so early in the morning?" I came in from the balcony and sat on the bed to watch. The workman was carrying only one tool—a short screwdriver with a cracked black plastic handle—but he seemed to know what he was doing. In quick succession, he unscrewed the latch, grumbled a few words to the floor lady, kicked off his shoes, and climbed up on the small table near the door. He used the screwdriver handle to knock something into alignment. That explained the cracks in the handle. He smacked his lips in satisfaction, climbed down from the table, put the screws back in the latch, nodded to me, and walked out the door. I'd never seen anything so efficient. The floor lady beamed.

"We would have done it yesterday if we'd known this room was going to be in use. They normally save this view for important guests." She gave me a crooked smile, friendly but leaving ambiguous whether she thought I met the standard. "From here, you can see mountains on either side of the road and watch the stream as it tumbles down over the rocks. It's nearly full now, after the rain. If it storms again tonight, we'll have a regular torrent. The noise might keep you up all night long. To some people, it's an angry sound, but I don't think it is. By our dormitory, up the road there, it sounds like a train. Most of the time, though, it is kind of sleepy. Like everything hereabouts."

She bowed and turned to go. Then she turned back. "Just a thought, but you might like to walk around the temple up the way. A pretty stroll on a morning like this. It should be almost perfect. Stick to the side of the road, once in a while a truck coming downhill loses its brakes. When you reach the temple, you can be alone if you want. Tell the guides you can manage by yourself. Though sometimes they feel lonely and like to talk to people." She paused. "They see a lot. And they take notes." She paused again. "On paper."

I nodded to acknowledge what she'd said but didn't pursue the opening. Nobody was that helpful without reason, and I didn't know what her reason was, so I thought I'd let things set until after lunch. Meantime, I could look around. "Until what time is the dining room open for breakfast?"

"Did you call ahead?" Her tone changed, and not very subtly.

"For what?"

"New policy. We only fix enough food for people who sign up ahead of time. Got to make a profit, you know." She was verging on stern. Suddenly, profits looked like a bad idea.

"All I want is some tea. Maybe some fruit."

She shook her head. "I'll check, but they only started this a month ago, and the manager is new." Her expression showed she hadn't made up her mind about him yet. "He's strict. Says if we make an exception for one person, we'll have to do it for everyone, and then where will we be?" She turned to go again, stepped partway into the hall, then stopped and stepped back inside the room. "The guides at the temple always have a kettle on." Her manner was helpful again, almost pleading with me to start asking her some questions. "They sip tea and chat most of the day. Nice girls, but they don't work all that hard, if you ask me." When I didn't reply, she bowed deeply to hide her disappointment and glided away.

The road to the temple ran beside the river, which was coursing full and fast over large boulders army engineers had dumped there to slow the current and keep it from tearing at the banks. There wasn't much danger of that on the far side, where the solid-rock base of the mountain rose steeply, almost straight up, from the water. The last of the infant clouds had vanished in the daylight, and the rocky outcroppings were easy to see from the road. Growing from them, trunks struggling to stay upright on the slopes, were groups of the dwarf pine trees I needed to reach. Maybe some mountains were easier than they looked. Not this one.

By the time I reached the temple, I was puffing. It seemed to me the construction engineers could have done with a little less steepness if they'd given it some thought. There was a small ticket-selling hut just beyond the empty parking lot, next to a colored map of the temple complex and the surrounding mountains. The wooden shutter on the front of the hut was propped open, and I could see two guides sitting inside, drinking tea and staring out at the scenery. One emerged from the side door to ask what I wanted. She was tall and walked with a measured gait, so that the skirts of her costume floated over the stone pathway. Her hair was pinned up with two combs. It made her neck seem long and gave her jaw more attention than it needed. But she had a smile that looked real, and her eyes sparkled even in the dappled light.

"Good morning. Tours don't begin until noon. The temple complex opens at eleven o'clock." She could see I was still breathing hard from the walk. "The hotel staff knows they're not supposed to send people up here so early. Why don't you sit on the bench under those trees and catch your breath." Her voice was pleasant, without the hard-driving edge of the guides in the capital. It seemed to fit with the trees and the grass and the flowers. Either that or I was lightheaded from the climb.

I thought she would go back to the kiosk to finish her tea, but instead she stood there, looking at me as if she'd asked a question that I was so far failing to answer. I had started to say something about the weather when a gust of wind blew closed the shutter on the ticket hut. It swung shut with a loud bang, there was a muffled scream from inside, and then the second guide burst out the door. She was shorter than the first guide; her hair was long, and her face was exactly like those in old folk paintings. Cute, like a kitten or a puppy, with big, wide-set dark eyes. "You'd probably get tired of her after a while," I could hear Pak saying to me.

The second guide propped the shutter open and walked over to us. The front of her skirt was wet. "I was pouring myself a cup and spilled the whole kettle when that shutter banged shut. Could have burned myself like a chicken." She was agitated. Her friend tittered, then caught herself and looked away. It was incumbent on me to say something polite if I had any thought of seeing the kitten again. All I could think was that this had the earmarks of another morning without tea.

The second guide glanced down at her skirt, which was clinging to her legs. "It's soaked through. I can't give tours walking around like this, none of the men will listen. I've got to hike back to the room and change. If I can find any, I'll bring some extra tea, too. What we had left is all over the floor."

Amazing, I thought, and kicked a pinecone halfway across the parking lot. One lousy cup of tea wouldn't do me any harm. I strolled over for a closer view of the low orange flowers that bordered both sides of the walkway leading to the temple grounds. The first guide floated beside me. "It's going to rain again later this morning anyway, so there won't be any tours." She brushed against my arm. "As long as you've walked this far up the hill, you may as well look around the grounds. When the rain starts, we can duck into one of the old buildings. The roofs leak a little, but you don't look too delicate to me."

The sky had lost the freshness of morning and was turning a hard blue. The light on the grass and the flowers was brilliant, but it stopped suddenly at the edge of the main path, which was deeply shaded by ten or fifteen old Chinese elms standing in a row. Their trunks curved gently near the ground, as if they had once seen court ladies gathering their skirts and longed to do that, too.

With the sun climbing above the peaks, the near side of the hills was no longer in shadow. The dwarf pine trees looked farther away, and smaller, while the rocks they were growing from had become larger and more foreboding in the light. The guide looked up at the mountain. "There is a legend about those trees. They were planted by the monks who had to flee the fighting here centuries ago. The story is that they deliberately planted the trees in the most inaccessible places, to be a constant reminder to any invaders that nothing could crush our spirit."

"Nice tale. But I think they only live to be about fifty years old, at most, then they reseed. Though how anything could reseed on those rocks is beyond me."

The guide motioned me over to a boulder sitting behind a low wooden fence. The face of the rock had been carved away and a poem in ancient Chinese characters chiseled on it, but these had been worn by the weather, making it hard to read more than one or two in each line. "If I told you this boulder has been here for a thousand years, would you tell me it is not so?" The guide's voice remained professionally pleasant; nothing about her tone suggested she was irritated. It was a simple question. But her gait had changed: She wasn't floating anymore, and her skirts brushed the stepping-stones.

"Nothing is impossible," I said. "Everything you tell me on this beautiful morning, I believe."

She walked ahead of me without saying anything more until we reached a low bench in the middle of a semicircle of tall plane trees. They all leaned slightly in the same direction. It was their effort to catch the sun but gave them the look of a group of strangers, each trying to hear the same conversation. The guide sat looking away from the eaves-dropping trees, her back to the mountain that rose above the river. In front of us, a stone's throw away, was a small wooden building surrounded by a hedge of roses.

"This is my favorite building in the complex. No matter what, it carries an air of tranquility." She spoke softly, her voice barely rising above the sound of the river and the birds. Almost as an afterthought she said, "There have been a lot of visitors here recently." She laid her hands calmly in her lap and put her face up to the sky. Her eyes were closed, but she wasn't resting.

I thought she was expecting me to say something, to pick up on her remark. Then I realized she was getting her thoughts in order. "Am I interested?"

"I know who you are, Inspector. Isn't that what we're best at, keeping track of other people? Surely you're not surprised that someone called to tell us you were coming."

"No, I suppose not."

She closed her eyes again. I wasn't sure if she was trying to remember a story she'd been given to tell me, or was searching her memory for some facts that had fallen into the dark places where they were sitting quietly until she found them. Facts are like that sometimes, especially unpleasant ones. I make it a point to give people the benefit of the doubt if they say they don't remember, even when I'm not positive I can afford to believe them.

"Busier than normal?" It might help to start where she left off. If there was a story line, she'd feed it to me no matter what I said.

She opened her eyes and turned to me. "I didn't say 'busy.' I said we'd had a lot of visitors."

Good, she was paying attention, that meant no story line. But she seemed uncertain, trying to keep her balance mentally. "You're right, that's what you said—a lot of visitors. The usual tour groups?"

She stood up and moved slowly from under the trees into a patch of sunlight. I stayed on the bench. It isn't a good idea to question people when they are moving around—breaks the concentration—but when she didn't come back to sit down, I got to my feet and walked beyond her to a bed of yellow mums that were starting to bloom. Chasing after her wasn't going to work. It would confuse our roles. If she had something important to say, something she was nervous about, she was going to have to come to me. "Interesting thing about flowers," I said. "No matter when you plant them, they open on schedule. Once in a while you get a bush or a tree that lags behind, or gets anxious. Flowers don't do that."

When I looked up, she was beside me. She had started floating again. That was good. "Two weeks ago, five Military Security agents were here. They climbed that hill." She didn't turn around or point, but she meant the hill behind us, the one with the small pine trees. "People who come to the hotel sometimes climb up there, though they usually need permission. Normally, I wouldn't pay much attention. It's the local security man who is nervous, because if there is an accident, he gets blamed."

"You know the local security man?"

She reached over to pull off several wilted flowers that had been broken at the stem. "You know better than to ask a question like that. How could I not know him? He's been here a long time. And he has a good singing voice, so we sometimes have him come to the bar in the hotel. I can usually tell if a tour group is going to be trouble later, in the bar. I give him a call and he sings karaoke for a few hours. The tourists like it. If anyone has too much to drink, he helps them to their room. Otherwise, they become too friendly with the waitresses. Nothing special most of the time, just annoying. Once in a while, there's real trouble."

"How long have you been a guide here at the temple?"

"You mean, was I a waitress in the bar before I got this job? I can sing a little, feed tidbits to the guests, But I'm not a prostitute, if that's what you're thinking." She floated down the path, as if to emphasize that she could break the conversation anytime she wanted. I turned and looked up the hill at the pine trees. She'd told me everything I needed to know for right now. She could tell me more about the hotel, the guests, and the Military Security team later.

One thing worried me. A team of five men was unusual. I tried to remember if I'd ever heard of anything like that. Normally, they work in threes, like the three men in the jeep at Manpo, or the three standing around afterward. Five either meant two teams had been joined for a special operation, or they had been moved in without coordination, under separate orders. Even so, in either case, there should have been six. The Military Security Command made its share of mistakes, and its operations were still unclear to me, but this much they did by the book. A team was three men, an iron triangle.

I needed a picture of Colonel Kim, and maybe one of his dead agent, Chong, to show to the staff. There was no reason to think either of them had been here, but I wanted to know if there was any connection between Military Security's operation up here and their efforts to get at Kang. Some of them might have regional responsibilities, but others were probably assigned to particular cases, and I had to start one somewhere. Maybe one of the guides or the floor lady would recognize them. He wouldn't want to do it, but Kang could get me the pictures. His department kept files; he'd told me they took photographs of the three-man team that broke into the consulate in Beijing. For that matter, maybe Kang knew something about why Military Security had been up here.

Before I set off down the road to the hotel, I needed only one more thing from the guide. "In all those visitors, all the continents were represented?"

She thought a moment. "Funny way to put it. We don't usually divide up the groups like that, but—no. None from Antarctica."

# 2

Song Chon Kun, the local security man, was about fifty years old, tall, very fit, a firm handshake and a winning smile. I did not like him. It did not help his case that I knew about his singing ability. His speaking voice was rich and melodious, and he used it dramatically. Another black mark. "Nice to see you up here, Inspector," he said, cocking his head slightly as if he expected me to break into an aria in reply.

"Business brings me here, not pleasure. Official business, the capital investigative body." I figured inflating my rank a little might wipe the smile off his face. He only beamed all the more.

"Then it is a true pleasure, a true pleasure." His hair was dyed, a shade too dark. Most young girls didn't have shining black hair like that, much less a middle-aged security officer at a resort hotel, never mind how easy his job was. "Anything I can do, anything at all. My humble resources are at your disposal."

This must be his Japanese upbringing. Either his resources were at my disposal or they were not. Humble didn't make a damned bit of difference. "I will need your discretion, your knowledge of the surrounding countryside, and your memories about anything unusual over the past two or three weeks. This pertains to a murder investigation in the capital."

Song's eyes narrowed for a fraction of a second. He realized I was not going to share very much with him, and he was not used to being squeezed for information. Hyangsan was rated as a special area, and that gave Song special privileges. He could sense I was threatening his cozy existence. His voice lost its golden cover for the briefest moment, then regained it as quickly. "Let's get away from the hotel and go down by the river, where we can talk."

We walked the whole way in silence. A little small talk about the weather wouldn't have cost either of us anything, but I figured he was sore at me. That was alright; it meant he was on edge, probably trying to figure out how much damage I could do if he didn't answer my questions. When we got to the river he faced the water, his back to the hotel. The water pounding over the rocks was even louder than it had been earlier in the morning and was throwing up a spray.

"I apologize, Inspector, for seeming rude, but I didn't want to speak until we were standing here. It makes it hard for them to calibrate the microphones up there on the balcony."

Alright, so I had misjudged him; his voice didn't detract from his critical faculties as much as I'd thought. "We don't go in much for technical stuff in the Ministry, so I assume they aren't our mikes," I said. On a hot July day the spray might have been refreshing. Now it was just damp.

Song took out his handkerchief and mopped his face. "Gesture toward the river or up the mountain, would you? Otherwise they're going to become suspicious."

I stabbed my finger at the top of one of the hills. Song laughed, a rich baritone laugh. "No need to be too theatrical, Inspector. Now, you have some questions for me? You are quite an expert on our pine trees, I hear." Okay, so I had doubly misjudged him. He had already talked to the tall guide.

"I take it those mikes aren't here all the time. Something special going on?"

Song's hand pointed for a moment at the largest boulder midstream and then moved languidly in a smooth motion toward a bird in the trees. "See that rock?" I saw that the top had been chipped recently. "Those fools wanted to put a remote microphone on there, disguise it with some leaves or something. I told them it was crazy, that as soon as it rained and the river rose, it would wash away. Two of them tried it anyway. One of them fell into the river and broke his shoulder. Had to be carted away. The other five decided to take my advice."

That explained why the guide saw five, not six, Military Security monkeys climbing the hill. There were two whole teams originally. "What are they doing up here now? They aren't checking up on tourists or the hotel staff with remote microphones." Song didn't respond. "So who is the target? And I'll know if you are screwing with me."

Song picked up a small stone from the riverbank and threw it into the water. "In the time I've been here, we had this sort of thing once before. Two years ago." He paused. "No, three. You remember the nephew of a Politburo member who held some position in the party's Youth League? He was forever bouncing up here to 'rest,' but he never rested. He was always meeting people, Chinese businessmen in plaid shirts, Koreans from Japan with extra-oiled hair. Automobiles would come up from Pyongyang, carrying girls, always discreet, never more than one in each car." Song started moving up the riverbank, in small steps, keeping his back to the hotel. "About three or four months after the first visit by this guy, a captain from Military Security showed up. Real mean son of a bitch."

Song's voice was too mellifluous for such vocabulary; it made his curses sound like compliments. "His name is Kim," I said. "Short-haired snake, eyes sort of sharp, like little kitchen knives."

"Yes, that's the one." Song looked over at me and then pointed downstream. "You know him, I take it."

I was soaked from the spray; the sky was clouding over and the wind picking up. "I don't suppose there is someplace other than this river-bank where we can talk?"

Song pointed up the side of the hill. "We could go up there, if you don't mind the climb. That's where the other five security—"

"Finish what you were saying about Kim first." I didn't want to get onto the subject of the pine trees just yet. "And get to the point."

Song shrugged. "It's your session. Whatever you wish." He thought a moment. "Kim walked around the grounds. Sometimes he'd corner one of the staff members. They were all terrified, the way he stared at them. I kept out of his way but picked up bits and pieces of what he was un-earthing. The nephew was involved in a smuggling operation. Cars mostly, used luxury cars from Japan that were driven across the border into China where they got double, even triple the price and paid no tax. There were rumors the operation was greased with South Korean intelli-gence money, Kim figured he would set a trap for the nephew, bag a Politburo member, and take over the operation for himself."

My shoes were wet, and it was always hard to dry them out com-pletely. I'd be walking in these hills feeling that dampness for days. "Then what?"

"Nothing."

"No, not nothing. The cars kept coming, didn't they?"

"Maybe."

"Every other Thursday, in the afternoon, another car."

"Who told you?"

"I do my job, you do yours, if you still have one when I'm through with you. When I ask you a question, don't tell me 'nothing.'"

Song's face got a funny look—some fear, a touch of loathing, then the sickening realization that his fate was in someone else's hands. Only I didn't want his fate in my hands.

"When did the cars stop coming?"

"Last week of June nothing showed up. Nothing at all in July. That's when the Military Security teams arrived. I figured something was wrong."

"Kim's paying you off, isn't he?"

Song looked away.

"I asked you a question."

"I don't work for him."

"But you take his money."

"You think things are easy here, Inspector?"

"You've kept this to yourself until now, didn't even let the Ministry have a hint, didn't send in an anonymous report, didn't ask someone up here for a beer. Nothing." If I didn't get into a hot bath and some dry clothes pretty soon, I'd catch a cold that would stay with me until April. I stepped over to Song, put my arm around his shoulder in what would look like a friendly gesture to whoever might still be interested in our conversation and squeezed until he winced. "I'm going back to my room. If you have anything else to tell me, anything you left out accidentally on purpose, you better spill it before I leave here, or you and your velvet throat are going to be singing with the canaries in a deep, dark mine with other greedy local police. They have a special place assigned for people who served in cushy spots like this."

I released my grip, turned toward the hotel balcony and nodded slightly, and then walked up the path to the hotel. By the time I reached the steps to the front door, it was raining hard. When I looked back at the river, Song was still there, gesturing now and then at the mountain in front of him. As far as I could tell, he wasn't singing.

## 3

There wouldn't be any hot water for a while, the floor lady said. She was in the elevator when I rode up. "How was the temple?" She pointed at my shoes. "Those are ruined," she said. "No way to dry them. And you'll have to find some way to keep warm. There's no heat this time of year." She could have sounded more apologetic, I thought. "The boiler went out this morning, again. They thought it was fixed, but they always say that. Spare parts this, and spare parts that. The guests aren't going to be happy. Bad for profits."

"Yeah, well, I'm a guest. I'm not happy. Do you have an extra towel, one that I can't see through when I hold it up to the light? You know, something that will actually absorb water?"

"I can find one, but meantime try not to drip on the furniture, would you? Every time you move, you drip. We'll have to take this mat out of the elevator and dry it." Someone at the hotel must have been overseas at a place where they put floor mats emblazoned with the day of the week in the elevator. In theory, the mats get changed every day. If guests lose track of time, they only have to look down at their feet, assuming they can read English.

When I stepped into my room, the glass door to the balcony was wide open, letting in torrents of rain. A small lake had formed on the carpet. The desk lamp had fallen onto the floor, and the lampshade was soaking up water like a sponge. The balcony door latch couldn't have broken again; I'd watched the workman fix it. When I walked over to close the door, I could see that the latch had been pulled down. It had been snapped shut when I left for the temple.

The floor lady walked in with a towel. She looked at the window and then glanced around the room. "You going to stand there dripping all over the floor, like I asked you not to?"

"Funny how this window unlatched itself after I left," Frankly, I didn't give a damn about her floor. "In most hotels, things stay latched. The laws of physics don't work around here, I guess."

She laid the towel on the bed. "I wouldn't know about any laws of physics. I don't control who comes and goes in these rooms." Her face was composed, as if she had made an important decision and felt comfortable with it. "The guide at the temple enjoyed talking to you. But I guess you didn't have time to finish your tour."

I decided to skip over what should have been a couple of sessions of questioning and get to the point. "Who is the maid on the fifteenth floor?" That got a blank look but no answer, so I repeated the question, this time with extra emphasis. "This hotel won't earn any profits if I have it closed, and I'll do that if I don't get cooperation. I can authorize a 'closure for cause' if necessary." I was making this up, but she wouldn't know it.

"No, you can't do that. This is a special tourist zone, and you people can't touch us without authorization." She had invented this on the spot, and it topped mine. The "you people" was surprising, but I figured it might be useful. She wouldn't be any more cowed by Military Security than she was scared of me, and with luck she might even be more annoyed at them.

"Let me rephrase my question. Do the guests on the fifteenth floor scratch the furniture with their equipment?"

"Damned right they do. Gear and boxes and wires all over the place. Usually I don't work on fifteen, but the woman who normally does says she can't stand it with them around. One time she accidentally opened the door to their room and they nearly murdered her. She said she hasn't seen that many weapons since she was in the army."

I looked up at the ceiling, then glanced around the baseboard. The floor lady shook her head. "These rooms are clean, though no one believes it. Military Security can't put anything in without special permission. We have to know. Otherwise we might rip the wires out by mistake. They tried it once and the manager nearly had a fit. Said they put back the baseboard so bad, the next guest in, an Iranian, filed a complaint. The only thing they are allowed are those gun mikes they set up on their balcony. We clean their rooms once a week."

"Rooms. Plural?"

"Yes, two rooms. The fifteenth floor has the best view, and the manager has called Pyongyang more than once to ask if they could be put on another floor."

"What about the rest of the fifteenth floor?"

"What do you think?" She put her hands on her hips and stood there defiantly. "We rent it out. They complained because you can see from one balcony to the next, but we told them if they didn't like it, they'd have to pay for the whole floor. That's a lot of rooms. And they'd have to disable the elevator button, too. You want to guess how many guests drink too much at the bar on the top floor, then stumble off the elevator on the wrong floor and end up fumbling with the knob to the wrong room? The halls are dark at night, so you can't read the numbers on the doors to save your life. Got to save electricity, you know what I mean?"

"Ah, yes, profits. Well, thanks for the towel. If the hot water comes on, maybe you can have someone ring me." From the way she frowned, I wasn't expecting hot water anytime soon.

There wasn't a sound as she shut the door behind herself. It occurred to me that if she could close a door so quietly, she probably could open one that way, too. Not like the Koryo, where the doors always clicked. I picked the lamp off the floor and set it up again on the desk, then unplugged it from the wall. Probably I should have done it the other way around. The chances of getting electrocuted were slim, but lately things weren't exactly working in my favor. I sat down on the bed and reviewed what I'd learned. Song was good and scared; I didn't trust him at all, but enough of what he told me fit with what the old farmer had described about the cars on the highway. Kim had taken over a car-smuggling operation. It had been regular, twice a month. Then something happened to throw off the routine. There were more cars than there should have been, at times they weren't supposed to appear. At least one of the drivers wasn't from Military Security. No one working for Military Security could be described as skinny. Muscular, maybe. Ugly, burly, thuggish. Not skinny. They all got plenty of food and plenty of exercise. This was starting to point in one direction. Kang. That car I was supposed to photograph, the reason Colonel Kim had arranged for me to sit on that hillside at dawn—Kang. The reason I was in Manpo—Kang.

I lay down. A few minutes later, as I was sinking into sleep, I heard the river thundering over the rocks, tearing at its banks, willing itself away to the freedom of the ocean far to the west.

# 4

Pak walked into my office and sat on the only chair not piled with papers. "I scrounged you a filing cabinet. Why don't you use it?" This was always his opening line, and he no longer expected an answer. He knew the first drawer held my vase, the one with the flying cranes, and the second drawer my collection of sandpaper. In the third drawer were the pieces of a simple bookshelf I kept hoping to build.

"We are near a dead end on this case. The hospital says it can't justify the refrigeration and is going to have to dump the corpse. The Minister says it's time to file this in the Unsolved drawer and let it be." Pak looked over at the file cabinet. "Where do you put the unsolved stuff, in the drawer with your bookshelf plans?" He put his feet on my desk and then pulled them off again. "Sorry, rude of me. I was trying to think."

When he walked in, I'd been making another rough sketch of a bookshelf on the back of another Ministry memo. We both knew there might never be time or materials enough to build anything. I put the sketch to the side and found my notepad. "We both know the Minister wants us to solve this case," I said. "The fact that the vice minister doesn't think we can do it makes it doubly important to the old man." Pak made a noncommittal noise. "And we both know who has ordered the Minister to close the file. My brother. My former brother."

Pak stared off into space. He didn't blink, and for a while I thought he had stopped breathing.

"Not much we can do, Inspector," he said finally. "We're spending our time shuffling a pretty pile of facts that don't add up, and I can't justify keeping you on this much longer."

I didn't have to reply, because my phone rang. It was the local security man, Li, who handled the countryside district south of Pyongyang. One of the farmers had found something, he said, and he wanted me to take a look before he made a formal report. I thanked him, said I would be right there, and hung up.

Pak had heard only my half of the conversation, but he didn't ask any questions. "Use my car again," he said. "Get back here by noon, though. Kang and I are having lunch. Noodles. He's paying. About damn time."

# 5

Li was waiting on the side of the highway, not far from the spot where I had been staked out with the camera. He waved me over and pointed to a small side road. It was only a wide dirt path that led through the corn-field and up into the hills, but it would hide a car from the highway.

"Back in," he said. "You may want to get on the highway again and into town real quick." He looked into my car and then clucked his tongue. "You armed? Probably not. We have some old automatic weapons in the security building, but the local commander has the keys to the gun locker. He and I are on pretty good terms." Li paused, thinking over what he'd just said. "I guess not good enough, though, not yet."

"Why would I need to be armed? What's this about?"

"Get the car out of the road first." There was a ripple of urgency in his voice that caught me by surprise. It was not like Li. Even when we were in the army together, he never showed emotion. Older than the rest of us, he never sang or danced or drank. Sometimes he sat by himself, looking off at the horizon. When we went on patrol, he was serious and wouldn't let us joke about anything. If I ever heard him laugh, I don't remember, but I don't think I ever heard him complain, either. After we got out of the army, we lost touch, but one day, going through reports by local security officers, I spotted his name, and after that we saw each other from time to time. Whenever he came to Pyongyang, which wasn't often, he'd drop by the office.

Li watched the highway while I backed the car into the field. Then he led me along a second narrow path up a hill until we were above where I had sat the morning I watched the black car speed away.

"You want to tell me why I need to be armed? Or why you mentioned your gun locker?"

Li didn't reply. If he'd looked out at the horizon, like he used to do in the army, I'd have figured he was absorbed in his own thoughts. That used to happen: One of us would say something to him, and there'd be no reply, so after a while we'd just go away and leave him alone. Now, though, he was staring down at the ground. He shook his head slightly, but I knew he wasn't replying to my questions. He was having a conversation with himself. He'd called and asked me to come out here, and now he wasn't sure what to say. Finally, he sighed, and that worried me more than anything else he might have said or done at that moment.

"You need to know this. Otherwise I wouldn't be telling you." He looked up but at that instant turned his head slightly, so his eyes never met mine. "The whole time you were watching, you were being watched." Li pointed to the remains of some food, a couple of cigarette butts, and a small pile of rocks. "That's a support for a field dish, holds a little satellite relay system. Someone was up here, watching you and relaying the info to someone else. Must have been quite a distance away. Otherwise he could have used a regular transmitter."

I remembered the stone coming down the hill, and the bird. "How do you know someone was here when I was down there?" I already knew Li was involved—that's how he got the money to pay the farmers to keep quiet—but I couldn't believe he was working for Military Security.

"There's too much territory for me to cover, even with the two trainees they threw at me last year when the highway started getting more traffic. I decided to do regular patrols but at irregular times. I remembered it from an old book on guerrilla tactics. We log the times and the particular run, so that theoretically we cover everything once a week. The whole point is, there's no regular pattern, which means sometimes we do the same route two days in a row. What we lose in territory, we make up for in luck. This time we were lucky. We did the route that goes by this hillock twice."

I put my boot on the stones and ground them into the dirt. "I thought we were friends, Li. We've known each other a long time. Maybe friendship doesn't mean anything anymore." Below, a convoy of dump trucks filled with people moved to the next section of fields to harvest. They turned down a road and in a moment were out of sight. "Do you really think I'm a fool? You don't make regular runs through here, and even if you did, you'd never find anything in this corn. Two rows over could be a thousand kilometers away. So what is this about?" I motioned at the hill slightly higher and behind where we stood. "Let's go."

When we reached the top of the hill, Li squatted down peasant style and lit a cigarette. He puffed at it a few times, then pinched off the lit end and put what was left behind his ear. "You're right. Someone told me to be here. From this spot, we were watching that guy watching you. He was no one from this side of the DMZ—too many gadgets. I'm not supposed to say anything, but I got to thinking about it. You may not believe me, but it's true."

"I didn't even know where I was going to set up that morning. How could anyone else know where I'd be?"

"We didn't, and neither did the other guy as far I can tell. Maybe they just guessed you wouldn't drive too far down the highway. This hill and the next one over are the best surveillance spots for a couple of kilometers. All the other hills are too small or too bare, and there aren't many spots to hide your car."

"They? They guessed? Who are we talking about, Li?"

Li glanced at his watch. "Don't ask me anything else. Won't be but a few minutes. Just keep your eyes down on the road."

"What am I looking for?" I knew the answer.

"A car."

"What if I say I'm tired of watching highways?"

Li stood up and moved along the path down the hill. "That child, Inspector. He was my sister's son." He paused and looked up at me. "I know what happened. I think you do, too."

The sound of two cars coming out of the tunnel and moving at high speed made us both turn toward the road. The lead car, half a kilometer away and coming at us like an arrowhead, was deep blue, smaller than the one I'd seen on the first morning but just as clean. The second car was bigger, black, and right behind, so close it seemed attached to the first. I'd never seen two cars going so fast that close together. The driver of the black car must have taken his foot off the gas. The blue car pulled ahead suddenly, and as it came abreast of us, there was a muffled explosion, the road heaved into the air, and the car careened into the field across the way. The second car braked sharply and stopped just before the crater left by the explosion. The passenger-side door opened; a man got out and ran to the driver's side of the blue car. He looked in the window, pulled a small machine pistol from under his jacket, and fired a burst into the car. He looked again, then fired another. As he ran back to the black car, he stopped and looked up the hill. He had short-cropped hair. I couldn't see his eyes, but I knew they were like knives.

The black car drove on the dirt shoulder for a few yards, crushing the wildflowers. Once it eased back onto the highway, the driver accelerated so rapidly he fishtailed across the road, then regained control and moved north again. Just as the car disappeared over a small rise, I heard the horn blare. Li was shaking; I couldn't tell whether it was with fear or with anger. "He wanted you to see that, Inspector. And he wanted me to see it, too. It's a warning: If we get in his way, we're dead men, for sure."

# 6

"You hungry yet, Inspector?"

"It was your satellite dish, must have been. Your people were watching that highway. Or someone working for you. That radio scanner, in the black car the first time, it was yours, too?"

"Told you, I'm only a note taker. Mind if I fix a sandwich?" He walked into the kitchen and turned on the light. "Could make you a cup of tea—Irish tea, if you don't mind."

"I've had coffee already." I heard him grunt in disappointment. "Okay, I'll try the tea."

"I thought you liked tea."

"Lost my taste for it, I guess."

"Cream?"

"Cream! Are you kidding? How about whiskey? I thought that was how you people drank tea." I followed him to the kitchen.

"Some do. Not me. Cream and sugar." He turned to watch me for a moment, just long enough to make sure I'd stopped at the kitchen door. "Only a habit, drinking tea like that, but it reminds me of home. You ever get lonely, Inspector, on the road?"

"Wouldn't you like to know. If I did, it would take a lot of loneliness for me to drink tea with cream and sugar." I took the cup from him and looked around the edge.

"No cranes, sorry."

"Tell me, Richie, why were your people watching the highway? Is that when I wandered into your sights? Were you expecting Kang to be out there?"

The Irishman cleaned the counter, washed his cup, and wiped the faucets and then the cupboard handles. "Three questions, for which you already realize you won't get answers. But you know what Kang was doing back there in Pak's office, don't you. He wanted to find out how much Kim knew. And, if Kang was operating true to form, he also wanted a good look at you. He'd been checking up, he told you that. But Kang doesn't trust paper or other people's reports. He wanted to see you for himself."

I gave a mock salute. "I am impressed. You are obviously thorough, a trait too often overlooked. You've been watching Kang awhile, I take it."

"Not long enough. We didn't know about Kim, but we knew Kang was worried. He was jumping around, moving his people and collecting his cash, folding up networks. We couldn't figure it out, until we got wind of this Japanese thing. Someone told me it looked like Kang was scared. Didn't sound right to me."

"Kang wouldn't panic. He lacked that gene. Up in Manpo, he told me the deal with Japan was about to cause trouble internally. Do you know what he meant? Had you already figured out what he was doing on the border?"

"Let's just say we knew that a settlement between your country and Japan after all these years strikes a lot of people as inconvenient."

*"They shouldn't worry."*

*"Oh?"*

*"Richie, compared with relations between my country and Japan, the Irish have a love affair with England. South Koreans, Chinese, Indonesians—no one likes the Japanese and no one ever will. I don't know why. Pak and I would talk about it sometimes. Pak said it was irrational."*

*"What happened to Pak? You said he's dead. How?"*

*"Ask Kim."*

*"Be serious."* His phone rang; he answered it quickly. *"I think so."* He hung up. *"You want to keep going?"* He looked at his notebook, then frowned at the tape recorder. It had been running the whole time. *"You had just seen a couple of cars."*

# 7

"Military Security mined the highway." I had run up the stairs and was out of breath, standing in the doorway to Pak's office. "They blew up a car, and Kim shot the driver in cold blood. He must have told Li to bring me out there to watch. The guy's a fucking sadist." Pak was looking at me curiously from behind his desk. I never run up the stairs. "This is Kang's business, not ours. Remember, I told you this wasn't my job, I told you when this whole thing started. It has something to do with that black car I was supposed to photograph. This time it was blue. Get Kang on the phone."

"Let's go to your office, Inspector." He looked out his window at the Operations Building. "The view is better."

When we got to my office, Pak pointed at my desk. "Inspector, sit down, shut up, and listen to yourself. Call Kang? You want me to use the telephone in the middle of this?" He picked up my phone and yanked the wire from the wall. If the phones were bugged, they would transmit even when they were hung up. We unplugged them from the wall receptacle on the rare occasions we didn't want to risk being monitored. Yanking the wire from the wall was not the preferred method, but it did the job. "That's much better."

"What's wrong with your office?"

"I think someone is keeping an eye on us, and maybe an ear, from the Operations Building. I just noticed it a day or so ago. Curtains moving in odd ways."

"They've been watching me, too."

"Kang and I are having lunch today, remember? You can join us. Make jolly at the noodle place. Lots of laughs. Afterward, we can go up to the monuments by the river to talk. A couple of drunken cadre going to snooze on the grass. They can't get in too close, unless they've decided it's time to throw a net on us."

"This is no time for a picnic. Something is about to happen, and for all I know it's going to happen today. You already know what it is, don't you? You knew even before you sent me up to Manpo."

"I don't know what I don't know, Inspector." Pak was staring out my window. "Do you think Li really understands what is going on?" He didn't sound like he was interested in the answer; his attention was still completely riveted on the street.

"He must have. He looked at his watch; he knew the schedule. I think he's known for a long time something was going on. They had to bring the local security man in on it, at least enough to make sure the road was clear each time one of those cars came up the road. Something happened last month, though. Too many cars, on the wrong days. Li is quiet, but he's smart. He must have figured it out. Maybe he said something to Kim. Maybe he told Kim to find another highway, it was too dangerous for the locals. To keep him quiet, they killed his sister's son."

Pak whirled around. "The boy who had his throat cut?" He closed his eyes and put his hand on the wall to steady himself. "Enough," he said softly, and turned back to the window. "Enough."

"I don't think Li knew exactly what was going to happen when he told me to come out there. He seemed nervous, not like himself, but that could have been because he was planning to tell me something he had been told to keep secret. And he knew what happens when you cross Military Security. But they overreached if they thought they'd keep him quiet by killing the boy." I waited for Pak to say something, but he didn't. "You alright?" I asked.

"Fine, Inspector. Keep talking."

"After he saw what Kim did, when Kim stopped and looked up the hill, he said to me that Kim was warning us not to get in the way or we'd be dead men."

Pak kept staring out the window. "He didn't say, 'I'm a dead man.' He said, 'We.' Why include you? Why does Kim think you're getting in his way?"

I shrugged. "Does it matter?"

"Okay." Pak finally convinced himself there was nothing happening outside. "We're clear at the moment." He moved back slowly from the window and leaned against my desk. "You're right. We may not have much time before they get here. We need to lay out what we know and see what we can figure out. It doesn't all have to fit, just enough to put them off balance for a few more hours. If they think we've filed a report implicating them, it will send them back to their cave while they figure out their next move. That's long enough for me to call the Minister."

"Why not call the Minister right now?"

"And tell him what? We're scared? I need something concrete for him to issue an order throwing the Ministry in front of Military Security."

"You want to start with the black car I couldn't get a picture of?"

"No, I'll take your explanation of the cars. Where does the corpse in the Koryo come into this?"

"At this point, the only connection is Hyangsan."

"Meaning? And I don't want to hear about teeny-weeny pine cones, either."

"I played your game of Continents with the guide at the temple at Hyangsan. She said all the continents had been there. We got a good enough reconstruction of the hotel records. Three Americans and a Chinese tour group on the third floor, four people—technicians of some sort—from Brazil on the sixth. A couple of Australian businessmen and an African cultural troupe were on the seventh. They had a small riot in the upstairs bar over one of the hostesses. Next morning, they all made up and everyone went on a tour of the temple."

"No Europeans?"

"Only one. A male. Partial registration was on the computer. Paper copies with signatures and passport notation are gone, but I found a night note from the floor lady. Eighth floor. The man had the room on the end of the corridor, came back real late with a couple of other people. Very drunk, could barely walk. I showed a picture of the corpse to the temple guide. She nodded."

Pak slammed his fist onto my desk. "There must be more records. Someone made a reservation for him at the hotel, he checked in somewhere, he checked out of somewhere, he took a plane or a train into here, crossed a border. Why are there no traces of this character?"

I pulled out my notes from Hyangsan. "The local guy up there, what's his name, the one with the golden voice."

"Song."

"Song told me girls came up when a Politburo nephew was there. His exact words were, 'Very discreet, one in each car.' "

"Prostitution? Why would anyone try to blow up a car on the main highway over that?"

"Not girls." I looked up at the molding along the ceiling and wondered if I'd ever get to it at this rate. "Not girls. Cars. They're smuggling cars, from someplace south, up to Hyangsan, then to Manpo, and then into China. They sell them at a profit, a big profit because they get around the Chinese import duties. One car may not be worth all that much, but if you do it several times a month, over the course of a year or two, it would be worth a bundle."

I took a piece of wood from the top drawer of my desk. I smoothed it between my fingers; it was oak. Good, friendly, strong, reliable oak. Pak shook his head. "If we were in the Sahara, you'd be worthless, completely worthless. Can't keep that badge on to save your life, but always got a piece of wood nearby." He sighed. "Keep going. It's cars. Not girls."

"It's cars, but it's not just cars. Song told me that Military Security was involved in this smuggling operation. I didn't believe him at first. Now I do. Remember when Kang and I met for a beer at the Koryo? He wanted me to think Military Security was trying to set him up that morning I missed taking the picture of the black car. Only I don't think they were trying to set him up. I think Kang has his own smuggling operation going. He and Kim are both running cars to China, but for different reasons, and they're stumbling over each other."

"Kim wouldn't like anyone cutting into his profits, especially the Investigations Department. But this can't just be about money."

"Kim must have made plenty already if he started this a few years ago. And for all the political crap they feed us at the Saturday study sessions, one thing they have right: having money makes you greedy for more. There's no sense in getting killed over money, though. They could just carve up the operation, agree to move on alternate weeks or something."

"Impossible. Kim hates Kang's guts. And if Kang is running cars, like you said, then it's not for the money, not for himself, anyway."

"Song also told me South Korean intelligence money is greasing things."

"Maybe, but if it is, only Kim is taking it. Kang wouldn't do that. I'm telling you, I know he wouldn't."

"Alright, tell me Kang didn't want me up on the border to protect a car-smuggling operation." Pak's face didn't reveal anything; he had closed his eyes. "Maybe the Finn was a bagman." I was thinking out loud. "He must have been on Kang's payroll. That's why there isn't any trace of him. Maybe Military Security found out and killed him. You think I'm crazy? There's a link. Kang is up to something in Finland. He told me so himself. If you ask me, he's trying to use us. He's trying to put us between himself and Military Security, have them stop for fresh meat while he gets a step ahead of them. You trust him, fine. I don't. I don't know him, and I don't trust him. Don't forget, I was standing on that hill next to Li after that car got shot up. I was standing there when Kim looked up the hill to make sure I had seen the whole thing."

"Kang has operations all over, that's his job. Don't worry about Kang's motives. He's okay." Pak opened his eyes. "I'd bet my life on it." He turned back to the window. "Car outside. Two cars, actually. What's our next move?"

I walked over to my filing cabinet, pulled out a pine dowel, and threw it to Pak. "Start sanding."

# 8

Pak wasn't paying much attention to what he was doing. Though his hands were moving the sandpaper over the wood, all of his energy was in listening for the sound of two people, maybe three, coming up the stairs. After a while, he put down the wood. "Buy a bookcase. Save yourself a lot of time." From below, a car door slammed, the sound echoed in the courtyard. Pak and I looked at each other. His face had gone a little pale. "In a minute or so, they'll knock on the door," he said. "They always knock. So polite all of a sudden, like lowering your voice during an interrogation: We're all gentleman, aren't we now, let's just go quietly, no fussing, down the stairs, into the car, care for a blindfold, glass of water, anything we can get for you?"

I shook my head. It wasn't like Pak to get so nervous. "Only one car door slammed. No one's coming up here. Maybe the guy got a leg cramp, sitting there all the time. You ever get cramps during a surveillance?" I started sanding again. "Relax, or you'll get the wood all riled up."

The knock on the door was like the crack of a rifle. The sound tumbled down the hall; then I couldn't hear anything but Pak's breathing. Pak stood up slowly and nodded to me as he walked out into the hall. For a moment I thought he was going back to his office to shoot himself. Then I heard the door open.

"We going to get noodles or aren't we?" Kang's voice, booming into the room, sunshine after rain. I put down the wood carefully, then folded the small piece of sandpaper, thinking that if I did something with my hands, they would stop shaking. I fumbled on my desk for the piece of oak again, but it slipped out of my fingers.

Kang stuck his head into my office. "Sorry to be late. A traffic jam in front of your building." I heard a car engine start up, then a second one. As I glanced out the window, two black cars moved slowly down the street, in the direction of the river. Kang stood with arms folded, watching me. "Nice weather. The hills on the east coast are very pretty this time of year." He nodded down toward the floor near my chair. "You dropped something."

"I'm staying, I'm not leaving town. They don't scare me." I looked down to make sure my hands were steady. "Let's get lunch. Pak thinks we should go up to the monuments afterward and drink ourselves silly."

Pak had put on a light jacket. I knew it was to cover his holster. If he was caught wearing a gun, they'd have an excuse to shoot him, but first he'd get one of them, because they'd never expect it of him. Pak didn't always play their game, but no one ever questioned his loyalty.

Kang reached into his waistband and produced a pistol. He slid it across the desk. "You might want this. You only need one shot."

I stared at it for a moment, then put it in my back pocket. "Remind me, or I'll pull it out instead of my wallet at lunch."

The noodle restaurant was half full, but it was still early. Most of the customers wouldn't come in for another hour, and they would spend the rest of the afternoon talking and enjoying the view, watching the boat full of tourists that plied up and down the river in good weather. The three of us ate in silence. The waitress tried to cheer us up with some small talk, but Kang gave her a sullen look and she slunk away. Afterward, we went out onto the balcony looking over the river and across to the tower on the other side.

"I always meant to take that boat," Pak said. "Maybe I'll write a list of things I meant to do."

Kang clucked his tongue. "Too soon to be morose. No one will make a move yet."

Maybe it was his tone of voice, but I felt a sudden surge of anger. "You are pretty calm about this. You've been awfully damn calm the whole time, even in Manpo after you killed Chong."

Pak's right hand moved slightly. I thought he might be going for his gun. "Chong? The guy they were asking me about?"

Kang didn't change expression. "The inspector didn't tell you about our adventure?" He laughed. "Did he tell you about his Finnish girl-friend?"

Pak's hand stayed put. "It must be raining Finns. We're drowning in them. Come to think of it, I never did get a report, Inspector."

"No time for that." Kang nodded at three men who had just stepped into the restaurant. One of them was Colonel Kim. He was wearing civilian clothes; the two others were in well-fitting Military Security uniforms, fine buttons and all. Kim glanced out the window at us. He caught my eye and held it, then looked away and followed the restaurant manager to a private room off to the side. The manager, a tall man with a sad face, was sweating profusely. He did not look happy to see Kim.

Kang had already started down the steps to the parking lot, two at a time. "I'll meet you at the monuments." He flashed that smile of his, the one with the teeth. "Should be a splendid view."

Pak started his car and then turned the ignition off. "What's going on? Why didn't you tell me about Chong?"

"Chong? Arab blood? I started to, but you said you didn't want to know."

He gave me an acid look. "I didn't need to know if you two were acquainted. That's a hell of a lot different from knowing one of my inspectors was present when Kang shot a Military Security operative. Did you at least report it to someone?"

"Ha! He didn't shoot him. It was a rock." Pak stared out the windshield. "Kang said not to report it. He had some sort of operation under way at a compound in the hills just below where it happened, and he didn't want activity."

"What compound?"

"I don't know. He said it was run by Military Security, and he wanted me to get inside, but then you found the Finn and I had to come home."

"Did Kang seem rattled that I ordered you back here?"

"Kang? You've got to be kidding. Even when those three guys were frying in the jeep—"

"What jeep?"

I paused. "Let me give you the whole story as we drive." When I finished, Pak pulled into a narrow side street where an ice cream vendor had set up in the shade of three enormous mulberry trees. A few of the customers looked over when the car stopped next to the curb, but on a sunny afternoon, eating ice cream beats staring at a parked car. After a minute, no one looked to be paying much attention.

"You go back to the office." Pak ran his fingers through his hair. "Take the bus, if it's running today. No one will be laying for you on a city bus. I saw the way Kim sneered at you in the restaurant. They may not be tailing us right now, but it won't take them long to locate our cars."

"This is what you meant, isn't it, about all hell breaking loose.

They're about to move in on Kang, and you think you're on the list, too. Have you been working for Kang? Military Security has no reason to get you. You weren't there when Chong was killed." Pak didn't say anything. "Does it go back farther? You and Kang?"

"What you don't know, Inspector, can't hurt you."

"I'm not worried about what I don't know. I'm worried about you. Why don't you go back to the office? Or better yet, get over to the Ministry. The Minister won't let Military Security into the building. I can get to the monuments from here on foot. There won't be any trouble there. I think they're still waiting for something. That look from Kim wasn't the one a snake gives before it strikes. More like an invitation to play a little longer. Come on, mouse, try to get away. Anyhow, I have some business with Kang."

Pak reached over and opened my door. "Nope. You're outvoted, comrade. The People's Committee of Ministry Unit 826 has just voted and recommends you go back to the office. Period."

"You're going to have to tell me sooner or later what this is about. You just can't leave me dangling. Kang says you two know each other a long time." I got out and slammed the door.

Pak started the engine. "Go back to the office, straighten things up. Get to my desk. It was used by the Japanese army, probably the security people. It's not the normal junk we have. Second drawer, there's a fitted compartment. Inside is an envelope. Use it when you need it. You'll know what to do with it when the time comes. If they took apart the desk, they'd find it. Otherwise it would sit there for years, and then it would be too late. In my filing cabinet, there are transfer papers for you, a residence card, and a temporary food certificate."

"For where?"

"Not Kanggye." He smiled. Then the smile disappeared. "Stay low. Sand your wood if that's what you need to stay sane. The unit where you're going won't ask questions. Don't raise any. And wear the fucking pin, will you?"

I started to say something, but the car pulled away. The people sitting on the curb across the street concentrated on their ice cream and pretended they hadn't heard a word.

# 9

Pak's phone was ringing when I walked in an hour later. As soon as I picked it up, the line went dead. My office had been searched. The sandpaper I'd left on the desk had been opened and then refolded the wrong way. Why had they driven away just after Kang came up? How did they happen into the same restaurant just as we were leaving?

The only thing I was sure of was that Pak was yelling at Kang this very minute, demanding to know why the Investigations Department had exposed one of his inspectors to danger without telling him, and warning that he was going to cut off cooperation with Kang once and for all.

Pak's phone rang again. I let it go several times before I picked it up. It was the vice minister. "Inspector, your phone seems to be disconnected." His voice was dangerously normal, like the lid on a bottle of poison. "Get over to the Ministry, now. The Minister wants to see you. There's been an accident." Before I could ask what he meant, he hung up.

The Ministry was a five-minute car ride away. On my bicycle it would take longer. The bicycle was leaning against the tree where I had left it. It looked like the back tire had lost more air, but there wasn't much I could do about that. At the first intersection, the traffic lady whistled for me to stop and use the underpass. I ignored her. She could blow her whistle until she was red in the face, because I knew she didn't have a radio, and by the time a patrol car appeared to ask her what was wrong, I'd be at the Ministry. I gave her a salute as I rode by.

The guards at the Ministry's gate waved me through without asking to see my ID. The vice minister was in the Minister's outer office, sitting on a couch with an assistant, going over some papers. He pretended I wasn't there. Finally, he stood up and nodded to me. "The Minister is on the phone. As soon as he gets off, we'll go in. You will stand and listen to what he says. Don't ask him any questions, and don't comment on anything he says. When he's done, come back out here and wait for me."

"What happened? You said there was an accident?" I realized I still had the pistol in my back pocket. A good reason to let the vice minister walk ahead of me.

"Inspector, do us both a favor. Say nothing." His lips quivered with the rage that had long ago boiled away all his other emotions. "You think you're above the rest of us. You think you can ignore the regulations, sidestep politics, forget to come to the study sessions for months on end. Sanding wood instead, like some backcountry carpenter. You don't even bother to read the editorials in the newspaper. Don't think it hasn't been noticed. Did you think you'd get away with it forever?" The vice minister's aide shot me a warning look. He never wanted trouble, always wanted things calm until he could get out of the room.

The double doors to the Minister's office opened. The vice minister went in first, I followed, and the aide stepped past me into the hall, but not before he had mouthed one word: "Pak."

The Minister looked up slowly as we walked in. His face was haggard, his eyes sunk into his head, his cheeks hollow. He rested his glance for a moment on the vice minister as if he wanted to say something, then thought better of it and turned to me. "Inspector, have a seat." He gestured to a chair in front of his desk. The chair looked as frayed as he did, though it had once been a handsome piece. The arms were carved in an unusual shape, sloping down slightly and then flaring at the ends, so that whoever was sitting there did not have to grip the arms but could relax. "Your grandfather made that for me." From the corner of my eye, I could see the vice minister stiffen, and as he did, the shadow of a smile played across the Minister's face. I sat down, favoring one side. I didn't want to blow a hole in grandfather's chair, or my leg.

"Everything he did, everything he made, was perfectly planned and crafted. Not that he was perfect himself. But he left behind an example of enduring value." The Minister paused a moment to consider his next remarks. "I'm sure he passed those traits, and those values, on to you. I've watched you for years, Inspector." He glanced at my shirt. The absence of the pin was noted with a cough.

The vice minister walked around the desk and put a piece of paper in front of the old man. The Minister read it quickly, and as he did his shoulders slumped. "On the road leading up the hill to the monuments, weapons were discharged," he said. This was very much the Minister's style. He never said "shots were fired," but rather "weapons were discharged." He looked back down at the paper. "Your chief inspector was hit several times. He died in the hospital a short time ago. He had a pistol in his hand, an Israeli army pistol. It had been discharged twice." The Minister paused. "You were seen at lunch with him, along with an official of the Investigations Department. Do you know anything about this?"

The vice minister looked sharply at me, warning me to keep quiet. He needn't have worried. I was stunned, feeling sick. Pak had insisted I go back to the office. Now he was dead.

The Minister stared into space briefly, lost in thought. "Chief Inspector Pak will be irreplaceable. He was truly one of our foundation stones. I don't know what we are going to do without him." He stood up and walked around the desk so he was next to me. "There will be a tough investigation, and I mean very tough, over what happened this afternoon. The only reason you aren't in custody right now is that I've personally intervened at the top." The Minister turned to the vice minister. "Would you excuse us a moment?"

The vice minister raised a hand in protest, "Sir, I hardly think it would be proper—"

The Minister interrupted. "You let me worry about that. I'm asking you to leave my office so I can speak in private with the Inspector. Are you going to do so, or shall I have you thrown out?"

The vice minister's face became a blank mask. He gave a wooden bow and moved across the carpet to the doorway. "I'll be in my office," he said to me, and then closed the doors with an ominously gentle touch.

The Minister leaned against his desk, looking even paler and more tired than he did when we walked in. "This is the end for me. But that's not important. Things are happening. You can swim with the tide, Inspector, I won't blame you. Or you can act. But you'll have to make up your mind quickly."

I glanced around the room. The Minister shook his head. "Don't worry. This room is clean. They try every now and then, but whenever we find their handiwork, I raise hell and they have to remove everything. Then they have to start all over. I'm surprised the walls are still standing, they've drilled so many holes for their microphones. It has become almost a joke at the parties."

"What happened to Pak?" I needed to know if he had been surprised or if he had surprised them.

"Pak and Kang were walking up the hill together. Six Military Security agents stepped out and ordered them to get on the ground. Pak drew his weapon and fired. He killed one of them before they shot him. Kang rolled behind some boulders and fled. They are looking for him now. My information is that you spent time with Kang on the border last week. It has also come to the attention of Military Security, believe me. This case with the dead Finn you've been investigating, it also has Military Security connections."

"I realize that."

"What you don't realize is that things are moving at the top." The

Minister looked at his watch. "In about two hours, the leadership meets to discuss final details on clearing away some old mistakes. These were bad mistakes, horrendous mistakes, Inspector. They will snap their fingers, and someone will take the blame. That's all I know, and now you know it. The vice minister hasn't been told any of this, not from me, anyway. Still, he's vibrating about something. He probably has his suspicions. Watch his tongue. It darts in and out like a snake's. Maybe he can smell the fear in the wind." The Minister put on a dark, well-tailored jacket and straightened his tie. "I have to go to a meeting. I may not be back." He shrugged. "Someone might need this job to be vacant. The vice minister thinks he's going to get it." The Minister laughed, and some of the gauntness left his face. "He's in for a surprise. If I am replaced this afternoon, you're on your own, Inspector." I stood up, and we shook hands. He stepped quickly through a side door, without glancing back.

# 10

There was a steady stream of military traffic on the streets, jeeps barreling past, heavy trucks in twos and threes driving so fast their engines were screaming. I'd decided there was no reason to see the vice minister. He wasn't going to do me any favors. He and Pak had been enemies; now he was mine as well. He'd try to get rid of me if he could, but from what the Minister had said, Yun was going to have trouble just watching his own back. Without Pak or the Minister, my own back was none too safe, either, but if I kept a low profile in the middle of this political typhoon, no one would notice me, except Military Security. Kim had put me in his sights, but first he wanted Kang.

I needed to get rid of the pistol in my back pocket. I needed to get to Pak's office before anyone else did, to look at his files. Riding my bicycle seemed like a bad idea—too many army vehicles with bad brakes going at high speed. It would take twenty minutes on foot, but I could go on the path by the river most of the way. The walk rarely was crowded, and I knew there were no patrols down there except at night, looking for drunks sleeping on the benches.

Walking gave me time to think. By the time I was nearing the office, I knew I had to forget the Finn. The Finn wasn't important; his identity wasn't important; in some ways, even his killer wasn't important. What mattered to me was Pak. Why was he dead? It wasn't an accident. It was almost as if he had set it up himself, part of a script he had written a long time ago but couldn't play out until now. He had trusted Kang, he had helped Kang, and Kang left him to die. There must have been some bond between them. Maybe there was something in the papers Pak told me to get from his desk. I stopped and looked at the river. Pak was gone. Any bond he had with Kang had died with him. Kang was smooth. Kang was clever. Kang used people, but he wasn't going to use me, not anymore. I needed to be alone with the man for just a few minutes. After he gave me some answers, I would deal with him.

The guard at the gate to our compound had been changed, but no one stopped me as I walked past. There were no cars parked outside. The street was deserted except for an old woman and a boy, who bounced a red ball against the compound's wall.

The drawers on Pak's desk were locked, but I knew he kept a key in the top drawer of his file cabinet. There was a pile of folders in the drawer. As I flipped through them, I saw they all concerned Koreans from Japan who had died over the years under suspicious circumstances. I recognized only one of the cases, a couple killed when their car was hit head on by an army truck that had crossed over the center line on the highway to Hyangsan. Two farmers had witnessed the collision. They said the truck didn't even apply its brakes. The incident happened just inside our jurisdiction, and Pak had insisted that we start an investigation, even though we weren't equipped to deal with traffic accidents. The day after I called around for information on the truck's unit, Military Security moved in, took over, and told us to drop the case. They never shared their findings, but Pak found out through his own channels that the truck driver was not disciplined and, six months later, received a promotion.

We closed the case, and I forgot about it. Pak, it was clear, did not. He had kept the files active, feeding in bits and pieces of information, mostly from sources I'd never heard of. I dumped the folders back and dug around for the key. It was buried in a corner, under a pile of pamphlets from Japanese travel agencies. Folded up with them was the front page of an edition of the party newspaper from a year ago. It carried a government statement on improving relations with Japan. Pak had underlined a few sentences in pencil, and at the bottom of the statement he had written, "Reckoning." There was another article, from a Japanese newspaper. I couldn't read it, but there was a picture of a small boy holding a cat.

For all these years that Pak and I had worked together, sometimes seven days a week for months at a time, I had fooled myself into thinking we knew each other's rhymes and rhythms perfectly. Yet here, in his desk, was evidence I didn't know him very well after all. He never said anything about it, but all these years he had been focused on Japan. Why? "All hell is about to break loose," that's what he said to me on the phone. He hadn't mentioned Japan, but Kang had. Solving "old problems" in return for overdue blood money. Pak was dead. Japan had something to do with it.

After I unlocked it, the second drawer on the desk rolled open smoothly without a sound. I felt along the bottom and then the underside. Nothing. I pulled the drawer out, turned it over, and looked for a slight irregularity in the grain. Nothing. There was no compartment. Then I spotted it, along the back panel—not a compartment, really, just a slit, barely enough for a thin sheet of paper. I looked around for something sharp to slip inside and pull out whatever Pak had kept there. It wasn't a single sheet but an envelope, made of a sort of thin, fine paper I'd never seen.

A jeep braked sharply; doors slammed. There was a loud exchange as our guards blocked the way. Another car pulled up, and I heard the gate clank open. I quickly replaced the drawer and locked it. I opened the file cabinet, threw the key into the back, and picked up the first thing I saw, a small notebook. The first few pages had some rough entries about the Finn at the Koryo, but otherwise it was blank. Worthless. That's why Pak had put it on top: wouldn't fool anyone but might slow them down. In the very back of the file drawer, there was a soft blue cloth bag. I pulled it open. It contained two bundles of hundred-dollar bills. What was Pak doing with so much U.S. currency? All of us kept a little bit, to use in the market or at the diplomatic store, but not like this. I jammed both bundles in my pocket, then put one back in the drawer, closed things up again, and scrambled to my office. Just as I sat down, two men burst through the door. A moment later, Colonel Kim strolled in.

"We seem to be meeting quite often these days, Inspector. Restaurants. The countryside." Kim looked around my office without interest, as if he'd been there before. "Please remain seated. We are going to remove your chief inspector's files. He won't be needing them." He stopped to watch me. I felt the blood go to my face and a crazy urge to kill him, right then, but instead I sat there without speaking, controlling my heartbeat. "By rights, you should come with us for questioning." He smiled at the word. "But for some reason, you have a curious, protected status. It won't last long, I assure you. In the meantime"—I could feel him measuring every detail of how I sat, when I blinked, the way I breathed—"you are free to go to back and forth between your apartment and this office. You understand, I'm sure."

I decided if I didn't answer he would think I was scared, so I said, "You have no control over me, Kim. Until I'm told otherwise by the Minister, I don't take orders from you. And I have work to do. Now, if you don't mind . . ." I picked up the sandpaper on my desk and began to sand the piece of wood for the bookcase that Pak had said I would never build. Kim turned to go, but before he did, I saw the knives in his eyes sharpen with anger. At least I had to hope that's what it was. Anger would make Kim stumble, and the more he stumbled, the angrier he would get. He would lose his focus; I'd seen it happen before with people like him. It was only when he was cold and restrained that he was deadly.

"Don't forget to lock Pak's cabinet when you're done," I shouted after him. "And don't mess up the notes about that Finn. We only just put things in there." I heard Kim shout some orders; furniture crashed on the floor, there were footsteps, and then the hall door slammed shut so hard it rattled the windows. After the jeep pulled away, there was silence, then soft footsteps in the hall. Kim stopped as he reached my door.

"Very good, Inspector." He stepped into my office. "Just sit. It will make things easier. Most people bolt like rabbits, or die of fear at their desks."

"You got what you needed, I assume."

"Yes, I have what I came for."

"That's good." I pushed the envelope across my desk. "Don't forget this."

"And what is that?" He wasn't curious, he was angry. He pointed at my desk as if there were something insulting on it.

I had no idea what was in the envelope, and if Kim even imagined that for an instant, I was dead. He would kill me right here, on the spot. I put my hand on the paper, touched it as if it were completely familiar to me. I couldn't let a muscle be out of place; Kim would sense it. Every movement had to tell Kim that he was in the one in danger, not me, that I was the one in charge, not him—and that this paper held his fate.

"We both know that important things are happening, Colonel. If they break your way, you can deal with me later. But if the situation breaks my way, and something has happened to me in the meantime, something with your fingerprints on it, you're finished. And they'll make sure it hurts." I didn't expect him to look worried or even thoughtful. I just wanted to keep talking, to keep touching the envelope, getting the connection established in his eyes and his ears. That envelope was his fate. Not mine, his. I put the envelope down again and moved my hand from it, as if I'd done that before, as if it weren't the first time I'd had it on my desk.

"Curious-looking paper. I didn't know your Ministry had anything like that. Special issue?"

"That's not for you to know. All you have to do is keep it safe. Surely you can do that, Colonel. I don't much care about the rest of the files, but this you deliver, safe and sound. It's sealed. That's how it stays. That's how you deliver it."

"I could just take it and you'd never know what happened. I could take it back and have my people open it, then seal it up again."

"You could also shoot yourself between the eyes. It would be quicker."

"I could kill you right now, you know, say you tried to run." He didn't sound troubled.

"Not now, Colonel. Later, if you like."

He took a polished gold case from his breast pocket, a remarkably thin case that fit perfectly in his hand. He removed a cigarette, looked at it thoughtfully, then struck a match on the side of my desk. The match flared; the sound seemed to grow beyond the flame, then stopped abruptly as he dropped it on the desktop, near the envelope. We both watched as the match consumed itself.

I could see that Kim was not sure of his next move. The envelope was not something he'd planned for. He looked around the room, then up at the ceiling. "Too bad."

"What?" I thought he meant that the envelope hadn't burned.

He struck another match and lit the cigarette, inhaling slowly so the tobacco at the tip glowed for a long time. "Too bad you'll never know what that molding was meant to be." He coughed, dropped the cigarette to the floor, and ground it under the heel of his boot.

I picked up the envelope and lazily fanned the cigarette smoke away from the desk. "Take it, Kim. Deliver it to one person and one person only."

"Are you giving me orders, Inspector? I think not." But there was no edge to his tone.

"A simple chain of custody. From me to you. From you"—I paused and then heard what I knew I'd say all along—"to my brother."

Kim's lips pulled back in a half snarl. "I don't work for you. And I don't work for your brother."

I dropped the envelope onto the desk. Kim stood there, rigid, his mind tumbling as he tried to regain his balance. He picked up the envelope with a quick motion. "What's in it?"

"Names, dates."

"Meaning you don't know."

"If I were you, Kim, I wouldn't start to gamble so late in my career." Kim was waiting. He was waiting for me to swallow too hard, breathe too deep, blink my eyes too fast—anything that would tell him that I was nervous, that I was lying, that I was a dead man.

I remembered my grandfather. I remembered the trees lining the road in front of our village. I remembered how, the first time the old man had taken me with him to Pyongyang, I'd watched the setting sun run alongside the train. It had turned red as it touched the horizon, then flared against the paddies so they sparkled like a jeweled necklace reaching to the hills. That calmed me. I could afford to blink my eyes. Kim turned toward the window, maybe to give himself a moment to think. It was the wrong move, and he knew it right away. In the half second it took him to turn back to me, it was too late. The rhythm had changed. I wasn't about to let it shift back again. The only thing to do was to press him, change the subject slightly, make him respond to me. "You made a mistake, Colonel. You thought you could scare me on that hillside."

"I don't know what you're talking about."

"You shot one of Kang's men, machine-gunned a wounded man. First you blew up the Reunification Highway."

"Inspector, I'm surprised at you. I'm operating under orders. The blue car was illegal. It was coming from the south. It might have been an enemy agent for all I knew. Maybe even an assassin. We protected the leadership. You were a witness to that."

"No, I saw something else."

"Is that right? You and who else?"

"You know who. The local security man, Li."

"Yes, Li. Must have been a shock to him. He died not long after. It looks like it was a heart attack. You knew him? My condolences. And you, Inspector, you worked for a man who was killed in a firefight with an operations team performing its duty to arrest an enemy of the state. Two enemies, actually."

"So, you finally made your move against Kang." I paused. It was time to double the bluff—and it better be convincing. "It may not be soon enough. A report on your car-smuggling operation is waiting to be passed up the line, along with evidence that it was carried out with the help of South Korean intelligence. Kang will gladly corroborate it. When I hear from my brother that you have delivered this envelope to him, I tell someone to pull it back. If I don't give the word, the report is released twelve hours from now. And if that report is released, it doesn't matter which way events break. You'll be dead either way. Any questions?"

Kim turned abruptly, his boots thudded down the stairs, the door slammed, and then it was quiet. From my window, I saw him leaning against his car, catching his breath, putting the anger back where it wouldn't get in his way. He climbed in and shut the car door carefully, and when the car finally started, it moved down the street so slowly it barely got out of first gear. The big engine throbbed, a low, menacing sound. Kim wanted me to hear it—the restraint.

I sat still for another minute, then walked into Pak's office. The cabinet was open, all of the drawers pulled out onto the floor; the desk was a mess. On top were the folders about the Koreans from Japan, with the papers scattered everywhere. The blue bag was ripped open, and the money was gone. The notebook on the Finn hadn't been touched. Kim was furious. I didn't have any evidence that he was taking money from the south, but he didn't know that. I had bought myself twelve hours to find Kang and make him pay for Pak's death. After that, I didn't care if Military Security found me.

# PART
# SEVEN

In late summer the rose blooms;
The perfumed morning floats above the hills,
And along the road where I wait,
Again to hear the song of a voice that is gone.

—Yang Hyong Jin (1715–1756)

I decided to take Pak's car. There was enough confusion on the streets that I knew I could get out of the city. Once on the highway, I'd be vulnerable to any traffic policeman or sentry who spotted my plates and logged them in, but that was later. It was a shock to find Pak's parking space empty. It was a bigger shock to realize I'd forgotten that Pak had driven his car to meet Kang. It was probably still on the hill near the Chinese war monument. There was no time to get over there. Even if there had been, Kim's people would have set up a cordon to see if anyone approached the car. Or Kang might have taken it, leaving his ancient Nissan behind.

Both sentries posted at the front gate watched closely as I stood in the empty parking space. Neither of them belonged to the Ministry. The sentries at our compound were assigned from the army, changed at irregular times and always from different units. It was a brilliant idea. With the constant rotation, we never got to know the guards, and they felt no loyalty to us. Whoever thought of it was obviously a genius.

This was the sort of idea that received a bonus. Like all good ideas rewarded with a bonus, though, it was flawed.

I sauntered over to the guards, smiling, and pulled out one of Pak's hundred-dollar bills. The guards yanked their heads back, suddenly interested in the top branches of the trees across the street. I dropped the bill close behind the guard on the right, the one who looked more alert. He moved his foot so his canvas shoe covered it, but he kept blocking what I needed, the phone to our duty driver. A moment later the phone rang. The guard reached back without turning his body, took the receiver from the hook, and held it out for me.

"Who is this?" The duty driver was speaking carefully. "I just received an order from the Ministry that no cars are to leave the compound."

"Good," I replied, loud enough so the guards could hear me without straining. "That means the duty car, too. Bring it around, so I can secure it."

"Inspector, is that you?"

"Just me."

There was a pause, and I could hear a chair scrape the floor. "Are you all right?" The bonus idea had another flaw. It covered the guards but overlooked duty drivers.

"I'm fine. Bring the car."

The phone clicked. The guard's hand appeared again, and I put the receiver in it. He was still looking at the trees, and said to no one in particular, "My stomach's bad. Must be the rice from overseas, they say it's been poisoned. Makes me have to go. I might need some relief." He gave a low whistle to the other guard, who nodded. Just then the sound of a car's engine came from around the corner. I reached into my back pocket for the pistol Kang had given me. If the car was a black Mercedes, I wasn't going to let them have the pleasure of taking me.

It was a Volvo—an old burgundy Volvo nosing down the street, its bad tires hissing on the pavement. I slipped the pistol back into place.

Pak had insisted we get a Volvo as a second duty car. "I don't want anything that even looks like a Mercedes," he said.

The car pulled up to the gate and waited. The guards stood at attention. They gave no indication of seeing or hearing anything. You can't forget what you never saw, and there's plenty you might never see if there's a hundred-dollar bill under your left shoe.

I climbed in, and the car started rolling again. We didn't pick up speed until we turned the corner onto the main road. There were more army trucks running in pairs. Every few blocks, one was stopped, hood up, engine smoking, a mechanic leaning against the cab, his cap pushed back, staring up into the sky and thoughtfully puffing on a cigarette.

The driver didn't say a word. I had the feeling he was worrying that with each passing minute, his fate was sealed tighter. I didn't need him and he didn't need me. "Pull over," I said, so suddenly it startled him. "Get out. Tell them I held a gun to your head." I took the pistol from my pocket. "This one."

The driver swung down a small street to an empty lot overgrown with weeds and stopped. He shoved open his door but didn't move. It flashed through my mind that I had been set up. I turned to look out the back window. The driver shook his head. "Relax, we're by ourselves." He tapped the gas gauge. "There is only half a tank, but I carry a spare can in the trunk. Pak told me it was against regulations, but he kept it off the books. The left rear tire is almost bald, and the high beams don't work except when it's foggy." I had thought he was scared, but his voice was steady. "I know what you think happened. Forget it. Kang says to meet him in Hyangsan. If that doesn't work, the fallback is Manpo. Been nice knowing you, Inspector." He climbed out, put his hands in his pockets, and strolled back toward the main road.

For the first kilometer I had to dodge military vehicles, none of them paying attention to traffic laws, mostly using horns instead of brakes, but they thinned out when I got past the last big intersection at the edge of town. All but a few of the trucks were directed off to the

right, toward the road that led out of town to a complex of army command bunkers. The traffic ladies were gone, replaced by soldiers wearing shiny helmets and carrying new automatic weapons. I went left onto
an old road, over some railroad tracks, and then made a sharp turn up
an embankment that formed the shoulder to the main highway. Either
the left rear tire would last or it wouldn't. I thought over what the
driver had told me. Why was he passing messages to me from Kang?
Who had slipped him into our operation? Maybe Kim and Kang were
working together after all, and that's why Kang got away. They killed
Pak. What did they want with me? If Kang was waiting at Hyangsan,
we'd end the game right there.

At the first checkpoint on the outskirts of the city, a young traffic
policeman with a long face stepped onto the road and waved me over.
"Going somewhere? You're almost out of your jurisdiction." He was
very tall and moved like a stork in a rice paddy, slowly, with an odd, deliberate majesty. His white uniform was spotless; the white hat fit perfectly on his head. I had no idea where they had found such a specimen,
or why he was assigned to a low-level traffic checkpoint. The tall ones
usually get better assignments.

"The local security officer in Pyongsong called with an emergency.
He said he had some information on a case." It was the best I could
come up with on the spur of the moment.

"He must have been lucky to get through. The phones are down.
There's a lookout for you, Inspector." He leaned down so his face was
even with mine. "You don't know me, but I know you. You're O
Chang-yun's grandson. Military Security doesn't want you to leave city
limits."

"So what now?" He was polite, but I had the feeling he was going to
be a problem.

"If I told you to turn around, that's what you'd have to do."

I started to turn the wheel, but he put his white-gloved hand on it.

"That's what you'd have to do if I told you. But like I said, the phones are down, and my radio doesn't always work. Mostly it's a miracle when it does." He pulled his head back and stood up. "Road is clear from here to the Sinuiju turnoff. You ever been to Sinuiju? Nice place. From there you can go into China real easy."

"No. I don't like border cities. You're not from one, are you?"

"Drive carefully, Inspector." I started to thank him, but he was already walking back down the road. In the mirror I could see him bend over and retrieve something from behind a tree. It was an old thermos with a black plastic cup. As I pulled away, he was pouring himself some tea.

The Sinuiju turnoff usually had a couple of sentries standing around. Sometimes they stopped a few cars to break the boredom, but they didn't exert themselves as long as there wasn't an inspection team in the area. They didn't even raise their heads as I went past. I wasn't surprised. If Kim was tracking my progress—and I didn't know if I could trust a traffic policeman who had a thermos—a black Mercedes would suddenly appear out of nowhere. Sometimes it seemed those cars just sprouted from the earth, spit up from hell.

Past Kaechon, there were convoys of big brown trucks with field workers standing in the rear. Whatever the alert in Pyongyang, it hadn't reached into the countryside yet, or no one wanted to get in the way of bringing in the crop. Gangs of women sat beside the road, resting from the harvest. A few had taken off their floppy hats and put them on the ground, where they fluttered with each passing truck.

The fields gave way to hilly wasteland, and coming around a curve I passed a young girl walking alone on a deserted stretch of road. She held a dainty white sun-parasol over her head and had a white bag purse slung over her shoulder. What really caught my eye was her blouse.

Crisp and new, but most of all red. Bright, bold red. She looked straight ahead, her free arm swinging at her side. I watched her in the rearview mirror for as long as I could. Where was she going all by herself, wearing a red blouse in the middle of nowhere? I almost stopped to offer a ride, but on second thought I decided she was one of those cranes on the celedon vase. Lifting in flight, going nowhere.

When I pulled across the tracks onto the final short stretch of road that led along the river to the hotel, the moon was rising, pale and brimming with the sorrow of early evening. The sight of the hotel did nothing to cheer me up. The last time I was here, I had seen it only during the day. In the sunlight, even if you weren't crazy about buildings that looked like wedding cakes, you could see that some effort had been made to fit the hotel into the landscape. At dusk, it looked like a spaceship that had wandered off course, or a big white bug feeding at the foot of the hills.

The lobby was almost dark and seemed deserted. As I stepped inside, I spotted two people sitting on a sofa against the far wall. When she saw me, Lena lit a cigarette and looked away. Song, the singing security man, started, muttered something, and then disappeared through a doorway marked NO ENTRANCE. The front desk looked unmanned, so I wandered over to the sofa. "Shocked to see me?"

"Not half as shocked as you are to see me." She blew some smoke off to the side. "There aren't any no-smoking rooms here, but the twelfth floor has a good view." She'd been drinking, enough so that she slurred a word here and there.

"So does the fifteenth floor, I hear." I sat down next to her. "Out of your neighborhood, aren't you?"

"My papers are in order, if that's what is worrying you."

"I'll bet they are."

"I'm glad to see you." She patted my hand. "Really I am." For some reason she switched to Chinese; maybe it was because knitting reminded her of her mother. "I hope the sweater fit."

I realized I had never even tried it on, but I knew enough not to say so. "Did you have dinner yet?"

"Still good at changing the subject, I see. Yes, I ate. They serve early. The dining room has closed." She looked at her watch. "And I must get to the bar upstairs in a minute, before it opens." She put out her cigarette slowly and then turned to me. "Tomorrow is promised as good weather."

Maybe I was tired, or maybe it was her perfume, but it took me half a second too long to realize what she meant. By then, she was at the elevator. There was a laugh from a chair hidden in the shadows behind a potted plant. The desk clerk emerged and moved behind the counter. When Lena stepped into the elevator and the doors closed after her, he laughed again. "You better fix that timing, friend, or you're going to be one lonely inspector. The rules are you must, I emphasize must, have a reservation to get a room, but what I just saw was so pathetic, I'm willing to bend them. Lucky for you we have a room or two left. Breakfast starts at seven. Tell me now or you don't eat." He handed me a key: 1504.

I dangled it in front of his face. "How about another floor?"

"Can't. We're full and you don't, I emphasize don't, have a reservation. When we're full, we use the fifteenth. Great views." He gave me a sly look. "Don't worry, the window won't swing open in this room. The bastards soldered them shut."

The floor mat in the elevator said it was Wednesday. Either they were two days late changing it, or they wanted to get a good jump on next week. The hallway on the fifteenth floor was pitch-black. The only way to find my room was by counting doorknobs. When I rattled the knob on what I assumed was 1502, I heard the safety clicked off a pistol. I didn't bother to apologize. At the fourth knob I opened the door, half expecting Kim to be sitting on the bed. Or Kang. The room was empty. Maybe they didn't know where I was. One of them would by tomorrow. Someone roaming through the parking lot would see my plates and phone them in. I thought about walking up to the temple in the moonlight but remembered the climb and fell asleep instead.

The knock on the door at four in the morning woke me. Something about that hour attracts hall walkers. I knew it wouldn't be Kim. He wouldn't knock, not after what happened during our last meeting. It was the local guy, Song. He looked uneasy as he opened the door, stepped in, and turned on the light. "Master key." He held it up for me to see.

"Good morning."

"I put new plates on your car, from Hamhung. Now it's part of the Hamhung group that's here to see the Friendship Exhibit, though there aren't many of those Volvos left. Sort of stands out. I don't really know if there are any in Hamhung, but no one's going to check right away. Too much trouble." He massaged his shoulder. "Don't thank me. It's my job."

"Did you have something else?"

"Kang was here, but he left all of a sudden. He said you'd know what to do."

"That's it?"

"Yeah. If I were you, I wouldn't stick around here, Inspector. The Military Security team down the hall is restless. They're packing their equipment. Somebody's coming up from Pyongyang tomorrow night to pick them up."

"Kim?"

"I don't know. I'll be glad when they're gone. And you with them."

"Any more cars with girls come up here?"

"I wouldn't know what you are talking about. Your old plates are in the trunk. Along with that gas can."

"How much gas did you take?" As I got out of the bed, he backed toward the door.

"Don't worry, you've got enough left."

"Anything else?"

"Yeah, I'd do something about that rear tire. That's what I'd do."

# 2

In the morning I went down to the front desk and asked the clerk to give Lena a message.

"She's in 614. Deliver it yourself if you want."

"I don't. I want you to give it to her." I handed him a sheet of stationery that had been in the room. There were no envelopes, so I folded it in thirds and then tucked in the edges. I didn't write anything. I figured the blue button I'd found on the floor in the closet in the Koryo would be enough.

# 3

The pine needles made a soft bed on the slope of the hill facing the temple. No one could see anything from below; the spot was screened by wild azaleas and a grove of scrub pine trees. Lena had circled around and approached me from behind. I heard her footsteps, but not until the perfume reached me did I turn to look at her.

She had on the same long skirt and the white blouse she'd been wearing the night I first saw her. The blue buttons were even brighter in the sun, but mostly it was her eyes that took the light.

"We missed our picnic last time," I said. "I thought we could try it here."

"If I'd known, I would have brought something." She was speaking Chinese, and I was never able to read much emotion drifting in the tones of that language.

"I have the black bread and blueberry jam." She didn't look amused, and I began to worry that the whole thing was a mistake.

"A small joke," I said. "Sorry. I did bring some rice cakes from the hotel and a couple of apples. They're tart this time of year."

"I see you have a bottle of beer, too. Do you have any glasses, by any chance?"

"No. We'll have to drink out of the bottle. Not so elegant, I guess. Next time I'll bring some cups that I made a few years ago, out of persimmon wood. Liquor takes on the flavor. So does tea. Do you like persimmon?" I reached in my pocket, then remembered all I had was a piece of oak. "Persimmon is pretty wood. Has a nice glow. But it hides itself. Some wood tells you almost as soon as you touch it what it means to become. Not persimmon. It's beautiful on the surface, almost unfathomable underneath. That's why furniture made out of persimmon often looks odd. Someone tries to shape it into something it was never meant to be."

"Is that the greatest tragedy you can think of, Inspector, being shaped into something you were never meant to be?"

"It is a sad thing, don't you think?"

"You're not married, are you, Inspector? I've heard you live alone. Didn't you ever want to be with someone?" It wasn't the question I was expecting.

"I'm fine. I'm with other people enough. I'm with you right now."

"That's not what I meant." She stopped and I waited. The silence grew, but there was nothing awkward about it.

"In the house where I grew up," I said after a while, "there were only two of us, my grandfather and me. Both my parents died in the war. My older brother went away to a school for the children of war heroes, but I was too young. Grandfather said that I had to be more filial than any kid whose parents were still living, I had to respect the memory of my father and mother with all my heart. If I'd been a tree, he used to say, I would have had to be the straightest one in the forest."

"Trees in the forest aren't alone. My father used to tell us that when you see a tree standing by itself, it's a sign that something sad will happen."

"Maybe my father would have said that, too. I don't know what he would have told me. It isn't something I wonder about." The silence fell between us again. I looked at her face and was surprised to find she was crying softly. I handed her a handkerchief. "I've heard that when a man and a woman part, he gives her a handkerchief." I paused. "I hope you won't keep that."

She laughed, the mixed-up laugh that sometimes comes from a woman who has been crying. "This is very nice of you, Inspector. It's the sort of thing I imagined you'd do. Maybe that's why I've thought about you so much since we met." She dried her eyes. "What do you want?"

"Wasn't this your idea?"

We sat down on the pine needles. She was close beside me but with enough distance to leave open what she had in mind. "That must have been long ago," she said. "A week, a decade. Time moves in funny ways in this country. Did I suggest a picnic? I must have been intoxicated with the idea of a quiet afternoon. Maybe I thought it would be like at home, by the lake. Maybe I thought you and I would have something to talk about. Do we? Pardon me for asking again, but what you do want? It's not an unreasonable question, under the circumstances. You didn't drive up to Hyangsan to see me. You didn't even know I'd be here."

"You're right. I was surprised. I'm just wondering, how is it that you happen to be so far away from where you normally stay?"

"This is a resort, as you may have noticed. There are tourists here, with dollars." She let the thought hang in the air. "Not very pretty, I realize. Do you still want to have a picnic?"

"Tell me about Finland."

"You mean, why would a Finn come here, to this country?"

"You know a guy named Pikkusaari?"

She turned her head away quickly. I hadn't even thought about that question. It just came out, like Lake Keitele.

"I don't know him well. He used to work for the Finnish National

Police. He and my father often did business, though he was very young at the time."

Now it was my turn to blink. Maybe she was making this up. She probably made a lot of things up, but I didn't follow that thought too far.

"Your father did business with the police?"

"No, Inspector, my father was a spy. I never knew exactly who he worked for. As a businessman, he traveled all over. He was gone every winter and spring, but every year on June 21, without fail, he always came home. We waited at the train station for him, my sisters and I. Pikkusaari came to see him a couple of times a month, in the summer. The two of them went for long walks beside the lake, moving slowly, their hands behind their backs. Sometimes they would be gone for hours. When they came back down the path, they looked exactly the same, moving slowly, hands behind their backs, as if they'd never said a word to each other the whole time. For all I know, they didn't.

"When they returned, Pikkusaari would always say, 'You're a lucky man, Ollie. You've a good wife and fine children. All you lack is a son. I wish I could say the same.' Then they would drink a bottle of vodka, sitting on the wicker chairs we put under the birch trees in the back of the house, and listen to old records. My father had a good collection of classical music, but he insisted it be kept for winter, when everything was dreary. Summer was for jazz, he'd say. With the record player perched on the ledge of the open window, the sound turned up, he liked to sit facing the lake, tapping his feet. Pikkusaari liked jazz, too, but he said he couldn't listen to it at home. His mother couldn't stand what she called 'that noise.'

"That's how they'd sit, my father and Pikkusaari, drinking and listening to jazz. Neither spoke, except to say something in English, 'Oh yeah,' or 'That's the stuff.' After a few glasses of vodka, Pikkusaari would stand up and start to dance by himself, perspiring, his face tilted toward the sky, eyes closed, his hands swaying over his head as he turned in small, tight circles. Where we lived was quiet, no other houses nearby, and the scratchy sound of jazz, a trumpet and then a piano wildly taking flight, would make its way down to the water, where my sisters and I lay on our backs on the pier, watching the clouds. Around nine or ten o'clock at night, with the summer sky still bright and small waves from the lake splashing against the wooden pilings, Pikkusaari would stagger toward his car. My father would call after him, 'You're drunk, you fool, drive slowly.'"

"Did your father ever come here?"

Lena shook her head. "To this godforsa . . . isolated country? He said it wasn't worth his time."

"Any Asians ever come out to see you at the lake?"

"My mother was Chinese, Inspector. It was rare enough among all those blondes. We always had visitors." She was dodging the question; I didn't know why. Or maybe I did, but I wasn't going to spoil the picnic. "If you must know, Pikkusaari came out the most. My mother said it wasn't to see my father really, but to see me."

"Fine. Enough questions. Let's just enjoy the view." As I moved closer to her, my hand touched hers. I could see the pulse in her throat, and the way the breeze floated strands of her long hair over her shoulders.

Then it was gone. She stood up and brushed the pine needles off her skirt. "I think we're out of luck again, Inspector. I have to be back in the hotel before dinner, to change and put on my makeup. Anyway"—she looked up at the sky—"it's going to rain." She pointed across the valley, where a huge cloud bank was piling up, dwarfing the hills and rapidly replacing the high blue of autumn with a heavy blackness that squeezed the light out of what might have been a glorious afternoon.

# 4

"People think I'm absentminded, that I forget things. Maybe. To me, it's more complicated. I know something, but I choose not to remember it. I can do both at the same time."

The Irishman looked tired, but I knew he was wide-awake. He turned off the tape recorder and put his hand over his eyes. "That's not good for a detective, is it? Detectives are supposed to see everything, remember everything."

"So you think. But knowing too much can only lead to trouble. You know what you need to know. I'm not talking about instincts. No, my instincts are fine. Sometimes they move sideways, like an ox stumbling across a muddy field, I let them move however they wish. People think instincts should be sharp, they should fly like arrows. I don't believe that. I think instincts should wander and meander, like streams coming down the mountain. An arrow can miss the target. A stream always knows where it is going, eventually."

"Maybe. But if you forget things, you make mistakes."

"And why not? Mistakes are good. The more mistakes, the better. People who make mistakes get promoted. They can be trusted. Why? They're not dangerous. They can't be too serious. People who don't make mistakes eventually step off cliffs, a bad thing because anyone in free fall is considered a liability. They might land on you." I stood up and stretched. "Listen, Richie, where I live, we don't solve cases. What is a solution in a reality that never resolves itself into anything definable? For you, life is optimistic, endless in possibilities, but you think the parts are limited and self-contained. That's why you make lists. You think it is possible to check off what is done. Me, I don't ever make a list. What if someone sees it? It would lack something important, surely, and that would be evidence to be used against me. Not today, maybe, but someday. For the same reason, I don't draw diagrams.

I don't connect dots. Unnecessary, because I know that nothing is a straight line. Everything is circles, overlapping circles that bleed into each other."

"Bleeding circles?"

"To solve a case you have to put the wind in a jar. For me, life consists of badly limited possibilities, but I know the parts are endlessly rearranged, always shifting, always changing. Nobody puts down their foot twice in the same place. I once heard a Westerner say, 'What you see is what you get.' We laughed for days about that at the office. Nothing is like that. Nobody is like that. But it's what you people want to believe. Straightforward, direct, what's the term?"

"Transparent."

"Ah, Richie, you are trying to read my mind. You shouldn't do that. No, not transparent. It doesn't matter. I'm not saying your way is wrong. It doesn't exist, not for me."

"So nothing is ever solved. That is a grand excuse if ever I heard one."

"An excuse? Could you live with uncertainty, moving shapes and shadows, morning, noon, and night, my friend? The mountains have become the only certain thing in my life. When they disappear, I die."

"Glorious words, Inspector. Put them to music and they'd make a fine, sad drinking song. But we're not here to sing, are we? You're to talk, I'm to listen." He wrote something in his notebook and then turned on the tape recorder but quickly turned it off again. "The tragedy, Inspector, is that you have poetry in your soul, but all my ears are trained to hear is facts."

"Don't worry about it, Richie. There's less poetry as you go along."

# 5

That night, I couldn't sleep. I was reading when Song stepped into the room, pale and scared. There was blood on his shirt, lots of it. "Come, quickly, to the temple." I didn't ask but followed him silently up the steep road; he walked so fast, it was hard to keep up. The rain had stopped, but there were enough lingering clouds to cover the moon. The road was dark, and the sound of the river, swollen with the afternoon's storm, echoed against the hills. At the gate to the temple compound, Song was waiting for me. "In there." He pointed. "The low building." He was hoarse, like someone who had been screaming. "I'm staying here." He looked down at his shirt. "You couldn't pay me enough to go back in there."

Before dawn I was on my way north to Kanggye, driving fast. That early, I didn't expect any other traffic. I stuck to the middle of the highway, because if I hit a pothole at the speed I was going, the car's frame would probably break apart. When the gas gauge showed empty, I pulled over. The gas can in the trunk was only half full; it might get me to Kanggye but no farther. Song owed me, for the gas, for everything. He knew he owed me, and he knew that someday I was going to collect.

# 6

The Inn of the Red Dragon in Kanggye was a wreck. The TV lay on its side, smashed. I stepped on the pages of a paperback book scattered over the floor. A moan came from the back room. The clerk was lying on a bed, his face to the wall. He rolled over when he heard me at the door. He had been pistol-whipped, badly.

"Welcome back, Inspector. I don't have any vacancies." It was hard to understand him because his face was so bruised.

"Who?"

He coughed and his body tensed in pain. Maybe a rib was broken, too. "What difference does it make? I don't keep score anymore. They asked about you."

"And?"

"I told them I didn't have any registration papers for anyone of your description."

"They believe you?"

"That's when they broke my ribs. What do you think?"

I turned to go. "I'll be back. I've got to get to Manpo."

He shook his head. "Too late. You'll never make it."

"I need some gas."

He wiped the blood that was oozing from his mouth. "Grandma Pak might have some gas coupons." He moaned again and rolled back to face the wall. "If she's still alive."


The place where Grandma Pak usually sat was empty. The blanket was still on the floor, along with her eyeglasses. The frames were bent and one lens was shattered. At least it wasn't a bullet hole. I looked along the bottom of the wall for a loose board, anything that might be a place to hide papers. In the corner was a different, older party newspaper. April 15, 1962. The editorial on the front chattered about loyalty in bold letters. Underneath the newspaper was a small wooden box. Loyalty covers a lot of sins, they like to say. Maybe that was what she figured.

The box felt worn and smooth, the corners rounded from being handled. It had been made without nails, from Siberian chestnut. It was notched along the top to make the lid fit perfectly; the grain on each side matched precisely all the way around. I didn't have to look twice to know whose hand it was from. My grandfather worked four months, morning and night, on that box. Most of the detail work was on the inside: a carving of a tiger on a rock, with a pine forest stretched below. You could even see the pinecones. I opened it up. There were some old train schedules and a black-and-white photograph of a young woman, her mouth set, staring into the camera with wide, dark eyes. Underneath were three gas coupons, the fancy ones with scenes of workers embossed on the front and farmers in a rice paddy on the back. They had expired twenty years ago. I put two in my pocket, then put the box in the corner again, under the newspaper. Maybe Grandma Pak would find her way back. I wanted the box there if she did.

# 7

The gas station at the edge of the city looked deserted; the front gate was shut tight. A sentry waved me away when I pulled up. An old man wearing a cloth cap looked at me from behind the bars of the gate. "Everything's closed. You can't get nothing here." I handed the coupons to him. He studied them closely, then said something to the sentry. The gate sagged so badly it took the two of them to swing it open.

The old man put out his hand. "Give me the keys. You can't drive in without a military pass. You can sit over there if you want." He indicated a concrete bench on a patch of dirt next to a low fence. He got in and started the car. "A Volvo. Not many of these left. None in Hamhung as far as I know. And only a few in Pyongyang." I watched the car pull up to the fuel pump at the far end of the compound. The sentry dragged the gate shut and locked it.

A rose bush grew along the fence behind the bench, climbing up from the ugly oil-stained pavement to make a thick wall. The flowers were red, a shade lighter than the girl's blouse had been. The bush was pruned and tended, fed and watered. Each leaf was a glossy green, free of pests or disease. At night, when the air was still and no trucks were spewing exhaust along the street, this spot must have been a perfumed silence.

The old man was standing next to me. "Even in this sadness, in this ugly time, the roses want to bloom," he said quietly. "Here are your keys. You better keep these gas coupons. Or maybe put 'em back where they came from." He touched the bill of his cap in a small salute and watched from the side of the road as I drove down the town's main street, past a half-ruined guesthouse called the Rainbow Inn and a park where a woman and a frail girl were sweeping imaginary leaves from the gravel walkway.

At the edge of town, the street made a sharp bend and gave way to a two-lane, rutted dirt track. I couldn't drive fast, but with a full tank of gas, I made it to just outside Manpo with only one stop. A bridge was down, and two soldiers were directing traffic through a field to a ford across the river. They weren't checking papers, but when I parked at the water's edge, waiting my turn, one of them looked at my plates, then stuck his head in the window. "You really from Hamhung?"

"Nah. Never been there." From his accent I could tell he wasn't from that part of the country. "Hamgyong people are kind of thick. I won this car in a card game with a couple of them." He laughed and waved me on, forgetting that he meant to bum a cigarette.

# 8

The four tables had been overturned, their legs snapped off and broken into pieces. Each of the vases was shattered, the flowers strewn around the room. On the rear counter, a pool of blood was soaking the pages of a book that lay face down.

Kang sat on the floor with his back against the wall. "I've been waiting for you, Inspector." He spoke each word distinctly. "What took you so long?" He saw me grip the pistol in my coat pocket.

"Don't worry. I'm not armed."

"Somehow, I don't believe you, Kang. I never should have."

He looked around the wreckage of the room. "Inspector, if you don't mind, I'm not in the mood for your moralizing. You know, I hoped you would get here first. But you were behind them each step of the way, weren't you?" He tapped his watch and held it to his ear. "Battery's gone." He smiled faintly. "Sound familiar?"

I took the pistol out of my pocket and held it at my side. "What happened here?"

"We don't have much time left. You're allowed one guess, Inspector." His smile faded. "They came looking for me. And now they're desperate. They know they have to get this done." He glanced back at the counter, as if he still couldn't grasp what had happened, but from the set of his shoulders, I could see that he knew.

"Do you know where they took her?"

"Somewhere her screams will be muffled." He looked up at the ceiling, but his eyes were half closed; he must have been watching something ugly inside his head, because he grimaced. "Do us a favor, Inspector. Shoot me. You hate me, and you'll be a hero. They'll give you a medal."

"You killed Pak. If you didn't squeeze the trigger, you caused it. Your whole network has been torn up by the roots, people flung like garbage across the landscape. So I will shoot you, Kang. But if I do it right now, your soul may float free. First, I want to know it's soaked in regret, that it will drag around the stinking mud into forever. I don't want to look up and think of you near the stars."

"That's your problem, Inspector, not mine. You have a funny urge to judge me. Go ahead, but we both know you can't. Pak was my friend. He told me to get away and leave him. It wasn't the first time."

The pistol jerked up in my hand and I fired one shot near Kang's head almost before I knew what I'd done. "Shut up." I could taste the anger; it was all I could do to keep from taking aim and firing again. I wouldn't miss the second time.

Kang didn't flinch. "Alright, you don't believe a word I say. In that case, there's not much to discuss."

"I've got most of this figured out, Kang. Only a few things I don't understand." I waited, but Kang was silent. "For openers, you set me up."

"Wrong," he broke in, and then stopped himself from saying more.

"Military Security was after you because you were poaching on their territory, smuggling cars. You tried to distract them by trailing me in front of them. You brought me up here to Manpo to meet Lena, threw me in her bed, and when that got you nothing, you dragged her down to Hyangsan to try again. That didn't work, so you killed her."

It was so quiet in the room that it felt as if I were alone. Kang didn't move; his breathing had become shallow and fast. "What are you talking about?"

"I ran across Lena at Hyangsan." I waited, but again Kang sat silently. "She said she was there for the tourists, but why all of a sudden would she go down there? Funny thing, you were there just before I arrived. Did you set it up, so I'd meet her again?"

Kang ignored my question; he didn't even seem to be listening anymore.

"We sat on a hillside and talked for a few minutes. About her father. And Pikkusaari. Interesting fellow, is our friend Pikkusaari. That night I got a frantic visit from the local security man. There were sounds coming from one of the buildings at the temple. He went in to check. Then he panicked and came for me. I went up there. Lena was inside, lying in the mud. She had been beaten." I paused because I could hardly speak with the picture in my mind. "She was still alive, but you couldn't recognize her face. It was gone. It took her a few minutes to die." I took a deep breath. "It was like watching an animal."

Kang's body slumped. His voice was drained, dead. "You can't believe I would do that. She was supposed to leave Hyangsan a few hours after I did. We were getting out of the country. I loved her. I wouldn't kill her."

"She wasn't going anywhere with you." The anger was building in my throat, but I knew Kang could hear the doubt creeping in. I could hear it myself. "Were you ever with her at the Koryo?"

"Go to hell, Inspector."

"Were you in that room in the Koryo on the eighth floor with her?"

"What business is it of yours?"

"A blue button in the closet of the room where the body was found. It was hers, wasn't it?"

"Congratulations, Inspector." Kang applauded gently. "Does that help you fill in some details of your investigation?" He stopped clapping and rested his face in his hands. When he looked up, he was in control of himself, but finally I could read his eyes. "She liked the Koryo. She said that room reminded her of an old movie. I always had a vase of flowers there for her." He stopped and looked at the crushed remains of the purple flowers on the floor. "We're about to get company, Inspector. They'll be circling back any minute, they always do. Have you any idea what is going on?"

"You mean the army trucks in Pyongyang?"

Kang's laugh was short and bitter. "So the answer is no, you don't know. You've been stumbling after that dead Finn the whole time." He kicked at a table leg lying at his feet. "This is what's about to happen. The furniture is being replaced. I mean all of it. The iron broom of history. Prisons emptied, old wrongs righted, intelligence operations gone awry dragged back into the sweet cleansing sunlight." Kang laughed again, with less bitterness. "Sunlight is our new god, Inspector. Don't you love the sun? All bad things happen in darkness, but only good can come of light." With an effort, he turned to look back at the countertop. I could see he was forcing himself to commit the whole scene to memory. "This took place in the light, Inspector. This, right here, all in the name of vanquishing evil. This is goodness in the flesh." He gestured around the room, his hands fluttering like a bird with a wounded wing, wondering how to land.

"Why do they want you so badly? It can't be just car smuggling. I saw Kim gun down one of your men two days ago. He gave me some story about enemy agents, but what he meant was, he had license to kill your people. It's something that happened a while ago, something you and Pak were involved in. Do you know what Pak had in his office? Files on Japanese. That's it, isn't it? This big decision on Japan, this all-hell-breaking-loose decision on Japan."

"Close, Inspector. Very close. But you're off in one respect. Your grandfather would have realized it immediately." Kang started to stand. My hand went to my pistol, and he settled back, though not in fear. "They could drag in anyone, actually. Anyone would do. But it would feel wrong somehow. They really think they can purge themselves of evil spirits, that they can be good and sound once the evil is chased down and destroyed. This is the day of reckoning. The leadership is looking for the magic key to the brilliant future. They think they have a chance to step across the river, watch a million ugly deeds from the past sweep off toward a deep, forgiving ocean. But those damned evil spirits are clinging to their trouser cuffs, muddy reminders of bad decisions, people who know the history and can't forget, files that can never be burned because they aren't on paper. They're here." Kang touched his chest.

"And you, you are the evil spirit?"

"Not only me. The whole department, and more. Even you, maybe. You are too much like your grandfather for them."

"They're going after your whole department?"

"We know too much, too much paper, too many orders stamped, signed, and dated about too many abductions."

"But that's not what is motivating Kim."

"No, it's something else. The man likes blood. He hates my people, and he wants to see them bleed. Military Security has been trying to sink its teeth into us for years. We operated outside their universe, in a reality they despise, and it drove them crazy that we were out of reach. We knew once they got an opening, they would exploit it for all they were worth to cut our throats." Kang paused.

"The man in the colonel's uniform, in the wrecked car on the high-way. It must have happened after I drove back into town."

"You almost saw it. The first car, the black one that you didn't get on film, was Kim's. Ours was not far behind. A few of my people were able to break out as soon as we realized what was happening, but I couldn't get everyone to safety all at once. That's why we started the car-smuggling operation, funds for the evacuation. There wasn't time for much organization, so we improvised. We didn't know Kim was using the highway, too, for his own smuggling ring. He was furious. You saw the results. It gave him extra incentive to go after my people when Military Security was given the order to roll up the Investigations Department. A handful of us are on the run. I should have been out days ago."

"But you're still here." I watched him sink down further against the wall. He'd almost given up; it was over and it didn't matter anymore. "You were waiting for Lena to join you." Nothing, he didn't move a muscle, but in his stillness I could see I was right. "You were going to Lake Keitele." I heard myself say it even before the thought had formed in my mind, because it was suddenly so clear. "And your daughter, that's really why she was here, close to the border. Because you knew the day would come. You've been getting ready for years. Even now, someone's waiting across the river for you. In a nice shiny black Mercedes. It's Pikkusaari, isn't it? And that other Finn, the corpse in the Koryo, he was part of your operation, too. That's why they dumped the body in that particular room. They knew you used it sometimes. It was Kim's way of playing with you, of telling you that he was closing in."

Kang shook his head. "No, not across the river. In Harbin."

I heard it click into place. Not organic, mechanical, just like Pak said. "Hyesan-Musan-Najin-Harbin. The train schedule, the one you took from me in the truck. That was your escape route, wasn't it? Where were you going to meet Lena, in Najin?"

"The clerk in Manpo was supposed to give me that schedule. Why he gave it to you, I'll never know."

"That's why they killed him. They were after you. How can you live with so much of other people's blood on your boots?"

Kang shifted his weight. It was more of an answer than I had expected.

"So what made you think you could sacrifice me and Pak? Because you did sacrifice him. He had an Israeli pistol in his hand when he died, only it wasn't his. The one he had was Czech, the same one in your shoulder holster right now."

For a moment I thought Kang wasn't paying attention. His head was cocked slightly, like a dog listening for something on the wind, far away. He looked at the front door, then turned to me. "It seems you're wrong about many things, Inspector. Pak was my friend."

"I heard you the first time."

"And you were so mad you couldn't shoot straight. So I'll say it again, and if you want to put a bullet in my heart, go ahead." He opened his jacket. I could see he hadn't unbuttoned the strap over Pak's pistol. "My heart is in the usual place." He paused. "Pak and I served together. Twenty-five years ago, a different time. We were in a squad run out of a little fishing port, at Sinpo. Remember in Manpo when I told you about those rumors my people had picked up on plans for a political settlement—and lots of money—if these old cases of abductions of Japanese were resolved?"

"You're wandering."

"You want to hear what I have to say, or do you want to pretend this is an interrogation? Pak and I were assigned to a routine agent operation in Japan. We did it all the time, almost with our eyes closed. Go in, insert an agent, get out. Only it didn't stay routine. It went bad. One night, the beach where we landed was supposed to be deserted, but it wasn't. Someone panicked, a little boy got hurt. We could see lights in the distance, police cars coming up the road. Pak argued with me to leave him behind, to cover our exit. I told him I wasn't leaving anyone, not even the boy. 'The boy needs a doctor.' He said it over and over. I can still hear him. 'Leave the boy.' But there were five of us in that team. We'd trained together for years. I was in charge, and I made the

decision. When we got back home, Pak resigned. He never blamed me.
I saved his life, against his will. He always said it was his fault for giving
me the choice. He raised the boy, his only son. On the list of cases the
Japanese want resolved, the boy is number one. They don't know he's
dead. As far as they're concerned, he's still a child."

"And when they have stories on him, the Japanese papers run a picture of a five-year-old kid, holding a cat."

A jeep pulled up in front of the shop. The doors slammed even before the squeal of the tires stopped. Kang moved closer. "Shoot me,
quick, or they'll say you were helping."

I turned and fired at the door. "Around back. Get out, now."

Kang didn't hesitate. He moved over the broken chairs, passed his
hand over the bloody book, and disappeared in the dark. There were
two shots in quick succession. Then the jeep started and drove away.

# 9

*"Jesus." The Irishman closed his notebook. "They aren't going to be
happy to hear this. Kang shot by Military Security. What a mess." He
turned off the tape recorder and tucked it in his coat pocket. "Hell, and
bloody hell."*

*"That's it. Nobody's happy these days." I pushed my chair back. "I'm
going tomorrow if I can get a reservation on the train. Unless it's already
tomorrow."*

*"I thought you had enough of trains."*

*"See you around sometime, Richie."*

*"Would that be an offer?"*

*"Hardly. I'm not the type to defect. And you know I won't work for
you. I wouldn't work for Kang. Why would I want to serve the queen." I
pulled an envelope out of my back pocket and threw it on the table. "A
present."*

"Isn't this is a little awkward, Inspector? I'm supposed to pay you."

"It's not money. It's a copy of Kim's passport. He travels under the name of Yun. And he's been promoted." The Irishman didn't move; he was the type who would wait until I left to reach for the envelope. "Go on, take a look. A good photo, he's not squinting. Easy to pick out of the crowd."

"Bad haircut?" He looked thoughtfully at me for a moment.

"He's yours, Richie. Your people can cold-pitch him. He'll have to report it. If he doesn't and they find out, he's dead."

"What if they don't find out?"

"Don't worry, they will."

"And if he does report it?"

"No one will believe he turned you down. They'll tear him to shreds trying to make sure."

The Irishman stood up. "Cheers, Inspector." He walked over to the floor lamp, switched it off, and then turned to me. "Icy outside, I'll bet. Watch your step."

My hotel was not far, but I took a few wrong turns, partly to see if I was being followed, partly just to walk in the night air. I figured the Irishman would sit in the dark awhile, sipping his tea, wondering what I hadn't told him. It was his job, to listen for what people didn't say. He must have heard loud and clear the word I never said—revenge. They'd probably look for Kim; maybe they'd find him, maybe they wouldn't. Trying to track him would keep them busy enough so they'd miss what else I had left out. It wasn't much.

It was quiet until dawn, not peaceful, but the heavy silence that weighs on the hours, so that you crave the smallest sound besides your own breathing, crickets or even just the wind to show that the night is rolling unbroken, that it will end. When the sun finally came through the rear window, I peered outside. The dirt path from the back door went down a small slope to a slender, solitary birch tree. A man slumped against it, his legs across the path and his feet, bootless, on the grass beyond. He gazed toward the mist lifting from the hills, only his eyes never blinked. A breeze came up, making the tree's top branches sway and the leaves dance with a sudden, nervous energy that scattered the light across the ground. I must have stared a long time, but not because I needed to be sure. From the moment the sun came through the window, I knew it would not be Kang.

The girl's book I left where it was, and the flowers, too. As I shut the front door behind me and turned toward the station, I thought I spotted a line of geese heading south. They were flying straight as an arrow, high in an autumn sky that was as blue as anything I'd ever seen.

JANUARY 2003, PRAGUE